Jack Higgins lived in Belfast till the age of twelve. Leaving school at fifteen, he spent three years with the Royal Horse Guards, serving on the East German border during the Cold War. His subsequent employment included occupations as diverse as circus roustabout, truck driver, clerk and, after taking an honours degree in sociology and social psychology, teacher and university lecturer.

The Eagle Has Landed turned him into an international bestselling author, and his novels have since sold over 250 million copies and have been translated into sixty languages. Many of them have also been made into successful films. His recent bestselling novels include, *The Killing Ground*, *Rough Justice*, *The Khufra Run*, *A Darker Place*, *The Wolf at the Door*, *Confessional* and *The Judas Gate*.

In 1995 Jack Higgins was awarded an honorary doctorate by Leeds Metropolitan University. He is a fellow of the Royal Society of Arts and an expert scuba diver and marksman. He lives on Jersey.

ALSO BY JACK HIGGINS

JACK HIGGINS

DRINK WITH THE DEVIL

HARPER

Harper
An imprint of HarperCollins*Publishers*
77–85 Fulham Palace Road,
Hammersmith, London W6 8JB

www.harpercollins.co.uk

This paperback edition 2012
1

First published in Great Britain by Michael Joseph 1996
Signet Edition 1998

Copyright © Harry Patterson 1996

Jack Higgins asserts the moral right to
be identified as the author of this work

A catalogue record for this book is
available from the British Library

ISBN: 978-0-00-792618-3

Set in Sabon by Palimpsest Book Production Limited,
Falkirk, Stirlingshire

Printed and bound in Great Britain by
Clays Ltd, St Ives plc

PUBLISHER'S NOTE

Drink with the Devil was first published in the UK by Michael Joseph in 1996 and later by Signet in 1998. This amazing novel has been out of print for some years, and in 2011 it seemed to the author and his publishers that it was a pity to leave such a good story languishing on his shelves. So we are delighted to be able to bring back *Drink with the Devil* for the vast majority of us who never had a chance to read the earlier editions.

To Denise
Best of girls

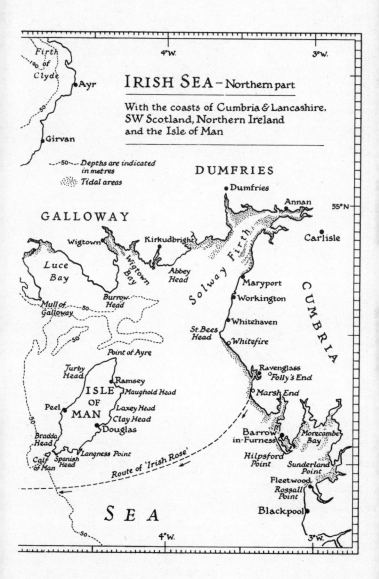

IRISH SEA – Northern part

With the coasts of Cumbria & Lancashire,
SW Scotland, Northern Ireland
and the Isle of Man

--50-- *Depths are indicated*
in metres
⋯⋯ *Tidal areas*

Firth of Clyde

Ayr

Girvan

DUMFRIES

Dumfries

Annan

55°N

GALLOWAY

Wigtown

Kirkudbright

Carlisle

Luce Bay

Wigtown Bay

Abbey Head

Solway Firth

Maryport

Burrow Head

Workington

Mull of Galloway

St Bees Head

Whitehaven

Whitefire

CUMBRIA

Point of Ayre

Ravenglass

Folly's End

Turby Head

Ramsey

Maughold Head

Marsh End

Peel

ISLE
OF
MAN

Laxey Head

Clay Head

Douglas

Barrow-
in-Furness

Morecambe Bay

Bradda Head

Langness Point

Hilpsford
Point

Sunderland
Point

Calf of Man

Spanish Head

Route of 'Irish Rose'

Fleetwood
Rossall Point

Blackpool

S E A

4°W.

3°W.

BELFAST

1985

1

Rain swept in from Belfast Lough and, as he turned the corner, there was the rattle of small-arms fire somewhere in the darkness of the city centre followed by the crump of an explosion. He didn't hesitate, but started across the square, a small man, no more than five feet five, in jeans, reefer coat and peaked cap, a seaman's duffel bag hanging from one shoulder.

A sign said Albert Hotel, but it was more a lodging house than anything else, of a type used by sailors and constructed originally by the simple expedient of knocking three Victorian terrace houses together. The front door stood open and a small, balding man peered out, a newspaper in one hand.

There was another explosion in the distance. 'Jesus!' he said. 'The boys are active tonight.'

The small man said from the bottom of the

steps, 'I phoned earlier about a room. Keogh is the name.' His voice was more English than anything else, only a hint of the distinctive Belfast accent.

'Ah, yes – Mr Keogh. Off a boat are ye?'

'Something like that.'

'Well, come away in out of the rain and I'll fix you up.'

At that moment a Land Rover turned the corner followed by another. They were stripped down, three paratroopers crouched behind the driver, hard young men in red berets and flak jackets, each one carrying a sub-machine gun. They vanished into the darkness and rain on the other side of the square.

'Jesus!' the old man said again then went inside and Keogh followed him.

It was a poor sort of a place, a square hall with a reception desk and a narrow staircase. The white paint had yellowed over the years and the wallpaper was badly faded, damp showing through here and there.

The old man pushed a register across the desk for Keogh to sign. 'RUC regulations. Home address. Next port of call. The lot.'

'Fine by me.' Keogh quickly filled it in and pushed the register back across the desk.

'Martin Keogh, Wapping, London. I haven't been to London in years.'

'A fine city.' Keogh took out a packet of cigarettes and lit one.

The old man took a room key down from a board. 'At least they don't have Paras hurtling around the streets armed to the teeth. Crazy that, sitting out in the open, even in the rain. What a target. Suicide, if you ask me.'

'Not really,' Keogh told him. 'It's an old Para trick developed years ago in Aden. They travel in twos to look after each other and, with no armour in the way, they can respond instantly to any attack.'

'And how would you be knowing a thing like that?'

Keogh shrugged, 'Common knowledge, Da. Now, can I have my key?'

It was then that the old man noticed the eyes which were of no particular colour and yet were the coldest he had ever seen and for some unaccountable reason he knew fear. And at that moment Keogh smiled and his personality changed totally. He reached across and took the key.

'Someone told me there was a decent café near here. The Regent?'

'That's right. Straight across the square to Lurgen Street. It's by the old docks.'

'I'll find it,' and Keogh turned and went upstairs.

He found the room easily enough, opened the door, the lock of which had obviously been forced on numerous occasions, and went in. The room was very small and smelled of damp. There was a single bed, a hanging cupboard and a chair. There was a washbasin in the corner, but no toilet. There wasn't even a telephone; still, with any luck, it would only be for one night.

He put his duffel bag on the bed, opened it. There was a toilet bag, spare shirts, some books. He pulled them to one side and prised up the thick cardboard base of the bag, disclosing a Walther PPK pistol, several clips of ammunition and the new small Carswell silencer. He checked the weapon, loaded it and screwed the silencer into place then he slipped it inside his jeans against the small of his back.

'Regent, son,' he said softly and went out whistling a small sad tune.

There was a public telephone by the reception desk, of the old-fashioned kind in a booth. Keogh nodded to the man, went inside and closed the door. He found some pound coins and dialled a number.

Jack Barry was a tall, pleasant-looking man whose horn-rimmed spectacles gave him a bookish look. He had the look also of the schoolmaster, which

was exactly what he had once been. But not now
– now he was Chief of Staff of the Provisional IRA
and he was seated by the fire at his Dublin home
reading the paper, his portable phone at his side,
when it rang.

He picked it up and his wife, Jean, called, 'Now
don't be long. Your supper's ready.'

'Barry here.'

Keogh said in Irish, 'It's me. I've booked in at
the Albert Hotel under the name of Martin Keogh.
Next step is to meet the girl.'

'Will that be difficult?'

'No, I've organized it. Trust me. I'm off to this
Regent Café now. Her uncle owns it.'

'Good man. Keep me posted. Use the mobile
number only.'

He switched off his phone and his wife called
again, 'Come away in. It's getting cold.'

He got to his feet obediently and went into the
kitchen.

Keogh found the Regent Café with no trouble.
One window was boarded up, obviously from the
bomb blast, but the other was intact, offering a
clear view of the interior. There were hardly any
customers, just three old men at one table and a
ravaged-looking middle-aged woman at another
who looked like a prostitute.

The girl sitting behind the counter was just sixteen; he knew that because he knew all about her. Her name was Kathleen Ryan and she ran the café on behalf of her uncle, Michael Ryan, a Protestant, and a gunman from his earliest youth. She was a small girl with black hair and angry eyes above pronounced cheekbones. Not pretty by any conventional standard. She wore a dark sweater, denim miniskirt and boots and sat on a stool engrossed in a book when Keogh went in.

He leaned on the counter. 'Is it good?'

She looked him over calmly and that look told him of someone infinitely older than her years.

'Very good. *The Midnight Court*.'

'But that's in Irish, surely?' Keogh reached for the book and saw that he was right.

'And why shouldn't it be? You think a Protestant shouldn't read Irish? Why not? It's our country too, mister, and if you're Sinn Fein or any of that old rubbish I'd prefer you went elsewhere. Catholics aren't welcome. An IRA street bomb killed my father, my mother and my wee sister.'

'Girl, dear.' Keogh held up his hands defensively. 'I'm a Belfast boy home from the sea who's just come in for a cup of tea.'

'You don't sound Belfast to me. English, I'd say.'

'And that's because my father took me to live there when I was a boy.'

She frowned for a moment then shrugged. 'All right.' She raised her voice. 'Tea for one, Mary.' She said to Keogh, 'No more cooking. We're closing soon.'

'The tea will do just fine.'

A moment later, a grey-haired woman in an apron brought tea in a mug and placed it on the counter. 'Milk and sugar over there. Help yourself.'

Keogh did as he was told and pushed a pound coin across. The woman gave him some change. The girl ignored him, reached for her book and stood up. 'I'll be away now, Mary. Give it another hour then you can take an early night.' And she went through to the back.

Keogh took his tea to a table by the door, sat down and lit a cigarette. Five minutes later Kathleen Ryan emerged wearing a beret and an old trench-coat. She went out without looking at him. Keogh sipped some more tea, then got up and left.

It was raining harder now as she turned on to the waterfront and she increased her pace, head down. The three youths standing in the doorway of a disused warehouse saw her coming as she passed under the light of a street lamp. They were of a type to be found in any city in the world. Vicious young animals in bomber jackets and jeans.

'That's her, Pat,' the one wearing a baseball cap said. 'That's her. The Ryan bitch from the café.'

'I can tell for myself, you fool,' the one called Pat said. 'Now hold still and grab her on the way past.'

Kathleen Ryan was totally unaware of their existence as they stayed back in the shadows. It was only the quick rush of feet that alerted her and by then it was too late, one arm round her neck half choking her.

Pat walked round in front and tilted her chin. 'Well, now, what have we got here? A little Prod bitch. Ryan, isn't it?'

She kicked back, catching the youth in the baseball cap on the shin. 'Leave me be, you Taig bastard.'

'Taig bastard, is it,' Pat said. 'And us decent Catholic boys!' He slapped her face. 'Up the alley with her. Time she learned her manners.'

She didn't scream for it was not in her nature, but cried out in rage and bit the hand that fastened on her mouth.

'Bitch!' Baseball Cap called out and punched her in the back and then they ran her along the alley through the rain. There was a stack of packing cases clear under an old-fashioned gas street lamp. As she struggled, two of them pulled her across a packing case and Pat moved up behind and racked her skirt up.

'Time you learned,' he said.

'No, time you learned!' a voice called. Pat turned and Martin Keogh walked up the alley, hands in the pockets of his reefer. 'Put her down. I mean, she doesn't know where you've been, does she?'

'Stuff you, wee man,' the one in the baseball cap said, released his hold on the girl and swung a punch at Keogh who caught the wrist, twisted and ran him face-first into the wall.

'You bastard!' the third youth cried and rushed him.

Keogh's left hand came out of his pocket, holding the Walther and he slashed the youth across the face, splitting the cheek from the left eye to the corner of the mouth. He raised the gun and fired, the distinctive muted cough of the silenced weapon flat in the rain.

Baseball Cap was on his knees, the other clutching his cheek, blood pouring through his fingers. Pat stood there, rage on his face.

'You bloody swine!'

'It's been said before.' Keogh touched him between the eyes with the silenced end of the Walther. 'Not another word or I'll kill you.'

The youth froze. Kathleen Ryan was pulling her skirt down. Keogh said, 'Back to that café of yours, girl. I'll see you soon.'

She hesitated, staring at him, then turned and ran away along the alley.

There was only the rain now and the groans of the injured. Pat said wildly, 'We did what you told us to do. Why this?'

'Oh, no,' Keogh said. 'I told you to frighten the girl a little and then I'd come and save her.' He found a cigarette one-handed and lit it. 'And what were we into? Gang rape.'

'She's a dirty little Prod. Who cares?'

'I do,' Keogh told him. 'And I'm a Catholic. You give us a bad name.'

Pat rushed him. Keogh swayed to one side, tripping him with his right foot and dropped one knee down hard in his back. Pat lay there sobbing in the rain.

Keogh said, 'You need a lesson, son.'

He jammed the muzzle of the Walther against the youth's thigh and pulled the trigger. There was a muted report and Pat cried out.

Keogh stood up. 'Only a flesh wound. It could have been your kneecap.'

Pat was sobbing now. 'Damn you!'

'Taken care of a long time ago.' Keogh took an envelope from his pocket and dropped it down. 'Five hundred quid, that was the price. Now get yourself to the Royal Victoria Casualty Department.

Best in the world for gunshot wounds, but then they get a lot of experience.'

He walked away, whistling the same eerie little tune and left them there in the rain.

When he reached the café there were no longer any customers, but he could see Kathleen Ryan and the woman Mary standing behind the counter. The girl was on the telephone. Keogh tried the door, but it was locked. Kathleen Ryan turned as the door rattled and nodded to Mary who came from behind the counter and unlocked it.

As Keogh entered Mary said, 'She told me what you did for her. God bless you.'

Keogh sat on the edge of a table and lit a cigarette. The girl was still talking. 'No, I'll be fine now. I'll be at the Drum in twenty minutes. Don't fret.' She put the phone down and turned, her face calm. 'My Uncle Michael. He worries about me.'

'And why not?' Keogh said. 'Desperate times.'

'You don't take prisoners, do you?'

'I could never see the point.'

'And you're carrying. A Walther, from what I saw.'

'Very knowledgeable for one so young.'

'Oh, I know guns, mister, I was raised on them. What did you do after I left?'

'I sent them on their way.'

'Home, was it, with a pat on the head?'

'No, the nearest casualty department. They needed a lesson. They got one. The one who seemed to be in charge will be on sticks for a while, if that's a comfort to you.'

She frowned, her eyes dark. 'What's your game?'

'No game. I didn't like what was going on, that's all.' He stood up and stubbed out his cigarette. 'Still, you seem fine now so I'll be on my way.'

He got the door open. She said quickly, 'No, hang on.' He turned and she added, 'You can walk me to my uncle's pub. That's the Orange Drum on Connor's Wharf. It's about a quarter of a mile. My name is Kathleen Ryan. What's yours?'

'Martin Keogh.'

'Wait for me outside.'

He did as he was told and saw her go to the phone again. Probably speaking to her uncle, he thought. A few moments later she joined him, this time carrying a large umbrella.

As she put it up against the driving rain he said, 'And wouldn't a taxi be safer?'

'I like the city at night,' she told him. 'I like the rain. I've got a right to go my own way and to hell with those Fenian bastards.'

'A point of view,' he replied as they started to walk.

'Here, get under this,' she said, pulling him

14

under the umbrella and taking his arm. 'A sailor, you said?'

'Just for the past couple of years.'

'A sailor from Belfast raised in London who carries a Walther.' There was a question in her voice.

'A dangerous place, this old town, as you saw tonight.'

'Dangerous for you, you mean, and that's why you're carrying.' She frowned. 'You're not a Fenian or you wouldn't have done what you did to that lot.'

'I'm not anybody's, girl dear.' He paused to light a cigarette.

She said, 'Give me one.'

'I will not and you with your green years ahead of you. God, but you're one for the questions, Kate.'

She turned to glance at him. 'Why do you call me that? No one else does.'

'Oh, it seems to suit.'

They were walking along the waterfront now, container ships anchored at the Quay and, further out, the red and green lights of a freighter moving out to sea.

Kathleen Ryan said, 'So, the gun? Why are you carrying?'

'Jesus, it's the persistent one you are. A long time ago I was a soldier. Did three tours of duty in this very town and there's always the chance of someone with a long memory and a grudge to work off.'

'What regiment?'

'1 Para.'

'Don't tell me you were at Bloody Sunday in Londonderry?'

'That's right. Like I said, a long time ago.'

Her hand tightened on his arm. 'God, but you lads gave those Fenians a roasting that day. How many did you kill? Thirteen wasn't it?'

The lights of the pub were plain across a cobbled quay now. Keogh said, 'How old are you?'

'Sixteen.'

'So young and so full of hate.'

'I told you. The IRA killed my father, my mother and my wee sister. That only leaves Uncle Michael.'

The sign said The Orange Drum and one was painted on the brick wall beside it with the legend Our Country Too. The girl put the umbrella down, opened the door and led the way in.

The interior was a typical Belfast pub with several booths, a few tables and chairs and a long mahogany bar. Bottles of every kind of drink were ranged on shelves against a mirrored wall. There were only half-a-dozen customers, all old men, four of them playing cards by an open fire, two others talking softly to each other. A hard-looking young man with one arm sat behind the bar reading the *Belfast Telegraph*.

He glanced up and put the paper down. 'Are you OK, Kathleen? Michael told me what happened.'

'I'm fine, Ivor. Thanks to Mr Keogh here. Is Uncle Michael in the back?'

At that moment a door opened and a man walked through. Keogh knew him at once from the photos Barry had supplied at his briefing in Dublin. Michael Ryan, aged fifty-five, a Loyalist of the first order who had served in the UVF and Red Hand of Ulster, the most extreme Protestant group of all, a man who had killed for his beliefs many times. He was of medium height, hair greying slightly at the temples, eyes very blue, and there was an energy to him.

'This is Martin Keogh,' the girl said.

Ryan came round the bar and held out his hand. 'You did me a good turn tonight. I shan't forget.'

'Lucky I was there.'

'That's as may be. I owe you a drink anyway.'

'Bushmills whiskey would be fine,' Keogh told him.

'Over here.' Ryan indicated a booth in the corner.

The girl took off her raincoat and beret and eased behind the table. Her uncle sat beside her and Keogh was opposite. Ivor brought a bottle of Bushmills and two glasses.

'Can I get you anything, Kathleen?'

'No, I'm OK, Ivor.'

He plainly worshipped her, but nodded and walked away. Ryan said, 'I've checked with a contact at the Royal Victoria. They just received three very damaged young men. One with a bullet in the thigh.'

'Is that a fact?' Keogh said.

Kathleen Ryan stared at him. 'You didn't tell me.'

'No need.'

'Let's see what you're carrying,' Ryan asked. 'No need to worry. All friends here.'

Keogh shrugged, took the Walther from his pocket and passed it across. Ryan examined it expertly. 'Carswell silencer, the new job. Very nice.' He took a Browning from his pocket and passed it over. 'Still my personal favourite.'

'Preferred weapon of the SAS.' Keogh lifted the Browning in one hand. 'And the Parachute Regiment.'

'He served with 1 Para,' the girl said. 'Bloody Sunday.'

'Is that a fact?' Michael Ryan said.

'A long time ago. Lately I've been at sea.'

'Belfast, but raised in London, Kathleen tells me?'

'My mother died in childbirth. My father went to London in search of work. He's dead now.'

Ryan had ejected the magazine from the butt of the Walther. 'And a good Prod. You must be because of what you did for Kathleen.'

'To be honest with you, religion doesn't mean a thing to me,' Keogh told him. 'But let's say I know which side I'm on.'

At that moment, the door was flung open and a man in a cloth cap and raincoat rushed in, a revolver in one hand.

'Michael Ryan, you bastard, I've got you now,' he cried and raised the revolver.

Ryan was caught, the magazine from the Walther on the table beside it. Keogh said, 'What do I do, shoot him? All right. Bang, you're dead.' He picked up the Browning and fired once. The man dropped the hand holding the revolver to one side. Keogh said, 'Blanks, Mr Ryan, I could tell by the weight. What kind of a game are we playing here?'

Ryan was laughing now. 'Go on, Joseph, and get yourself a drink at the bar.'

The supposed gunman turned away. The old men by the fire continued their card game as if nothing had happened.

Michael Ryan stood up. 'Just a test, my old son, in a manner of speaking. Let's adjourn to the parlour and talk some more.'

There was a fire in the grate of the small parlour, curtains drawn as rain drummed against the window. It was warm and comfortable and Ryan and Keogh sat opposite each other. The girl came in from the kitchen with a teapot, milk and cups on a tray.

Ryan said, 'If you're a seaman you'll have your papers.'

'Of course,' Keogh said.

Ryan held out his hand and Keogh shrugged, opened his reefer and took a wallet from his inside pocket.

'There you go. Ships' papers, union card, the lot.'

The girl poured tea and Ryan examined everything closely. 'Paid off the *Ventura* two weeks ago. Deck hand and diver. What's all that?'

'The *Ventura*'s a supply ship in the North Sea oilfields. Besides general ship's duties, I did some diving. Not the really deep stuff. Just underwater maintenance, welding when necessary. That sort of thing.'

'Interesting. A man of parts. Any special skills from the Parachute Regiment?'

'Just how to kill people. The usual weaponry skills. A considerable knowledge of explosives.' Keogh lit a cigarette. 'But where's all this leading?'

Ryan persisted. 'Can you ride a motorcycle?'

'Since I was sixteen and that's a long time ago. So what?'

Ryan leaned back, took out a pipe and filled it from an old pouch. 'Visiting relatives, are you?'

'Not that I know of,' Keogh said. 'A few cousins

scattered here and there. I came back on a whim. Nostalgia if you like. A bad idea really, but I can always go back and get another berth.'

'I could offer you a job,' Ryan said and the girl brought a taper from the fire to light his pipe.

'What, here in Belfast?'

'No, in England.'

'Doing what?'

'Why, the kind of thing you did tonight. The kind of thing you're good at.'

It was very quiet. Keogh was aware of the girl watching him eagerly. 'Do I smell politics here?'

'Since nineteen sixty-nine I've worked for the Loyalist cause,' Ryan said. 'Served six years in the Maze prison. I hate Fenians. I hate the bloody Sinn Fein because if they win they'll drive us all out, every Protestant in the country. Ethnic cleansing to the hilt. Now if things get that bad I'll take as many of them to hell with me as I can.'

'So where's this leading?'

'A job in England. A very lucrative job. Funds for our organization.'

'In other words we steal from someone,' Keogh said.

'We need money, Keogh,' Ryan said. 'Money for arms. The bloody IRA have their Irish American sympathizers providing funds. We don't.' He leaned forward. 'I'm not asking you for patriotism. I'll settle for greed. Fifty thousand pounds.'

There was a long pause and Ryan and the girl waited, her face sombre as if she expected him to say no.

Keogh smiled. 'That's a lot of money, Mr Ryan, so you'll be expecting a lot in return.'

'Back-up is what I expect from a man who can handle anything and, from the way you've carried yourself tonight, you would seem to be that kind of man.'

Keogh said, 'What about your own people? You've as many gunmen out on the street as the IRA. More, even. I know that from army days.' He lit a cigarette and leaned back. 'Unless there's another truth here. That you're in it for the money, you're in it for yourself.'

Kathleen Ryan jumped up. 'Damn you for saying that. My uncle has given more for our people than anyone I know. Better you get out of here while you can.'

Ryan held up a hand. 'Softly, child, any intelligent man would see it as a possibility. It's happened before, God knows, and on both sides.'

'So?' Keogh said.

'I can be as hungry as the next man where money is concerned, but my cause is a just one, the one certainty in my life. Any money that passes through my hands goes to the Protestant cause. That's what my life is about.'

'Then why not use some of your own men?'

'Because people talk too much, a weakness in all revolutionary movements. The IRA have the same problem. I've always preferred to use what I call hired help and for that I go to the underworld. An honest thief who is working for wages is a sounder proposition than some revolutionary hothead.'

'So that's where I come in?' Keogh said. 'Hired help, just like anyone else you need?'

'Exactly. So, are you in or out? If it's no then say no. After what you did for Kathleen tonight you'll come to no harm from me.'

'Well, that's nice to know.' Keogh shrugged. 'Oh, what the hell, I might as well give it a try. A change from the North Sea. Terrible weather there at this time of the year.'

'Good man yourself,' Ryan smiled. 'A couple of Bushmills, Kathleen, and we'll drink to it.'

'Where are you staying?' Ryan asked.

'A fleapit called the Albert Hotel,' Keogh told him.

'Fleapit indeed,' Ryan toasted him. 'Our country too.'

'May you die in Ireland,' Keogh replied.

'An excellent sentiment.' Ryan swallowed his Bushmills in a single gulp.

'So what happens now?'

'I'll tell you in London. We'll fly there – you, me and Kathleen. There's someone I have to see.'

Keogh turned to the girl. 'An activist, is it? A little young, I would have thought.'

'They blew up my family when I was ten years old, Mr Keogh,' she said fiercely. 'I grew up fast after that.'

'A hard world.'

'And I'll make it harder for the other side, believe me.'

'You hate well, I'll say that.' Keogh turned back to her uncle. 'So that's it, then?' He shook his hand. 'What am I really getting into? I should know more.'

'All right, a taster only. How well do you know the north-west of England? The Lake District?'

'I've never been there.'

'A wild and lonely area at this time of the year with the tourists gone.'

'So?'

'A certain truck will be passing through there, a meat transporter. You and I will hi-jack it. Very simple, very fast. A five-minute job.'

'You did say meat transporter?'

Ryan smiled. 'That's what this truck is. What's inside is another matter. You find that out later.'

'And what happens afterwards?'

'We drive to a place on the Cumbrian coast

where there's an old disused jetty. There will be a boat waiting, a Siemans ferry. Do you know what that is?'

'The Germans used them in the Second World War to transport heavy equipment and men in coastal attacks.'

'You're well informed. We drive on board and sail for Ulster. I've found a suitable spot on the coast where there's a disused quarry pier. We drive the truck off the boat and disappear into the night. All beautifully simple.'

'So it would seem,' Keogh said. 'And the crew of this Siemans ferry? What are they doing?'

'Earning their wages. As far as they are concerned it's just some sort of illegal traffic or other. They do it all the time. They're those sort of people.'

'Crooks, you mean.'

'Exactly. The boat is tied up near Wapping at the moment. That's why we're going to London. To finalize things.'

There was a pause and then Kathleen Ryan said, 'What do you think, Mr Keogh?'

'That you'd better start calling me Martin as it seems we're going to spend some time together.'

'But do you think it would work?'

'Its greatest virtue, as your uncle says, is its simplicity. It could work perfectly, just like a Swiss watch. On the other hand, even Swiss watches break down sometimes.'

'Oh ye of little faith.' Ryan smiled. 'Of course it will work. It's got to. My organization needs the means to buy arms for our people. It's essential. There's a passage in the Koran that says there is more truth in one sword than ten thousand words.'

'I take your point.' Keogh stood up. 'It's late. I'd better get back to my hotel.'

'Join us here for breakfast in the morning,' Ryan told him. 'We'll catch the noon plane. I'll take care of the tickets.'

'I'll say goodnight, then.'

'The bar is closed. Kathleen will let you out. I'll keep your Walther here. No way of passing through airport security with that, but it doesn't matter. Our London connection will provide any weapons we need.' He held out his hand. 'I'll see you in the morning.'

The girl opened the door and rain drove in on the wind.

'A dirty old night,' she said.

'You can say that again.' Keogh turned up his collar. 'An Ulster fry-up will do me fine for breakfast especially if you cook it yourself. Two eggs and don't forget the sausage.'

'Go on, get on your way.' She pushed him out

and laughed that distinctive laugh of hers and closed the door.

Keogh had difficulty finding a phone box. Most of them seemed to be vandalized. He finally struck lucky when he was quite close to the hotel. He closed the glass door to keep out the rain and rang the Dublin number. Barry was seated at the desk of his small study with his Chief of Intelligence for Ulster, a man named John Cassidy, when he took the call.

'It's me,' Keogh said. 'Worked like a charm. I'm in it up to my neck. Ryan's taken me on board.'

'Tell me everything.'

Which Keogh did in a few brief sentences. Finally, he said, 'What could be in this meat transporter?'

'Gold bullion if it's the job I'm thinking of. It was put to the Loyalist Army Council about a year ago and thrown out as being too risky.'

'So Ryan has decided to do it on his own initiative.'

'Exactly, but then he always was the wild one. That's why I wanted you in there when I got the whisper through an informer that he was up to something.'

'Up to something big,' Keogh told him.

'That's right. Stay in close touch. You've got

those alternate numbers for the mobile phone and watch your back.'

Barry leaned back thoughtfully and lit a cigarette. Cassidy said, 'Trouble?'

'Michael Ryan up to his old tricks.' He ran through what Keogh had told him.

Cassidy said, 'My God, if it is gold bullion, the bastards would have enough money to arm for a civil war. What are you going to do?'

'I don't need to do a thing except have a suitable reception committee waiting when that boat delivers the truck somewhere on the Ulster coast. Then we'll have enough money to start a civil war.'

'And you're certain of knowing the time and place?'

'Oh, yes. The man on the other end of the phone just now is one of our own. He's infiltrated under a false identity. He'll be going along for the ride every step of the way.'

'A good man?'

'The best.'

'Would I be knowing him?'

Barry told him Keogh's real name.

Cassidy laughed out loud. 'God save us, the Devil himself, so God help Michael Ryan.'

* * *

There was no one at the reception desk when Keogh entered the hotel. He went up the stairs quickly and unlocked the door to his room. It was unbelievably depressing and he looked around with distaste. It certainly wasn't worth taking off his clothes. He switched off the light, lit a cigarette, lay on the bed and went over the whole affair.

The astonishing thing was, as had been said, the simplicity of it. He'd have to consider that again once Ryan had taken him fully into his confidence, of course. Not a bad fella, Ryan; a man hard to dislike. And then there was the girl. So much hate there in one so young and all blamed on the bomb which had killed her family. He shook his head. There was more to it than that, had to be, and, finally, he drifted into sleep.

Kathleen Ryan took a cup of tea in to her uncle just before she went to bed. Ryan was sitting by the fire smoking his pipe and brooding.

'You think it will work?' she asked.

'I've never been more certain, and with Keogh along . . .' He shrugged. 'Fifty million pounds in gold bullion, Kathleen. Just think of that.'

'A strange one,' she said. 'Can you trust him?'

'I've never trusted anyone in my life,' he said cheerfully, 'not even you. No, don't you fret over Keogh. I'll have my eye on him.'

'But can you be sure?'

'Of course I can. I know him like I know myself, Kathleen, my love. We're cut from the same bolt of cloth. Like me he's got brains, that's obvious. He's also a killer. It's his nature. He can do no other, just like me.' He reached up to kiss her cheek. 'Now off to bed with you.'

She went out and he sat back, sipping his tea and thinking of a lonely road in the Lake District, a road that not even his niece knew he had visited.

LONDON
THE LAKE DISTRICT

1985

2

If there is such a thing as an Irish quarter in London it's to be found in Kilburn along with a profusion of pubs to make any Irish Republican happy. But there are also the Protestant variety, identical with anything to be found in Belfast. The William & Mary was one of those, its landlord, Hugh Bell, an Orange Protestant to the hilt, performing the same function in London for the Loyalist movement as Sinn Fein did for the IRA.

In the early evening of the day they had arrived in London, Ryan, Keogh and Kathleen sat with him in a back room, an assortment of handguns on the table. Bell, a large, jovial man with white hair, poured himself a whiskey.

'Anything you like, Michael and there's more where that came from.'

Ryan selected a Browning, hefted it and put it

in his pocket. Keogh found a Walther. 'Would you have a Carswell for this?' he asked.

'A man of taste and discernment I see,' Bell observed. He got up, went to a cupboard, rummaged inside and came back. 'There you go. The latest model.'

Keogh screwed it on to the end of the Walther. 'Just the ticket.'

'And the young lady?' Bell asked.

'My niece doesn't carry,' Ryan told him.

The girl bridled instantly. 'I'm as good a shot as you, Uncle Michael, and you know it. How am I expected to protect myself? Kick them in the balls?'

Bell laughed. 'I might have a solution.' He went back to the cupboard and returned with a small automatic. 'Colt .25, quite rare. Slips in a lady's handbag or stocking quite easily.'

'And no bloody stopping power,' Ryan told him.

'Enough if you're close enough,' Bell said.

The girl took the weapon from him and smiled. 'This will do me just fine.' She slipped it into her handbag.

Ryan said, 'All right. What about the *Irish Rose*?'

'Sieman's ferry, tied up in Wapping near the Pool of London. Captain Frank Tully, but you know that. The kind of rat who'll do anything for money. The worst kind of drugs, anything that pays. He's twice run arms for the IRA to the Republic.'

'What about his crew?'

'There's four.' Bell opened a drawer and took out a piece of paper. He put reading spectacles on the end of his nose. 'Mick Dolan and Jock Grant – they're from Liverpool. Bert Fox from London and a Kraut named Muller – Hans Muller. They've all got form – all been inside.'

'Well at least we know what we're dealing with,' Keogh observed.

'That's right,' Ryan told him. 'Just your average scum.'

Bell said, 'These aren't good people, Michael. I hope you know what you're doing.'

'I usually do.' Ryan grinned and took a folded piece of paper from his pocket. 'These are my requirements. See if you can fill the bill.'

Bell had a look. 'Stun grenades, smoke grenades. That's fine. Two AK assault rifles. OK. Semtex? Is that essential?'

'I might have to blow my way into my target.'

'All right, I'll see what I can do.'

'That's it, then.' Ryan smiled at his niece and Keogh. 'Something to eat and then we'll go and see Tully.'

It was very cold on the Thames, Tower Bridge on the right and the floodlit Tower of London just beyond it. A couple of ships passed from the Pool of London, red and green lights clear in the evening darkness as the taxi stopped at the end of Cable Wharfe and Ryan, Kathleen and Keogh got out. The taxi moved away and they walked along the waterfront.

The ferry was moored at the far end, cables reaching to the pier and in the sickly yellow light of two lamps they could see the legend on the stern plain. *Irish Rose*.

'Enough to make a man feel at home,' Ryan said.

'I'm not sure that's the right word for it,' Keogh told him.

They started up the gangway and a man in reefer coat and peaked cap appeared. 'And where do you think you're going?' he asked in a hard Liverpool voice.

'We're expected,' Ryan said. 'Tell Captain Tully.'

The man laughed out loud. 'Captain Tully? Is that what he calls himself?' He laughed again. 'All right, this way.'

The boat was very flat, the central section including the wheelhouse rising up from the deck three quarters of the way along. She was about five hundred feet in length.

'What do you think?' Ryan whispered to Keogh as they followed.

'That they weren't designed for heavy weather,' Keogh told him.

They went up a ladder to the wheelhouse, stopped on the landing below. Their escort opened a door and stood to one side.

'Here we are then.'

'Thank you, Mr Dolan.'

The man who sat behind the chart table wore a seagoing officer's coat, had hair down to his shoulders and a face that was so ravaged by drink and bad living that it was impossible to determine his age.

'Mr Ryan, here we are again.' He stood up and extended his hand. 'And who might this gorgeous young lady be?'

'My niece, Captain Tully. You might well remember that. This is my associate, Martin Keogh.'

'Mr Keogh.' Tully shook his hand enthusiastically. 'A real pleasure.'

'I'm sure it is,' Keogh told him.

'To business then,' Tully said.

Ryan opened the briefcase he was holding and took out a folded chart. 'There is your destination. Marsh End, south of Ravenglass on the Cumbrian coast. You have two days. Can you manage that?'

Tully unfolded the chart and examined it. 'No problem. What then?'

'I'll arrive by truck which we'll take across to Kilalla on the coast of County Down.' He took out another chart. 'There's a disused quarry pier there. We put the truck on shore and you sail away.'

'We do indeed, Mr Ryan. There is, of course, the small matter of recompense.'

Ryan took a large envelope from the briefcase and passed it across. 'Fifty thousand pounds there. Another fifty on the termination of the contract at Kilalla. Satisfactory?'

'Oh, very, Mr Ryan, I can assure you of that.'

'Excellent, then we'll see you on Friday morning at Marsh End.'

'No problem,' Tully said. 'We won't let you down.'

'Good. We'll be off then.'

As they walked along the waterfront Kathleen Ryan said, 'I didn't like anything about that bowser.'

'You aren't expected to.' Ryan turned to Keogh. 'What about you?'

'He'll cut your throat if he thinks there's a pound in it.'

'Which is why I have you along, so let's get back,' and Ryan walked to the corner and waved to a taxi.

The man who had greeted them at the gangway was Dolan. When he went back into the chartroom he found Tully examining the charts Ryan had given him.

'What do you think?'

'It's big,' Tully said. 'Fifty thousand now and another fifty when we hit the Ulster coast. Whatever is in that truck must be worth more.'

'So?'

'The number he gave me to contact him. It's a pub in Kilburn called the William & Mary, I think I'll go up there and have a nose around.' He folded the charts. 'You look after things here.' He moved to the door and turned. 'This could be a big pay day, Mick.'

'Well I'm with you on that,' Dolan said. 'Whatever it takes.'

'Good man,' Tully said and went out.

The saloon bar of the William & Mary was packed, men standing shoulder-to-shoulder at the bar as they drank. It was a cheerful enough scene and very noisy as Tully peered in through one of the windows.

He decided to take his chances round the back and followed a narrow alley that brought him to a high wall, a gate opening into a yard. There was a chink of light showing at a window, curtains partly drawn. He approached cautiously and peered inside.

Ryan, Bell and Kathleen sat at a table, a map unfolded before them. Keogh stood by the fire. Ryan laughed as Bell said something to him, but Tully couldn't hear what it was. It was then that he noticed the back door in the shadows. He tried the handle gingerly and the door opened to his touch.

He found himself in a narrow corridor. There was no light on and he groped his way forward, aware of coats hanging from a peg rack. At that moment a door opened, light flooding out, and Bell appeared. Tully froze, trying to bury himself in the hanging coats and Bell called, 'I'll only be a minute.'

He went down the corridor, opened a door and went inside. A few moments later there was the sound of a toilet flushing. He returned, went into the back room and closed the door. Tully went forward and put his ear to the door and was instantly aware of everything being said inside.

'Right, then, cards on the table,' Ryan said. 'It's time you knew what the rest of us do, Martin.'

'I'm all in favour of that,' Keogh told him.

'I put this job together a year or so ago. Hugh here helped with the planning of the English end of things. Unfortunately the Army Council turned it down flat, thought the whole thing too risky.'

'Bunch of old women,' Bell said.

'So what's it all about?' Keogh demanded. 'What's on the meat transporter?'

It was Kathleen who answered. 'Gold, Martin. Gold bullion. Fifty million pounds.'

'God save us,' Keogh managed to look astonished. 'And why would it be transported in such a way?'

'Let me explain,' Ryan said. 'Bullion used to be landed at London Docks on the Thames, but over the past twenty-five years the waterfront has been in decline. Shippers prefer Amsterdam. However bullion deliveries were rerouted to Glasgow.'

'How long has this been going on?'

'Five years. Ever since they built a new smelter at Barrow-in-Furness. See it there on the map right at the bottom of the Lake District? Mainly ship-building there. The latest atomic submarine came out of their yards.'

'So what's the smelter got to do with things?'

'They melt the gold down and re-process it into smaller ingots. The banks prefer it that way. Gold is heavy stuff.'

'I see,' Keogh said.

Ryan continued. 'The transporter travels from Glasgow to Carlisle then cuts across to Maryport on the coast and follows the coast road down to Barrow.'

'And we hit it somewhere on that road?'

'Exactly. This coming Friday.'

'But how do we stop it and, what's more to the point, how do we get in?'

It was Bell who answered. 'It's no ordinary truck. There's a driver and two armed security guards in the cabin behind him. The truck looks standard, but it's reinforced in every possible way and there's a battery of electronic security devices and a first class radio system.'

'And how do you handle that?' Keogh asked.

Bell opened a drawer in the table and took out a black hand-held computer with several rows of buttons and a read-out screen.

'I know this looks as if you use it to turn your television on and off, but it's a bit of pure genius called a Howler. You see, privileged information again, we know the code for the security system of the truck. The Howler has already selected it. You press the red button three times and the entire security system in the truck, electronic door locks, radio, the lot, are neutralized. That means the doors are open.'

'And where in the hell did you get that?' Keogh asked.

'Oh, a young electronic whiz kid at Queen's University in Belfast who is sympathetic to our cause.'

Keogh nodded slowly. 'And the driver and the guards? What happens there?'

'A stun grenade should take care of them.' Ryan

looked bleak for a moment. 'Mind you, I'll kill them if I have to. This is serious business.'

Keogh nodded. 'All right, what happens after the heist?'

'We drive it to Marsh End where the *Irish Rose* will be waiting.' He smiled. 'We'll be well out to sea and on our way and the police running round in circles.'

There was a long silence while Keogh brooded. Finally he nodded. 'You know, you're right. It could work.'

Ryan laughed delightedly. 'Good man yourself, Martin. Let's have a drink on it.'

Bell got up, opened a cupboard and took out a bottle of Bushmills and three glasses and at that moment there was a crash in the yard outside as a trash can went over.

When Ryan suggested the drink, Tully decided it was time to go. He opened the back door, closed it softly behind him and started across the yard. It was then that he blundered into the trash can, dislodging the metal lid which clanged as it fell to the stone flagging. He carried on, got the gate open and ran along the alley. As he reached the far end Keogh emerged into the alley but by then it was too late as Tully crossed the busy main road and was lost in the evening crowd.

When Keogh returned, Bell had turned on the yard light and was standing at the back door with Ryan and the girl.

'Was there someone?' Ryan demanded.

'Oh, yes,' Keogh said. 'And you're not going to like it one little bit. I just caught a glimpse of him as he turned into the road. It looked remarkably like Tully to me.'

'The bastard was checking up on us,' Ryan said and led the way back into the parlour.

'So what do we do now?' Bell demanded. 'This blows everything.'

'No, I don't agree,' Keogh said. 'He wants to see the affair go through because he wants the rest of his money.'

'That makes sense.' Ryan nodded.

'I'd say he was simply sniffing around to find out more.'

'Which means he's a shifty swine,' Kathleen put in.

'Who now knows more than he did before, if he overheard our discussion.' Keogh pulled on his reefer coat.

'Where are you going?' Ryan demanded.

'Back to the *Irish Rose*.' Keogh took out his Walther and checked it. 'I'm going to do some sniffing around myself.'

'I'll come with you,' Ryan told him.

'No need, I can handle it.' Keogh smiled. 'After all, that's what you're paying me for.'

As he turned for the door, Kathleen Ryan said, 'Take care, Martin.'

'Ah, but I always do, girl dear.' He smiled and went out, there was the sound of the yard gate opening and closing and he was gone.

It was raining again as Keogh paid off the taxi and turned along Cable Wharfe. It was a place of shadows, a touch of fog in the air. He kept to those shadows by the old disused warehouses and paused when he was close to the gangway. There was no sign of life. He thought about it for a while then decided to take a chance and darted across to the stern of the ferry which at that point was lower than the wharf.

He dropped down to the deck, paused for a moment, then moved through the darkness to where the central section and the wheelhouse reared into the night. There was a light up there. Keogh went up an iron ladder to the landing below the wheelhouse, then approached, crouching. He could hear voices, smell cigarette smoke. They were all in there, Tully and his crew. Keogh stood, protected by a life raft, and listened.

He heard the man Dolan say, 'Gold? Are you kidding us, Frank?'

'No. I'm bloody not. The truck that we pick up at Marsh End will be loaded with the stuff. They're going to knock it off on its way to the smelters in Barrow-in-Furness.'

'But who are *they?*' Dolan demanded.

'Well, they're Irish, that's for certain. I'd have said IRA, but I don't think so.'

'Why not?'

'Two things. Our destination, Kilalla. That's Ulster, not the Republic. Another thing. The William & Mary in Kilburn. That's a Prod pub, not Catholic. I think they're probably the other side.'

'Loyalists?' Dolan asked.

'Same difference, as far as I'm concerned,' Tully told him. 'I couldn't care less which side they're on. All I'm interested in is that gold.'

There was a stirring amongst the crew. Dolan said, 'You mean we're going to knock it off?'

'Who knows?' Tully laughed. 'After all, lads, anything can happen at sea, but let's get moving. Prepare to cast off. We've only got two days to get up there.'

Keogh crouched behind the life raft as the crew emerged and descended to the deck. He stayed there thinking about it then stood up and moved to the wheelhouse door.

Tully, leaning over the table, was aware of a small wind that lifted the chart for the Cumbrian coast a little. He looked up and found Keogh leaning against the door lighting a cigarette.

'As they used to say in those old Agatha Christie plays, all is revealed. I was outside, old son, and I heard your little speech to that motley crew of yours.' Tully tried to open a drawer and Keogh's hand came out of his pocket holding the Walther. 'Don't be stupid.'

Tully glowered at him. 'What do you want?'

'Well, I know you were at the William & Mary. By rights I should put a bullet between your eyes, but I'll settle for the fifty thousand pounds Ryan gave you earlier.'

'You can go to hell.'

Keogh raised the Walther and fired. There was the usual dull cough and the lobe of Tully's right ear disintegrated. He cried out sharply and clutched at the ear, blood spurting.

'That was for starters,' Keogh said. 'Come on, the envelope.'

Tully got the drawer open with his free hand, took out the envelope and tossed it over. Keogh put it in his pocket. Tully took a handkerchief from his pocket and held it to his ear.

'My God, look what you've done.'

'So what's the difference?' Keogh said. 'You couldn't look worse than you do.'

'Fuck you.' Tully opened a cupboard one-handed, took out a bottle of Scotch and pulled the cork with his teeth. He took a long swallow. 'Now what?'

'Now nothing,' Keogh told him. 'I'll see you at Marsh End on Friday.'

Tully looked astonished. 'You mean it's still on?'

'Too late to get anyone else now,' Keogh told him. 'This is what I call an "I know that you know that I know" situation, so behave yourself and you'll get this envelope back plus the other fifty thousand pounds when we reach Kilalla.'

'Sod you!' Tully said.

'Yes, I know that,' Keogh told him, 'but you will be at Marsh End on Friday.'

'Yes, damn you, I will.'

'Good man yourself. Now you can escort me to the gangway and we'll say goodnight.'

The engines rumbled into life at that moment. Tully led the way out, negotiating the ladder with difficulty, blood streaming from his ear. Only Dolan and the German, Muller, were working on deck. Muller was casting off and Dolan was about to haul in the gangway. He looked up in astonishment.

'Here, what's going on?'

'What's going on is that you leave the gangway alone until I've gone down it,' Keogh said.

Dolan tried to rush him and Keogh swiped him across the face with the Walther. Dolan staggered back with a cry of pain and Keogh went down the gangway. He turned at the bottom and smiled up at Tully.

'To our next merry meeting at Marsh End.'

'Bastard!' Tully called.

Keogh laughed and walked away through the rain.

Jack Barry was sitting at the desk of his study when the portable phone went.

Keogh said, 'It's me.'

Barry said, 'Where are you?'

'Wapping High Street in old London Town.'

'So what's happening?'

'You were right about the gold.'

'Is that a fact? Tell me.'

'It's complicated, but here goes,' and Keogh went through the whole business step-by-step.

When he was finished, Barry said, 'Christ, but it's the ruthless bastard you are. Will Tully play?'

'He will. A hundred thousand pound pay day. He isn't going to turn that down.'

'Right. Let's say everything works. What happens on board the *Irish Rose* once you put to sea? They'll try to take you.'

'Of course, but we'll be prepared.'

'You, Ryan and his niece? God save us all.'

'Oh, He will, He will. What about the Kilalla end?'

'Oh, I think I can promise you an interesting reception. A considerable contribution to IRA funds. It could win us the war.'

'Just think of that,' Keogh told him, 'and it's only taken seven hundred years.'

Barry laughed. 'Go on, dark hero, get on with it and keep in touch,' and he switched off his phone.

In the parlour at the William & Mary, Ryan and Kathleen sat at the table and listened to what Keogh had to say. Keogh helped himself to a Bushmills on the side.

Bell said, 'You shot him?'

'Only a little.' Keogh sipped a little Bushmills. 'The lobe of his right ear.'

Kathleen's face was infused with excitement. 'That taught the bastard a lesson.'

Ryan said, 'You think he'll still come?'

'Of course he will. He wants his hundred thousand pounds.'

'But he'll try for more on the run to Ulster?'

'Yes, well we know that so we'll just have to be prepared, won't we?'

'I suppose so.' Ryan took a deep breath. 'We'll catch the Glasgow Express in the morning. We'll leave at Carnforth and take the local train to Barrow.'

'Then what?'

'We'll be met,' Ryan told him. 'Something else I didn't tell you. I have a cousin who runs a sheep farm in the Lake District not far from Ravenglass. But enough of that now. I'm for bed. We'll need an early start.'

As the *Irish Rose* moved down the Thames, Tully stood at the wheel, his head disembodied in the light of the binnacle. His right ear was covered by a taped bandage. The door of the wheelhouse opened and Dolan entered with a mug in one hand. He put it down by the wheel.

'Tea,' he said. 'Are you OK?'

'I'm fine,' Tully told him.

'So what about that little bastard?'

'Oh, when the right time comes I'm going to cut his balls off.' Tully reached for the mug and drank some tea. 'There's an old Sinn Fein saying: Our day will come. Well mine certainly will where Keogh's concerned.'

He swung the wheel and increased power.

3

The Glasgow Express wasn't particularly busy. Keogh sat opposite Kathleen at a corner table. Ryan took the one opposite. Almost immediately he opened his briefcase and took out a file. He started to work his way through it, reading glasses perched on the end of his nose.

The girl took the copy of *The Midnight Court* from her carrying bag and an Irish dictionary which she put on one side. A strange one, Keogh thought, a strange one indeed. He sat there gazing out of the window wondering what she would say, what her reaction would be if she knew he was everything she hated. A Roman Catholic and an IRA enforcer. God, but the fat would be in the fire the day that got out.

About an hour out of London an attendant appeared pushing a trolley with tea, coffee, sandwiches and newspapers. Ryan stopped working and took a coffee. The girl asked for tea and so did Keogh. He also bought *The Times* and the *Daily Mail* and spent the next hour catching up on the news.

There wasn't much on the Irish situation. A bomb in Derry which had taken out six shops in one street, a tit-for-tat killing of two Catholics on the Falls Road, retaliation for the shooting of a Protestant in the Shankill and an Army Air Corps helicopter flying in to the command post at Crossmaglen had come under machine-gun fire. Just another day, they'd say in Ulster.

And then, half-way through *The Times*, he came to an article entitled HOW LONG, OH LORD, HOW LONG? It was written by a retired Member of Parliament, once a Minister at the Northern Ireland Office, who not unreasonably felt that sixteen years of bloody war in Ireland was enough. His preferred solution was an independent Ulster as a member of the British Commonwealth. Incredible how naive on the subject even politicians could be.

Keogh closed the paper, lit a cigarette and sat back, watching the girl. To his amusement he saw that she frequently consulted the dictionary. She glanced up and saw him smile.

She frowned. 'What's so funny?'

'Not much. You just seem to be having some difficulty with that.'

'It's not easy. I only started learning three months

ago. There's a phrase here that's damned difficult to work out.'

Keogh, a fluent Irish speaker, could have helped, but to disclose the fact would have been a serious error. People who spoke Irish were Catholics and Nationalists, it was as simple as that.

Ryan had finished the file, put it back in his briefcase and leaned back in the corner, closing his eyes.

'He seems tired,' Keogh observed.

'He does too much, almost burns himself out. He's a believer, you see. Our cause is everything to him. Meat and drink.'

'You too, I think.'

'You have to have something to believe in in this life.'

'In your case, the death of your family gave you that?'

'The murder of my family, Martin, the murder.'

There was no answer to that, could never be. Her face was white and intense, eyes filled with rage.

Keogh said, 'Peace, girl dear, peace. Go on, read your book,' and he picked up the *Daily Mail* and started on that.

Another half hour and the attendant returned. They had more tea, and ham sandwiches. Ryan was still asleep.

'We'll leave him be,' the girl said.

They ate in companionable silence. When they were finished Keogh lit another cigarette. 'Sixteen, Kate, and the whole of life ahead of you. And what would you like to do with it if peace ever comes to Ireland?'

'Oh, I know that well enough. I always wanted to be a nurse, ever since my time in hospital after the bomb. I was at the Royal Victoria for three months. The nurses were great.'

'Nursing, is it? Well, for that you need to pass your exams and you not even at school.'

She laughed that distinctive harsh laugh of hers. 'You couldn't be more wrong, mister. Most people do their ordinary level exams at sixteen. I did mine at fourteen. Most people do the advanced levels at eighteen. I did mine four months ago in English Literature, French and Spanish. I have a thing for languages, you see.' There was a kind of bravado in her voice. 'I'm qualified to go to university if I'm so minded and I'm only sixteen.'

'And are you?'

She shrugged. 'I've more important things to do. For the moment, our struggle is all that matters. Now shut up, Martin, and let me get on with my book,' and she returned to *The Midnight Court*.

*　　*　　*

They got off the train at Carnforth. It was desolate enough, hardly anyone about, rain drifting across the platform.

Ryan checked his watch. 'There's a local train to Barrow-in-Furness leaving in forty minutes. We'll get a cup of tea. I need to talk to you both.'

The café was deserted, only an ageing woman serving behind the bar. Kathleen Ryan went and got the tea and brought it back on a tray.

'I mind the time when this station was open for business twenty-four hours,' Ryan said. 'Steam engines thundering through one after another.' He shook his head. 'Everything changes.'

'You know the area well?' Keogh asked.

'Oh, yes, I've visited the Lake District a number of times over the years. I was up this way only four weeks ago.'

His niece said in genuine surprise, 'I didn't know that, Uncle Michael.'

'You thought I'd gone to Dublin,' Ryan said. 'Well I didn't. I was up here arranging things and there's a lot more you don't know and now is the time for the telling.'

'Go on,' Keogh told him.

Ryan produced the Ordnance Survey map of the area which they had consulted in London and unfolded it.

'There's Ravenglass on the coast. A bit of a

winding road from Barrow to get there. Maybe thirty-five miles. Marsh End is about five miles south of Ravenglass.'

'So?' Keogh said.

'See here, to one side of Ravenglass, the valley running up into the mountains? Eskdale, it's called. I've got what you might call friends there.'

'But you never told me that,' Kathleen Ryan said in astonishment.

'I'm telling you now, am I not? Now, this is the way of it. My own cousin, Colin Power, had an English wife, a farmer's daughter from Eskdale. Colin was a tenant farmer in County Down, but when her parents died, the farm in Eskdale was left to his wife, Mary.'

'So they moved over?'

'Exactly. This was twenty years ago. They brought with them a young boy, Colin's nephew, Benny. He had brain damage from birth. His parents wanted to put him in a home, but Mary, having no child of her own, took him on and raised him.'

'And they're up there now in Eskdale?' Kathleen demanded.

'Right at the head of the valley. A remote, desolate place. Folly's End, it's called, and that's an apt name for it. Too much rain, too much wind. The sheep don't thrive.' Ryan shrugged. 'It was too much for Colin. He died of a heart attack five years ago. Only Mary and Benny to run the place.'

'A lot of work for two people, I would have thought,' Keogh said.

Ryan laughed out loud. 'Just wait till you see Benny.' At that moment the local train pulled in at the platform and he glanced through the window. 'That's us. Let's get moving,' and he stood up and led the way out.

There were only a handful of passengers getting off the train at Barrow-in-Furness. They went through the ticket barrier, passed into the concourse and stood outside.

A voice called, 'Uncle Michael, it's me,' the words heavy and slurred.

There was an old Land Rover parked on the other side and the man standing beside it was quite extraordinary. He was at least six feet four in height and built like an ox with enormous shoulders. He wore a tweed cap and a shabby tweed suit with patches on the elbows. He rushed forward eagerly, a childlike expression on his fleshy face.

'It's me, Uncle Michael,' he said again.

Michael gave him a brief hug. 'Good man yourself, Benny. Is your aunt well?'

'Very well. Looking forward to seeing you.'

The words came out with difficulty, slow and measured.

Ryan said, 'My niece, Kathleen. You and she will be second cousins.'

Benny pulled off his cap revealing a shock of untidy yellowing hair. He nodded, beaming with pleasure. 'Kathleen.'

She reached up and kissed his cheek. 'It's good to meet you.'

He was overcome, nodding eagerly and Ryan introduced Keogh who held out his hand. Benny's grasp was so strong that Keogh grimaced with pain.

'Easy, son – easy does it.' He turned to Ryan. 'I see what you mean about running the farm. This lad must be up to the work of ten men.'

'At least,' Ryan said. 'Anyway, let's get going.'

Benny took Kathleen's suitcase and Ryan's and raced ahead to the Land Rover. Ryan said to Keogh and Kathleen, 'He could beat five men in any bar room brawl but in the heart of him he's a child. Mind that well and give him time when he speaks. Sometimes he has difficulty getting the words out.'

Benny put the luggage in the back and Keogh slung his duffel in. Benny ran round to open the front passenger door. He pulled off his cap and nodded eagerly again to Kathleen.

'In you go, Kate,' Keogh told her. 'Make the big fella's day. We'll sit behind.'

They all got in and Benny ran round and climbed behind the wheel. He started the engine and Ryan said, 'A great driver, this lad, make no mistake.' He patted Benny on the shoulder. 'Away we go, Benny. Is the truck all right?'

Benny nodded. 'Oh, yes.'

He turned into the main road and Ryan's niece said, 'What truck would that be?'

'Later girl, later. Just sit back and admire the scenery. Some of the best in England.'

When they reached the coast road it started to rain. Ryan said, 'It does that a lot up here. I suppose it's the mountains.'

They lifted up on the right, a spectacular sight, the peaks covered by low cloud. On the left the sea was angry, rolling in fast, whitecaps everywhere, a heavy sea mist following.

'The Isle of Man out there and then dear old Ireland,' Ryan told them.

Keogh said, 'I don't know whether you've had a forward weather forecast for Friday, but one thing's for sure. If it's rough weather that Siemens ferry is in for one hell of a ride.'

'We'll just have to see, won't we?' Ryan told him.

About forty-five minutes out of Barrow they came to an area where there were marshes on their left stretching out to sea, vanishing into the mist.

There was a sign up ahead and Ryan touched Benny on the shoulder.

The big man slowed down and Ryan said, 'Marsh End. Let's take a quick look, Benny.'

Benny turned down a track and drove slowly along a causeway through a landscape of total desolation, reeds marching into the mist. There was an old cottage to the right and then a jetty about one hundred yards long stretching out into the sea. Benny cut the engine.

'So that's it?' Keogh said.

'That's it.' Ryan nodded. 'Only something like the Siemens with its shallow draught could get in.'

'You can say that again. When the tide's out I'd say it's nothing but marsh and mud flats.'

Ryan tapped Benny on the shoulder. 'Off we go, Benny,' and the big man nodded obediently and reversed.

Towards the upper end of Eskdale Valley, mountains rearing before them, Benny turned into a broad track and dropped down into a low gear. There were grey stone walls on either hand, sheep huddled together in the rain.

'A desolate sort of place,' Keogh said.

Ryan nodded. 'A hard way to make a living.'

They came to a wooden signpost that bore the

legend Folly's End. 'And that just about sums it up,' Ryan observed.

A moment later and they came to farm gates wide open and beyond it the farm, two large barns, the farmhouse itself, all built in weathered grey stone. Benny turned off the engine and got out. As they followed the front door opened and a black and white sheepdog bounded out. A moment later a woman appeared. She wore a heavy knitted sweater, men's trousers and green Wellington boots. Her hair was iron grey, the face strangely young looking. Ryan went forward as she held her arms open. They embraced warmly and he turned.

'Here you are then, my cousin, Mary Power.'

The beamed kitchen had a stone-flagged floor, a wood fire burning in an open hearth. She served them herself, ladling lamb and potato stew from a large pot, moving round the table, then sat at the end.

'It's good to see you, girl,' she said to Kathleen. 'When you reach my age relatives are hard to come by.'

'And it's good to meet you,' Kathleen told her.

'And you, Mr Keogh, what would your speciality be?' Mary Power asked.

'Well, I like to think I can turn my hand to most

things.' Keogh spooned some stew to his mouth and smiled. 'But I'll never be the cook you are.'

Ryan pushed his plate away. Mary Power said, 'More?'

He shook his head. 'Tea would be fine.'

She got up and started to clear the plates and Kathleen helped her. Keogh said, 'Could we all know where we stand here?'

'You mean where Mary stands?' Ryan said. 'Simple. She's backing me to the hilt on this. If things go well, she gets a hundred thousand pounds. That means she can kiss this place goodbye and go back to County Down.'

She showed no response at all, simply took plates to the sink then reached for the kettle and made tea. 'Everything's in order. The truck is in the back barn. I've aired the cottage at Marsh End and there's a fire in the stove. Somebody will have to stay there.'

Ryan nodded and accepted a mug of strong tea. 'Perhaps Kathleen could stay with you and Martin and myself could make out at the cottage.'

'Fine.' She opened a tin box and took out a cake. 'Try this. I made it myself,' and she reached for a knife and cut it into slices.

There was a motorcycle on its stand just inside the barn, a black leather biker's jacket draped across it, and there was a helmet. Keogh recognized it at once. 'Heh, where did you get this beauty, Benny, a Montesa dirt bike?'

'You know this model?' Ryan asked.

'Of course. Spanish. They'll do half a mile an hour over very rough ground if you want them to.'

'And is that good?' Kathleen asked.

'It is if you're a shepherd operating in hill country,' Keogh told her. 'These things will go anywhere.' He turned to Ryan. 'You bought this for Benny?'

'Not really. A bit small for him. I thought it might suit our circumstances. I'll explain later.' He said to Mary, 'Let's have a look at the truck.'

She turned to Benny. 'Show us, Benny.'

He nodded eagerly, almost ran to the back of the barn, tossed some bales of hay to one side then felt for a hidden catch. The wooden wall swung open. Inside in an extension of the barn stood a large truck painted green and white.

The legend on the side of the truck read SHELBY MEAT IMPORTERS. Keogh said, 'Is this what I think it is?'

'An exact replica of the truck we're going to heist.'

'So what's the point?'

'A decoy, that's all. Benny will dump this down

65

on the coast road, all doors locked and so on. That should hold the police up nicely while they try to get inside. It'll give us extra time, if we need it, to get away with the real McCoy.'

'Very ingenious. And Benny can handle this?'

'Benny can handle anything with an engine, like you wouldn't believe. Benny should be a Formula One driver only he's too big.' Benny nodded delightedly.

'Right, let's go back inside and have a cup of tea and then Benny can take us to the front line, so to speak.'

The coast road was down below, a secondary road joining it at the side of a wood. The Land Rover pulled in and Ryan got out with Keogh and Kathleen and Benny followed.

'So this is it?' Keogh asked.

'That's right,' Ryan told him. 'Four o'clock, Friday afternoon, give or take fifteen minutes, and the transporter reaches this junction. Take my word for it, all carefully checked.'

'There's one thing I don't understand,' Keogh said. 'It's all right saying the Howler takes out the truck's security system, but how do you get the damn thing to stop in the first place?'

'A good point, but that's where Kathleen comes

in.' Ryan put an arm around her. 'I'll explain when we get back.'

The second barn was filled with farm machinery. There was also an old Ford van.

Ryan said, 'Now if you were driving along a country road and you saw that van burning and a young girl lying in the road, blood on her face, would you stop?'

'I'd have to say I would,' Keogh said.

'And so will they.' Ryan put an arm around Kathleen. 'A chance to earn your Oscar, girl.'

'I won't let you down.'

'I know you won't. Now let's go in and we'll take it step-by-step.'

'As I told you, the transporter reaches the junction at approximately four o'clock on Friday.'

They were all there in the kitchen. Mary and Kathleen at the table with Ryan, Benny at the door and Keogh by the fire.

Ryan said, 'Kathleen and I will drive to the scene of the action in the Ford van. You follow on the Montesa. I've got a couple of two-way radios in the case. You'll have one with you. You'll carry on a couple of miles and wait for the transporter.

When you see it you call me. Use Eagle One as a call sign, I'll use Eagle Two.'

'What do I do then?'

'Overtake the truck and join us. We'll set fire to the Ford and Kathleen lies down in the road and does her thing. I've some of that false blood actors use. She'll put it on her face.'

'Then they stop, or we hope they do, and you use the Howler to screw up the transporter's whole security system.'

'They'll be cut off from the world.'

'And if they fight?'

'No problem. I've got two AK rifles in my case, stun grenades and gas grenades. Even Semtex and pencil timers, but the doors will be unlocked anyway thanks to the Howler. Fifteen minutes after we leave the farm, Benny will drive the replica transporter down to the coast road where he'll dump it and clear off back to the farm on foot.'

'So, we neutralize the guards. What then?'

'You and Kathleen get the hell out of it on the Montesa, all the way to the jetty at Marsh End. I'll follow in the truck.'

'But why can't we all go together in the truck?' Keogh asked.

Ryan put an arm around Kathleen again. 'Because the truck's the vulnerable end of things. If anything goes sour that's where it will. I want her out of it. If things do go wrong then, as long as you and Kathleen get to the *Irish Rose*, there's always the chance of getting away.'

Kathleen said, 'What do you think, Martin?'

Keogh said, 'That it's going to be one hell of a Friday.'

In Kilburn, just before evening, Hugh Bell was sitting at the desk in his office when the door opened and the barman looked in.

'Some gentlemen to see you, sir.'

He was pulled to one side and a very large man in a navy blue raincoat entered, hands in pockets.

'So there you are, you old bastard.'

'Scully. What do you want?' and Bell knew fear.

'I've brought an old friend to see you.'

He stood to one side and a small man entered. His face was thin and wasted, he wore wire spectacles beneath an old trilby hat and a fawn raincoat.

'Mr Reid,' Bell said, his mouth dry.

'Nice to see you, Hugh.' The Belfast accent was very pronounced. 'A word would seem to be in order.'

'A word?' Bell said. 'I don't understand.'

'You don't?' Reid took off his hat and sat at the table. 'And me all the way from Belfast on behalf of the Army Council.'

'But what would they want with me?'

Reid took out an old silver case and selected a cigarette. Scully lit it for him with his lighter. 'Don't fence with me, Hugh. The other year Michael Ryan put up a hare-brained scheme to knock off some bullion truck up in the north-west of England. Don't deny it because you were involved. The Army Council turned it down.'

'That's true,' Bell said lamely. 'I do recall something of that.'

'Don't bullshit me, Hugh. Things get out as things always do and the whisper is that Michael is going ahead with this job on his own initiative right now.' He smiled thinly. 'It would seem obvious that you would be the man to know the truth of the matter.' He turned. 'Wouldn't you agree, Scully?'

'Oh, I would indeed, Mr Reid.' And Scully's smile was terrible.

He was in deep trouble, Bell knew that, but also knew that disclosing what he did know would do him no good at all. When Scully was brought in, it always meant a bad end to things. He was not known as the Shankill Butcher for nothing. Bell made his decision and took a deep breath.

'Sure and I can't deny I know something of the matter, Mr Reid. Michael did come to me the other day and discussed certain aspects.'

'The word I got was that a bullion truck would be heisted, is that true?'

'Well, it was in the original plan submitted to the Army Council.'

'And trans-shipped to somewhere in County Down. Do you know where?'

'God save us, but I don't.'

'Scully!' Reid said.

The big man took a Browning from his pocket and advanced. Bell said hurriedly, 'No need for that. I know where Ryan is staying here in London. I'll take you there now.'

Scully relaxed and Reid smiled. 'Very sensible, Hugh.'

'I'll get my coat.'

Bell went into the bedroom, picking up his jacket, put it on, then, quickly opening the opposite door, darted along the corridor, exited into the alley at the side of the pub and ran for the main road.

When the phone in the hall rang at Folly's End it was Mary Power who answered it. She came into the kitchen and said to Ryan, 'It's for you. Mr Bell.'

Ryan went out to the hall and picked up the phone. 'Yes, Hugh?'

'We're in trouble. Reid turned up from the Army Council with that sod Scully. They know, Michael, they've heard a whisper.'

'Did you tell them anything?'

'Did I hell. I ran for my life, but they knew the plan. I mean they would, wouldn't they? You submitted it to them originally.'

'The original plan was sketchy, Hugh. No mention of Folly's End or the precise target and, at that stage, the boat was only an idea. Did you tell them about the *Irish Rose*? Did you tell them we'd be putting in at Kilalla?'

'Of course not.'

'Good. Then we'll get on with it. Keep your head down and mind your back, Hugh. Go to ground for a while.'

After replacing the phone he stood there in the hall, lighting a cigarette and thinking about it. No point in alarming anyone. No point at all.

He returned to the kitchen. 'Hugh Bell. Nothing important.' He smiled at Keogh. 'I'll stay up here in case there are any more calls from Hugh. You'll have to spend the night at the cottage down at Marsh End on your own. No room here. Take the Ford van.'

'I'll be on my way then.' Keogh swallowed his tea and got up. 'I'll see you in the morning.'

Bell didn't know where he was going. He hesitated and started across Kilburn High Road. At that moment, an old Mercedes limousine turned out of a side-street, Scully at the wheel, Reid beside him.

'He's there,' Reid said, 'crossing the road. Get him.'

Scully gunned the motor. Bell, alarmed at the sound, turned. He tried to run and slipped in the rain. The Mercedes hit him at fifty miles an hour, bounced him into the gutter and moved on.

A woman screamed as a crowd converged. A uniformed Woman Police Officer pushed her way through, but by the time she knelt down beside Hugh Bell he was very dead indeed.

4

The morning was bleak, heavy clouds draped across the mountains. After breakfast, Ryan sat at the table drinking tea and thinking about things, wondering about Bell and Reid and that bastard Scully. On the other hand, there shouldn't be any danger from them as long as Bell kept out of their clutches. The original plan submitted to the Army Council had been simply the idea of the thing. That he knew of a truck somewhere in the north-west of England that carried bullion, that he thought it could be lifted and taken to Ulster by boat. So Reid was at a dead end without Bell.

He decided to take a chance, went out into the hall and phoned the William & Mary. The barman answered at once.

Ryan said, 'Ryan here, Angus. I was wanting a word with Hugh. Is he there?'

'He's dead, Mr Ryan. Killed in Kilburn High Road last night.'

'What happened?' Ryan said.

'He was knocked down crossing the road. Hit and run accident. The police found the car that did it abandoned a few streets away.'

'Have they traced who was in it?'

'The police sergeant who called earlier said it had been stolen in Hampstead a year ago. He thinks it must have been standing in some garage.'

'All very unfortunate,' Ryan said.

'Indeed it is, Mr Ryan. Will you be coming in?'

'No, I've got business to attend to.'

'Well if you let me know where you are and give me a phone number I'll keep you posted.'

It was enough. Ryan smiled softly. 'I'm away now, but just one more thing, Angus. Put Mr Reid on the phone.'

'Mr Reid? I don't understand,' Angus said.

'Stop arsing around and put him on.'

Reid, who had been standing beside Angus listening in, took the phone from him and shoved the barman across to Scully.

'Michael, old son. Don't you think it's time to be reasonable?'

'Was it you or Scully at the wheel? Not that it matters. When the time comes you're my meat.'

'You always did have a touch of the theatrical about you, Michael. So you intend to carry out that hare-brained scheme of yours?'

'Goodbye, Reid,' Michael Ryan said and put down the phone.

He opened the back door, lit a cigarette and stared into the rain thinking of Hugh Bell, good friend and comrade in arms for so many years. At least Scully hadn't had the chance to squeeze the truth out of him. There was some comfort in that.

The kitchen door opened and Kathleen looked out. 'There you are. Is everything all right?'

'Fine.'

'I thought I'd take Martin something to eat down at the cottage. Benny says he'll drive me.'

'That's fine. I want to go over the planning again so don't mind me.'

'I'll see you later then.'

She went back into the kitchen and Ryan stayed there, looking at the rain, thinking about Reid and Scully. They would have to go back home now, nothing else for it. There would be a confrontation eventually, had to be, but he would handle that when the time came.

He thought of Reid, the skull-like face and wire spectacles and his smile was terrible to see. 'You little bastard,' he said softly. 'You want it all yourself, don't you? Well I'll see you in hell before I allow that to happen.'

Keogh hadn't bothered with the bedroom of the small cottage at Marsh End, simply built up the fire and lay on the couch. He slept surprisingly well, got up at seven and put the kettle on.

He stood at the open door looking out at the rain and noticed the creek on his right hand. On impulse, he went back inside, stripped, found a towel in the small bathroom and ran naked across the yard.

He draped the towel over a bush and plunged into the creek, swimming strongly to the other side, passing into the reeds for a while, disturbing wildfowl and birds of every description which rose in clouds into the rain, calling angrily. The salt water was cold and invigorating.

'What a grand way to start the day,' he said softly as he emerged from the creek and reached for the towel.

He went back to the cottage, towelling himself vigorously, then he dressed and made a cup of tea. There was milk, bread, eggs and bacon in the larder. He stood there, sipping tea, wondering whether to leave. He looked out and saw the Land Rover with Benny and Kathleen.

*   *   *

In London at the William & Mary Reid and Scully were getting ready to leave. Their search of Bell's small office had yielded no clues.

Scully said, 'Nothing, Mr Reid; what do we do?'

'We go back to Belfast,' Reid said. 'Don't worry. Ryan has got to come home and no place for him to hide. We'll bide our time, but we'll get the bastard in the end.' He raised his voice. 'Angus, get in here.'

Angus stumbled through the door. 'Yes, Mr Reid.'

'Anything – anything at all you can tell me?'

'They took a train, that's all I know. I did hear the Glasgow Express mentioned.'

'Glasgow?' Scully said. 'Why would they go there?'

'Not Glasgow, you fool. That line goes up through the north-west. They'll get off somewhere.' He turned back to Angus. 'Anything else?'

'I don't think so.' Angus brightened. 'Oh, yes. The other week I overheard Mr Bell on the phone. It must have been a shipping office because he said he needed to charter a flat bottom ferry. The kind that could transport vehicles. After a while I heard him say the *Irish Rose*, Captain Tully and it's here in London.' Angus nodded. 'Yes, that's what he said.'

'Did you hear him mention that name again?'

Angus nodded. 'Just before they left I was in the stillroom checking bottles. I heard Ryan say to Mr Bell the *Irish Rose* is well on her way by now so we'll see her Friday morning.'

'But he didn't say where?'

'Definitely not.'

'All right,' Reid said. 'You've got my number. You phone me in Belfast if you hear anything.'

'Yes, sir.'

'Another thing. Keep your mouth shut. Give me any trouble and I'll send Scully to give you a seeing to. They'll find you in the Thames with your balls cut off.'

Reid went through the door and Angus, plainly terrified, stood back. Scully patted his face. 'You mind what Mr Reid says, there's a good boy,' and he went out.

Keogh ate the ham sandwiches Kathleen had brought, sitting at the end of the table, and she sat opposite, a mug of tea in her hands. Benny had gone back to the farm. Keogh finished it and lit a cigarette.

'How are you? How do you feel?'

'About the job, you mean?' She shrugged. 'I'll be fine. I've done things for Uncle Michael before; dangerous things. I can look after myself.'

'At your age you shouldn't have to.' He stood up. 'Come on. We'll get a breath of air.'

The mist drifted in, creating a strange and

sombre world. Reeds lifted on either side of the creek, water gurgled in the mud flats and as they walked along the broad track, birds lifted in protest on either hand.

'A strange place this,' Keogh observed.

'Yes, I'm not sure that I like it.' She frowned. 'It makes me feel uneasy.'

'I know what you mean.'

They reached the jetty and paused. The tide was out and iron girders were exposed, corroded by rust.

'I wonder what it was built for?' she said.

'God knows. Been here for years. Victorian from the look of it, but it still looks substantial enough.'

They walked along it, waves lapping around the girders below with a hollow booming sound. There was no rail at the end, only at the sides. Keogh peered over and noticed a jumble of granite blocks in the shallows.

'There's your answer,' he said. 'They must have shipped granite from here in the old days.'

'I see.'

She stood to one side, hands gripping the rail and looked out to sea, a strangely forlorn figure in her raincoat and beret.

Keogh leaned on the rail beside her. 'What do you want, Kate? What do you really want out of life?'

'God knows. All I've ever known was the

Troubles. I was born the year they started. All I know is the bombing and the killing. My family, friends, all gone.' Her face was bleak. 'Life is supposed to be for the living but all I see is death. Does that make any sense to you?'

'Perfect sense.' Keogh nodded. 'The terrible thing and you so young.'

She laughed. 'You're not exactly a greybeard yourself.'

'A very old thirty-two,' he said and he laughed.

Steps boomed along the jetty and they turned and saw Ryan coming towards them. 'God, what a lousy day,' he said.

Keogh pointed down into the water. 'It's to be hoped the tide is in at the right time tomorrow.'

'It will be, I've double-checked and it's a high one.' He took out a cigarette. 'One more thing. Hugh Bell is dead.'

'My God,' Kathleen said, 'how did that happen?'

So Ryan told them.

As they walked back along the jetty Keogh said, 'Reid can't touch you once you're back home with that transporter. All right, maybe your Army Council don't like people going their own way and acting without orders, but you'll be a bloody hero to them. They'll welcome you with open arms when they hear about the bullion.'

'Let's hope so. It's Reid I'm concerned about. Unless I miss my guess he'd like to have it all for himself.'

'Well fuck him,' Kathleen said angrily.

'You mind your tongue, girl,' Ryan told her.

'But if he doesn't know about Kilalla he isn't a threat,' Keogh said.

'Not when we land, but later,' Ryan shrugged. 'Who knows? Anyway, let's go back to the farm. I've got the Land Rover at the cottage.'

Mary Power provided a simple meal at one o'clock – vegetable soup, a cheese salad and the inevitable tea. Afterwards, as she cleared the table, she said to Benny, 'Mind your chores now. The sheep in the North meadow need seeing to.'

He nodded eagerly, got his cap and went out. A moment later Keogh, standing at the window, saw him cross the yard, a sack across his shoulders against the rain, the dog at his heels.

'He's a worker, that lad, I'll say that for him.'

'And in the mind still a child,' she said. 'He has to be told everything.'

Ryan finished his tea and stood up. 'I want to look at the ambush site again. We'll go in the Ford van, me and Kathleen. You follow on the Montesa. I'll give you one of the radios. When we get there you carry on up the road a mile or two then contact me. Use the call sign Eagle One, like I said. I'll be Eagle Two.'

'Fine by me,' Keogh told him.

As the Ford turned into the track towards the road leading down Eskdale, the girl was at the wheel. She glanced at her uncle.

'You know I'm not even licensed to do this. I'm under age.'

'And you handling a wheel to the manner born since you were fourteen. I mind that night when I took a bullet and crashed my car near Kilkelly.'

'And you phoned me from a roadside phone box and told me to get the boys to come and get you.'

'And came yourself, you little Devil and in a stolen car.'

'Well who showed me how to hot wire a stolen car?'

'I know and to my shame.' He laughed. 'The state I was in when you got there. Soaked to the skin in a stinking ditch, a bullet in the shoulder and then you crashed through that RUC road-block.'

'Great days, Uncle Michael.'

'Were they?' He lit a cigarette and opened the window. 'Sometimes I'm not so certain any more. I must be getting old.' He smiled suddenly. 'One thing I am sure of. You're a remarkable girl,

Kathleen, and you deserve better. Dammit, you could be an early entrant for the university.'

'Oh, hold your tongue,' she told him. 'I've more important things to do with my life.'

He sat there, thinking about it and a moment later they reached the junction and pulled in.

Keogh followed two hundred yards behind. He was wearing the biker's black leather jacket and the helmet. In spite of the rain, he was enjoying himself and the Montesa responded well.

The Ford van turned into a layby a few yards from the junction. Keogh raised a clenched fist in greeting and carried on.

Ryan sat in the van, the two-way radio in his hand, opened the door and looked out at the layby. 'This will do fine. After all, we don't want to block the road so effectively and this thing burning so that I can't get by in the transporter.'

At that moment Keogh's voice crackled over the radio, 'Eagle Two, this is Eagle One. Are you receiving me?'

'Loud and clear,' Ryan said. 'Anything to report?'

'Nothing but birds, the sea and this bloody rain. Can I go now?'

'I'll see you back at the farm. Over and out.'

Ryan switched off the radio and smiled at Kathleen. 'I've seen enough, girl, so back to Folly's End it is.'

Mary Power served the evening meal at seven o'clock – roast lamb, potatoes, carrots, cabbage. What fascinated Keogh was the vast amount of food Benny managed to put away.

'Jesus, but you'd think it was going to be his last meal on top of earth,' Keogh said.

'Well if he does the work of three men he's entitled to eat three men's food,' Kathleen put in.

'But not to forget his manners,' Mary Power said and she reached over and hit Benny over the knuckles with a wooden spoon. 'Now be a good boy and go and do the milking.'

He pulled on his cap, bread and cheese in one hand. 'Yes, aunty,' he mumbled and went out.

'Away into the parlour with you and I'll serve tea in there,' she told them.

Kathleen Ryan started to clear the plates and Keogh said firmly, 'My turn. Off you go with your uncle, there's a good girl.'

'Good girl yourself,' she said, but went anyway, following Ryan out.

'No Irishman I ever knew would volunteer to do the work of a woman so I take it you wanted to speak to me,' Mary Power said.

'Something like that.' Keogh stacked the plates for her. 'Are you happy with everything so far?'

'Happy?' She filled the sink with hot water and slid the plates in. 'I've forgotten what that word means. My husband and I came here full of hope, but this is only a place to die in. Subsistence farming of the worst kind. The land is a cruel master here.'

'I can see that.'

'So, when Michael came to me with word of this ploy he wanted to organize it was like a line thrown to a drowning man. If it comes off, Benny and I can go back to Ulster.'

'And if it doesn't?'

'We'll be trapped here forever. Michael made it clear there would be no police trouble whatever happens. Nothing to connect us with you lot.'

'And with luck that's the way it should stay.'

'Let's hope so. Politics mean nothing to me, but Michael is a good man and I trust him.'

Keogh left her there and went into the parlour. The girl sat in the window seat with her copy of *The Midnight Court*. Ryan was filling his pipe by the fire and lit it with a taper.

'A good woman that,' Keogh said. 'She's had a bad time.'

'The worst,' Ryan told him. 'But better times coming, God willing. We'd better check the weaponry in the barn after we've had our tea.'

'That suits me fine,' Keogh said.

'And me,' Kathleen put in. 'I'd like to try out that Colt pistol Mr Bell gave me.'

'Well, we'll see,' Ryan told her and at that moment Mary Power brought in a tray with the tea things.

Later in the dimly lit barn, Keogh and Ryan laid out the weaponry from Ryan's big case. There were the two AK assault rifles, spare clips, the stun and smoke grenades and the Semtex with its timing pencils. There was even a spare Walther in a leather ankle holster.

Keogh checked it out. 'Where did that come from?'

'Oh, I thought it might come in useful. I always liked the idea of an ace-in-the-hole,' Ryan said.

Keogh examined each AK separately, running his hands over the various parts expertly. He loaded one and passed it to Ryan. 'That latest silencer they have is pretty damn good. Try it.'

He took a wooden plank to the other end of the barn, propped it against the bales of hay and came back. Kathleen and Benny stood watching.

Ryan raised the AK and fired three single shots, there was the familiar crack the weapons always made in the silenced mode and three bullet holes appeared in the plank.

Keogh loaded the second AK and passed it across. 'And that one.'

Ryan pressed the trigger again and achieved the same result. He lowered the weapon and placed it on the trestle table. 'That's all right then.'

Kathleen came forward holding the Colt .25 automatic. 'Now me.'

Keogh said, 'It's all yours.'

She raised the Colt in both hands, took careful aim and fired, kicking up straw to one side of the plank.

'Try again,' Ryan told her.

The anger showed on her face, but she took aim again and achieved the same result.

She was furious now and Keogh said, 'Look, most people can't hit a barn door with a handgun so don't take it to heart. Come with me.' He stopped six or seven feet away from the plank. 'I wouldn't try it from any further away than this, if I were you. Just point and shoot.'

She tried again, clipping the plank with one shot, but her second was on target. 'Much better,' Keogh said. 'But holding the barrel against the target and pulling the trigger gets an even better result.'

He turned and walked back and Ryan was laughing. Even Benny was smiling and she was annoyed. 'Well, what about you, small man? Lots of advice for others, but little on display from yourself.'

Keogh turned, face calm and it was as if she

was only noticing for the first time how cold his eyes were. His hand went under his jacket at the rear, the Walther swung up, he fired six times, double-tapping splinters flew from the plank and it toppled over.

Benny had his hands over his ears in spite of the silencer and Kathleen Ryan's look of astonishment was something to see. Keogh didn't say a word, simply ejected the clip and re-filled it.

It was Michael Ryan who put it into words. 'Here endeth the lesson. Now let's turn in. It's going to be a hell of a day tomorrow.'

About forty miles south of Marsh End and some five miles off the coast, the *Irish Rose* was on course, rolling heavily in a troubled sea, winds four to five. In the wheelhouse the German, Muller, was at the wheel. Tully sat at the chart table, a cardboard box in front of him and the crew crowded round.

'Seven or eight handguns in there so take your pick. I want every man armed.'

Dolan took a Smith & Wesson .38. 'This will do me fine.'

The others helped themselves. Jock Grant, the engineer, said, 'What's our estimated time of arrival?'

'About eleven o'clock in the morning, but I can't be sure. I mean I don't know this Marsh End place so navigating could be awkward and we need to go in on the tide.'

'So what happens?' Dolan asked.

'I don't know, is the answer. When Bell first spoke to me he said we'd to be ready to leave late afternoon. He said the tide would be turning then and the timing was essential. We'll go in and wait. I mean, Ryan's bound to turn up to finalize things.'

'But he's bound to expect trouble after what happened,' Dolan persisted.

'Look, he doesn't have any choice. Once he has that truck, he's got to get it away. I'll tell him it was all a mistake, that I didn't mean any harm, that I was just making sure everything was on the level, that's all. What happens when we get to sea is another matter.'

Dolan said, 'But that little Keogh bastard is red hot. I mean, look what he did to your ear.'

'I'm not forgetting, but just remember, there's five of us and only Ryan and Keogh and the girl, and she's the key. If we can get our hands on her, Ryan will cave in soon enough. We'll have to make it up as we go along. We won't hit the Irish coast till dawn. I'll think of something, but to start with, everybody behaves.'

'I don't know,' Bert Fox sounded dubious. 'It could get nasty.'

Tully exploded in anger. 'The biggest pay day ever. Are you in or out? Make your minds up.'

It was Dolan who spoke for all of them. 'We're with you, Mr Tully, no question. Isn't that right, lads?'

There was a chorus of approval and Tully said, 'Get back to work.'

They all went, leaving Muller at the wheel. Tully went out on the bridge and stood there staring into the darkness. He touched his bandaged ear which still hurt like hell and it was Keogh he was thinking of and what he'd do to the little bastard when the time came.

5

The following morning when Keogh rose at seven the weather seemed to have deteriorated. There was heavy mist now over the marsh and when he opened the front door, the rain was relentless.

He made a cup of tea and shaved at the kitchen sink. There was a small portable radio on the windowsill. He switched it on and managed to find the early morning BBC news broadcast. He continued to shave and was wiping his face clean when the weather forecast came on and he listened intently. For the Irish Sea it was winds three to four with some sea fog and rain squalls.

Which could have been worse. He finished his tea and started to dress when there was the sound of a vehicle outside. He pulled on his boots and went to the window and saw Kathleen getting out of the Ford.

Keogh took his reefer down from a peg and

opened the door. 'Another dirty old morning,' he said cheerfully.

'We thought you'd like a proper breakfast. I've come to fetch you.'

'Now isn't that the kind thought?' He got into the passenger seat. 'First we'll take a run to the end of the jetty. I'd like to see how things are.'

'Fine by me.'

She drove along the broad track and moved on to the jetty, stopping just before the end. Keogh got out and went and peered over and she joined him.

'Only a few feet of water down there at the moment,' he said. 'The tide must be way out.'

'And that's bad?'

'They wouldn't get in. Still, it's supposed to start turning around about ten-thirty.' He looked out to sea. 'Pity about this damn mist. *Irish Rose* could be hove-to out there, but we can't see.' He smiled suddenly and squeezed her shoulder. 'Never mind, it's going to be fine. I have a good feeling about it. Now let's get that breakfast.'

And the *Irish Rose*, Muller at the wheel, was indeed hove-to about a mile out. Tully stood on the bridge with Dolan, peering into the mist.

'God damn this weather,' Dolan said. 'Can't see a thing.' He turned to Tully. 'Is it off?'

'Is it hell,' Tully said. 'If there's one thing I do well it's navigate, you know that. No, we wait for the turn of the tide and go in.' He turned fiercely. 'Nothing stops me getting my hands on that truck. Nothing,' and he went into the wheelhouse.

It was about half-ten and Keogh and Ryan were in the barn carefully checking the weapons again. Keogh picked up the Walther in the ankle holster.

'Can I take this? I've always liked an ace-in-the-hole myself.'

'Be my guest.'

'I'll put it on just before we leave,' and he put it in the pocket of his reefer.

'Everything else goes with us in the large case,' Ryan said. 'I'll bring it with me in the transporter.'

'Just in case we have to impress our friend Tully?'

'Exactly.'

Kathleen looked in. 'I'm going down to Marsh End in the Ford with Benny. He thinks he's lost some sheep and they might have wandered that way.'

'All right,' Ryan told her. 'But if there's any sign of the *Irish Rose* don't go near. Martin and I will be along in a wee while in the Land Rover.'

'I'll see you there,' she said and went out.

* * *

Kathleen left the Ford outside the cottage and she and Benny walked down the track into the marsh. It was still raining heavily and very misty. Suddenly there was the sound of a sheep baaing over on the right. Benny paused, a curiously intent look on his face and then he smiled and nodded and moved off at surprising speed considering his size and Kathleen went after him.

There were five sheep, standing in water up to their bellies, marooned from the look of it, as miserable as any living creature could be. Benny laughed, waded through the creek, picked one up and carried it across to dry land.

'Good,' he said.

Kathleen nodded. 'I'll walk down to the jetty,' and she turned away as he waded back to the other sheep.

She walked along the track, cocooned in mist and somewhere a dog barked and then the *Irish Rose* emerged as she went forward, moored stern first against the end of the jetty. The ramp wasn't down yet for the tide was still too low and a boy of perhaps twelve in a hooded anorak stood watching. He had a fishing rod in one hand and a small terrier at his heel.

The legend *Irish Rose* was plain across the stern and the boy moved forward to examine it. As he did so, Tully vaulted over the rail.

'Now then, you little bastard, what do you want?'

He grabbed the boy by the front of his anorak and shook him and Kathleen Ryan ran forward. 'You great bully, let him go.'

She struck out at Tully who released his grip in astonishment and the boy turned and ran away followed by the dog.

Tully grabbed for the girl's wrist. 'So it's you, is it?'

'Leave me be.'

She slapped his face and Dolan and Fox appeared at the stern, laughing. 'A hot one there, Captain. Needs sorting out. Are you up to it or do you need help?'

Tully was angry now as she slapped at him again. 'You little bitch. I'll teach you.'

He had both her wrists now and pulled her towards him and somewhere there was a terrible cry and Benny arrived on the run. He grabbed Tully from behind, pulling him away and threw him to the ground. Then he turned to the girl.

'You go now.'

Tully scrambled up and punched him in the back. Benny swung an arm backwards and knocked him down again with casual ease and Tully cried out, 'Dolan, get down here.'

Dolan and Fox vaulted the rail, Fox carrying

an iron bar. Benny took a fist in the face from Dolan with no apparent ill-effect, but punched him in the breastbone in return, knocking him on to his back.

Kathleen screamed, 'Stop it!'

Fox rushed in wielding his iron bar. Benny actually took the blow on his left arm, twisted Fox's wrist so that he dropped the bar. Then he gave him a slap back-handed that spun Fox around and sent him on his face.

'Benny, look out!' Kathleen called.

Tully had got to his feet and picked up the iron bar. He swung at Benny's skull, but the big man turned just in time so that it bounced off his shoulder. He tore the iron bar from Tully's hand then wrapped his great hands around his throat and actually lifted him off his feet.

There was a shot, flat in the rain and Keogh and Ryan ran out of the mist. 'Benny, no!' Ryan called out.

Benny paused, still holding Tully off the ground, then gently lowered him. Tully collapsed groaning, sitting on the ground, head on his knees.

'What brought this on?' Ryan asked.

She told him. When she was finished Keogh said, 'So some boy saw the boat. So what? It might mean something later, but not now.'

'I agree.' Ryan turned to Benny. 'Good lad, Benny, for looking after Kathleen. Back to the farm with you now.' He nodded to her. 'Go with him. We'll sort things here.'

'I'm sorry, Uncle Michael.'

'Not your fault, girl. It comes from having to deal with scum.'

She took Benny's hand and led him away. Tully, Dolan and Fox were on their feet, distinctly the worse for wear. Ryan stood looking at them.

'What a sorry bunch of shites you are. Go on, get on board before I forget myself and shoot the lot of ye.'

In the wheelhouse Tully sat at the chart table, the rest of the crew grouped around him. Ryan said, 'The only reason I'm talking at all is that I need you. We'll be back here between four-thirty and five with the transporter so you be ready for sea, do you understand?'

The crew shifted uncomfortably. It was Tully who said, 'Yes, we'll be ready to go.'

'You came snooping at the William & Mary,' Ryan said, 'so Mr Keogh informs me. Now why would you do that?'

'I was worried,' Tully said. 'I just wanted to make sure everything was kosher.'

'It's kosher enough for me to promise to blow your fucking head off if you try anything on the trip to Kilalla. Do you hear me?'

'Yes.'

'Good, we'll be off now and you be ready to leave at the appropriate time.'

He went down the ladder followed by Keogh and then crossed to the rail and dropped down to the jetty.

'What do you think?' Keogh asked.

'Oh, they'll try to cut our throats half-way across.'

'And doesn't that bother you?'

'Why should it? That's why I have you along, Keogh.'

Dolan said, 'Who was that bloody great ape, King Kong?'

'I don't know,' Tully replied and massaged his neck. 'I thought I was on the way out.'

'So what happens now?' Fox demanded.

'We wait. We do as we're told. Just remember one thing. When we put to sea King Kong won't be along for the ride. The boot will be on the other foot then.'

Just before three, Keogh stood beside the Montesa in the barn and pulled on the biker's leather jacket. He lifted the dark cord slacks he was wearing above the right ankle and strapped the Walther into place. He slipped the silenced version into the back of his waistband under the jacket and was ready to go.

Kathleen was wearing a denim jacket and jeans and she carried the Colt .25 in an inside pocket. Ryan inspected the inside of the weaponry case, then snapped it shut and put it in the back of the Ford.

He turned to them, embracing Mary Power, then took Benny's hand. 'We're going now, Benny, you understand?'

Benny nodded eagerly. 'Yes, Uncle Michael.'

You do as Aunty Mary tells you.'

'Yes, Uncle Michael.'

'You're a good lad.' Michael Ryan turned to Kathleen and Keogh. 'Time to go then, the moment of truth.'

And it was just like the test runs, Keogh told himself, trailing the Ford on the Montesa and the damn rain. Didn't it ever stop up here? The Ford pulled into the layby, he swerved to one side and halted. Ryan was round the back of the Ford, the door wide and opening the big case. He took out one of the AK assault rifles, stock folded, came across, unzipped Keogh's leather jacket and shoved it inside.

'On your way, boy.'

Keogh gunned the engine, reaching eighty in fifteen seconds, arriving at the junction in three minutes. He pulled in and waited.

When the green and white transporter with SHELBY MEAT IMPORTERS on the side drove by, so exactly the same as the replica, it had a dreamlike quality to it as if it was not really happening and he hurriedly switched on his radio.

'Eagle One to Eagle Two. Target on course.'

There was a pause and then a crackle. 'Eagle Two – message received. Come home.'

Keogh put the radio away, gunned his engine and went after the truck fast. For a few seconds he trailed it, then pulled out to overtake, one arm raised in salutation, went round a bend ahead and disappeared.

'Crazy bastard,' the transporter driver said to the two security guards sitting in the cabin behind him. They wore blue serge suits, for uniforms would have given the game away, but each man carried a Browning in a shoulder holster.

'Probably kill himself one of these days,' one of them said. 'Guys like that usually do.'

'Well that's his business,' his friend told him. 'So let's have a cup of coffee.' He opened a Thermos and somewhere up ahead there was the muffled sound of an explosion and smoke lifted into the air.

'Jesus, what's that?' the driver demanded and they went round the corner leading to the junction.

Keogh swerved into an open field gate, got off the motorcycle and pushed it up on its stand. The suitcase containing the weaponry was on the ground by the wall and he saw Kathleen at the side of the road smearing the false blood on her face as Ryan ran to the back of the Ford. A moment later there was a muffled explosion and flames flickered around the vehicle. A larger explosion followed as he ran and black smoke lifted into the sky.

The transporter came round the corner and skidded to a halt at the horrific scene. Keogh pulled out his AK and unfolded the stock, but it wasn't necessary. Ryan switched on the Howler and punched the buttons.

'The door,' he cried to Keogh. 'The door.'

Keogh ran to the off-side door, pulled on the handle and it opened to his touch. He was aware of the driver, the two behind, one already with a gun in his hand. Ryan lobbed in a stun grenade. It was enough. A moment later, he had the driver from behind the wheel, dazed and bewildered. Keogh pulled out the two security guards. They dragged them behind the field wall and secured them with the plastic handcuffs.

Kathleen was on her feet, wiping the blood

away. Ryan said, 'Good, you got your Oscar.' He ran to the back of the truck and opened the doors, revealing the containers inside.

'Would you look at that now? Keogh said.

'Would you, indeed.' Ryan picked up the suitcase with the weaponry and shoved it up into the cabin of the transporter. 'Go on, Martin, get the hell out of it.'

Keogh folded the AK and put it back inside his biker's jacket. 'Come on, girl,' he said to Kathleen.

He flung a leg across the motorcycle. She jumped onto the pillion behind him and put her arms around him. As they drove away, Ryan switched on the engine of the transporter and followed, leaving only the burning van hissing in the rain and the three men slowly regaining their senses behind the wall. It was almost half an hour later that a local farmer in his station wagon came upon the scene of destruction.

When Keogh and Kathleen on the Montesa reached Marsh End and turned along the track to the jetty, the *Irish Rose* already had the ramp down. Tully was waiting on deck with Dolan and Fox and Keogh ran the Montesa straight on board and braked to one side. Kathleen slid from the pillion and Keogh dismounted. He had the AK out in seconds and unfolded the stock.

'There's no need for that,' Tully said. 'Did it work?'

'Like a dream.'

'Then where is it? We've got to get out of here. I've got the engines turning over and a man on the wheel.'

'Take it easy,' Keogh said. 'He'll be here. Go and make sure everything's ready.'

Tully turned away reluctantly and Keogh smiled at Kathleen Ryan and took out a cigarette. 'We did it, Kate, we did it.'

She was incredibly excited. 'I know, I know, Martin, but where is Uncle Michael?'

'He's coming, girl dear. That transporter isn't as nippy as the Montesa.'

But it was another agonising twenty minutes before the green and white transporter appeared from the mist, came along the jetty and bounced on board. It rolled to a halt and braked and Ryan got out.

'I thought I'd had it. The damned engine died on me.'

Already Dolan and Bert Fox were hurriedly clamping the huge wheels to the deck.

Kathleen said, 'What happened?'

'There's an automatic choke system. It was jammed full on. Must have been the blast from the stun grenade. Once I'd got it in I managed to get going again.'

Tully called from the bridge. 'Can we go, for Christ's sake?'

Ryan waved. 'As soon as you like.'

The *Irish Rose* slipped out into the estuary and fled into the mist, leaving the land behind.

'We did it,' Ryan said.

'We certainly did.' Keogh offered him a cigarette. 'Only one matter of interest still to be resolved.'

'And what's that?' Ryan asked, accepting a light.

'Oh, exactly at what point on the way to Kilalla they intend to hit us.'

'Well, the best way of handling that is to impress them,' Ryan said. 'Get your AK out and I'll do the same. Conspicuous display at all times.'

'And I'm carrying too,' Kathleen said. 'I've got my Colt in my inside pocket.'

'For God's sake stay out of it, girl, and leave it to Martin and me.'

He got back in the cab, opened the case and took out the other AK. He got down again, held it against his thigh and moved to the rail. There were a couple of ship's boats on either side at the stern suspended in davits and an inflatable in yellow plastic with an outboard motor.

'Handy that for his illicit runs ashore,' Ryan observed.

'The outboard looks pretty good to me,' Keogh said. 'Close to brand new.'

'Probably stolen, if I know Tully.'

'So what do we do now?' Keogh asked.

'Give him time. He's got to work the ship. We'll wait till we're a few miles out to sea then we'll have words.'

He looked up at the wheelhouse and saw Tully looking down at them from the stern window. Ryan waved, grinning.

In the wheelhouse Muller was again at the wheel. Tully sat at the chart table, Dolan standing beside him. Grant and Fox were below in the engine room.

'You see what they're carrying?' Dolan demanded.

'Yes, AKs.'

'Those things could cut us to pieces.'

'I know. We've got to box clever. Hide your gun in the chart drawer, Muller's too, then go below and tell Fox and Grant to stow theirs somewhere in the engine room. I'll keep mine in my pocket.'

'But I don't understand.'

'Look, it's obvious he's leaving us to make our way out to sea. After a while, he'll be coming to see me and armed like that there's nothing we can do. They'll search the lot of us at gun point and won't find anything.'

'Except yours.'

'Which might make Ryan think that's all there is.' Dolan looked dubious and Tully pushed him. 'Go on, get moving. I've got a course to lay.'

Dolan went out and Muller said in his heavily accented English, 'So, we still go to Kilalla?'

'Well we can't exactly turn due south. Ryan's no fool. For the time being we'll simply make for the coast of County Down in a general way until we see what happens.'

'With guns such as they have it could be difficult.'

'You worry too much,' Tully said. 'It's going to work and I'm going to take that truck from them one way or another, I promise you.'

Ryan waited for an hour before making his move. 'Right,' he said, 'you stay up in the cab, Kathleen, nice and comfortable, while Martin and I go and sort out the bad guys.'

'I could die for a cup of tea.'

'Well if you look in the case, besides the weapons, you'll find a damn great Thermos flask, courtesy of Mary Power and there's an old cake tin in there too. No cake, just ham and cheese sandwiches.'

'Uncle Michael, you're the wonder of the world. You think of everything.'

'Not this time. Thank Mary Power.' He turned to Keogh. 'Here we go, Martin, moment of truth.'

Tully watched them coming, Ryan in the lead, and debated for a wild moment about trying to shoot him as he mounted the steel ladder to the bridge but hastily abandoned the idea as Keogh stood back, AK raised to cover Ryan. Ryan reached the bridge safely and stood outside the open door, covering Tully, Muller at the wheel and Dolan.

'Top of the morning,' Ryan said and raised his voice. 'Come away up, Martin.'

Keogh joined him a moment later. 'There you are, Tully, how's the ear?'

Tully glowered at him. 'It's been better.'

'I'm sorry to hear that.'

'Search them,' Ryan told him.

Keogh quickly ran a hand over Muller then Dolan. He found the Smith & Wesson revolver Tully had in his pocket.

'Very naughty,' Ryan said. 'I'm surprised at you.'

'I'm the captain,' Tully protested. 'What do you expect?'

'Oh, almost anything from you. Where are the other two?'

'Grant and Fox are in the engine room.'

'We'll pay them a visit and take another look at this pig boat on the way.'

'As you like.' Tully shrugged and went to the voice pipe and whistled. Fox replied and Tully said, 'Mr Ryan wants a look at the engine room. We're on our way down.'

'Good,' Ryan said. 'Let's get moving.' He nodded to Dolan. 'You too.'

From the deck below the wheelhouse a companion-way led to a narrow passage, door on either side. One of the doors had TOILET painted on it. Keogh opened it and found a stall lavatory, a washbasin and shower.

'Is this for the whole boat?'

'No, I have a separate one,' Tully said. 'It goes with my cabin. That's under the wheelhouse.'

'And these other doors?'

'Crew quarters.'

Keogh opened the doors and had a glimpse of untidy bunks and general disorder. 'What a stink. Doesn't anybody wash on this boat?'

Tully was enraged, but kept his mouth shut. Ryan said, 'So where's the engine room?'

'End of the passage.'

'Right, lead the way the both of you.'

Tully opened a door at the end and the throbbing of the engines became very pronounced. They went down a companionway and found themselves in the engine room itself, Grant and Fox oiling the pistons and other moving parts.

They paused in their work and Tully said, 'Is everything OK?'

'As much as it ever will be with this old bag of bones,' Grant told him.

Keogh said, 'Hands high, boys.'

Ryan raised his rifle and, sullenly, they did as they were told. Keogh retired, satisfied. 'Clean as a whistle.'

'Fine,' Ryan said. 'We'll go back then.'

6

The sea was building up as they went out on deck and the *Irish Rose* was already beginning to roll from side to side. Rain swept in, clearing the mist a little. They went back up to the wheelhouse, climbing the ladder one-by-one.

Tully sat down at the chart table. 'So, what now?'

'I've done a boat crossing from the Lake District coast to Ulster twice over the years,' Ryan told him.

'Is that a fact?'

'Yes, so I know where the Isle of Man is – halfway between the two and we pass south, skirting what they call the Calf of Man?'

'If you say so.'

'Oh, but I do and there it is on your top chart. I'd say we should be seeing the lighthouse there at midnight.'

'So what?'

'That should give us a landfall at Kilalla around three.'

'It depends on the weather.'

'And so it does, but keep on course. I have a marine compass in any case and I'd be very hurt if I discovered we weren't proceeding in a westerly direction.'

'All right,' Tully said sullenly. 'Now what happens?'

'Well, as there is nowhere else I'd particularly like to spend the night on this disgusting pig boat we'll use the cab of the truck. It even has a bunk behind the driver's seat.' He turned to Keogh. 'Give him your radio, Martin.'

Keogh took it from his pocket and put it on the chart table. 'There you go.'

'What's this?' Tully demanded.

'Two-way radio. I have one too so we can keep in touch, us down there and you up here. Another thing. You have one of your men standing on the deck down there where I can shoot him if anything untoward happens.'

'You bastard.'

'I always was, but I keep my word and I'm going to give you a chance to be sensible.' He took an envelope from his pocket and threw it down. 'That's the fifty thousand pounds Mr Keogh took from you.'

Tully was truly shocked. 'My God!'

'Count it when we're gone. It's all there.' Ryan smiled looking like the Devil himself. 'No bloodshed, no aggravation and you get another fifty thousand at Kilalla in a few hours. Think about it.' He nodded to Keogh. 'Let's go. You first, Martin. I'll mind your back and you cover me.'

They went down the ladder one after the other and Tully opened the envelope and examined the money. 'Damn him!' he said.

'What's he playing at?' Dolan asked.

'He's giving me a way out, isn't he? Play the game and settle for a hundred thousand.'

'And will you?'

'There's fifty million pounds in gold sitting out there, Dolan, fifty million.'

'All right,' Dolan said, 'but these are hard bastards.'

'Well so am I.'

Tully sat there frowning and examining the chart. Dolan said, 'Have you any ideas?'

'Not at the moment. If we don't pass the Calf of Man he'd know it. On top of that he's got a marine compass.' He shook his head. 'No, we'll have to stay on course and wait for our chance. There's bound to be one. Maybe in the early hours of the morning when we're closer to Ireland.'

Dolan nodded. 'They'll be tired then.'

'And seasick with any luck. I didn't tell the

bastard, but I checked the weather forecast and it's deteriorating. Winds gusting to seven around midnight and you know what this old tub is like in rough weather.'

'The original beast.'

The radio crackled and Keogh's voice sounded. 'As the song says, is that the captain of the ship?'

Tully pressed the answer button. 'What do you want?'

'A man on deck.'

'All right.' Tully turned to Dolan. 'Down you go, Mick, two hours then I'll have Muller relieve you and you'd better take an oilskin, you'll need it.' He smiled savagely. 'See, it's started to rain again.'

Dolan's shift being over it was Muller who stood by the ladder, clearly visible in the sickly yellow glow of the deck lights, a miserable looking figure as he tried to shelter from the rain under the lower canopy of the wheelhouse.

'Now isn't that the great sight!' Keogh demanded as he devoured one of Mary Power's ham sandwiches.

Kathleen laughed as she passed him a cup of tea. 'You're a terrible man, Martin.'

Ryan said, 'His bad luck he's on the wrong side. Here, I'll put the heater on for a while.'

A warm glow spread throughout the cabin within seconds. 'God, but that's nice,' Kathleen said.

Ryan took another sandwich. 'You'll be fine back there in the cabin. Nice and cosy on that bunk bed. You get your head down and get some sleep.'

'What about you and Martin?'

'Oh, we can snatch an hour or two just sitting here. We'll take it in turns.'

They finished eating and she put the rest of the sandwiches and the Thermos away and looked out into the darkness where the sea was angry, white-caps driving in, rolling the *Irish Rose* from one side to the other.

Kathleen clutched at Keogh's arm. 'Exciting, isn't it?' he said sardonically.

'Damn you, Martin, I'm bloody terrified and you know it.'

'It always gets worse before it gets better, that's the way of it,' he teased her.

She punched him in the shoulder. 'You can stop that.'

Ryan looked at his watch. 'Nine o'clock. Get on the bunk and try to sleep. You'll be better off.'

'Yes, well, first I want to go to the toilet.'

'The one thing we don't have,' he said.

'It's all right for you and Martin. You can stand at the side of the truck. I can't do that.'

'Dear God.' Ryan picked up the radio and called the wheelhouse. 'Tully, come in.'

'What do you want?' Tully demanded,

'My niece wants the toilet. Keogh is going to escort her and just to keep you in order he'll take Muller with him.'

'All right,' Tully said.

Keogh opened the door on his side and stepped down, his AK at the ready, the stock unfolded. The wind was much stronger now, driving in the rain as he approached Muller.

'The lady needs the toilet so you lead the way and watch yourself.'

Muller glared at him, but did as he was told, opening the door to the companionway and leading the way down. Keogh followed, the girl at his heels. He kept Muller covered while she went inside.

When she came out Keogh said to Muller, 'Go on, you first.'

Muller did as he was told sullenly and took up his station under the wheelhouse canopy whilst Keogh and Kathleen returned to the truck and climbed inside.

'Lie down now,' Ryan told her. 'There are blankets there. Try and sleep.'

She did as she was told and Keogh and her uncle sat there, looking out as rain streamed down the windscreen and the ship rolled.

'Better than a roller coaster this,' Ryan said.

'The Germans built them for inshore work,' Keogh told him. 'The bottom's almost flat.' He lit a cigarette. 'I've been thinking. Very convenient, Tully having the one pistol.'

'I know. I wouldn't believe that for one minute.'

'That ploy of yours, giving him the fifty thousand back. Will it work?'

'I'd like to think so, but I doubt it. He's a greedy animal, that one, but it was worth the try.'

'So what's your best guess?'

'Oh, he'll stay on course because I can check with my marine compass. I should imagine he'll wait till we're close to the Irish coast. The early hours would be best. They'll expect us to be tired so I suggest you get your head down for a while and I'll keep watch.'

And Keogh, with the soldier's habit ingrained of snatching an hour of sleep when he could, simply leaned back in his seat, closed his eyes and was asleep in the instant. His breathing deepened and Ryan watched him for a while. Hell on wheels, this one, and capable of anything, but who are you, Martin? he thought. Who are you really? He sat there, the AK in his lap, watching Muller, occasionally glancing up at the light in the wheelhouse, and waited.

* * *

Keogh came awake with a start, Ryan's hand on his shoulder. He checked his watch and saw that it was midnight. 'You should have wakened me, Michael. You need your sleep too.'

'Less than you do. I'm older. Will you look over there.'

Keogh saw the light at once, flickering out there in the darkness. 'Would that be the Calf of Man?'

'That's right and we're dead on course. I've checked with the compass.'

'So far so good then. I'll just step out for a moment. Call of nature.'

He opened the door and stepped down, the wind so strong that it bounced against him. It was Dolan on duty again and Keogh waved cheerfully.

'Try to smile, you miserable sod,' he called and relieved himself at the side of the truck.

He climbed back inside and Ryan said, 'Now me,' and got out on his side.

Tully, watching all this from the stern window of the wheelhouse, suddenly clenched his fists, excitement surging through him. 'That's it. Christ, that's it.' He turned to Muller. 'I'll take the wheel. Relieve Dolan. Tell him to get up here. Go on, it's important.'

Muller did as he was told and a few moments later Dolan came in, water streaming from his oilskins. 'What's up? I only did an hour.'

'I think I've got it,' Tully said. 'That girl is going to want to go to the toilet again, she's bound to.'

'So what?'

'Well try this for size. Keogh held Muller at gunpoint while she went in?'

'That's right.'

'What would happen if there was someone waiting in there with a shooter? Someone who'd bring her out with the barrel under her chin? What would Mr Bloody Keogh do; what could he do?'

'My God, it's a thought,' Dolan said.

'Yes, well you can't do it. They'll miss you if you're off the deck too long so get down to the engine room and get Fox. Grant will have to manage on his own. Tell Fox to get his shooter and go to that toilet now. He can sit there and wait.'

'How long for?'

'As long as it bloody well takes. Now get out of here,' and he hung on to the wheel as a sudden squall hit the *Irish Rose* from the north.

It was just after two, the wind very strong now and Ryan checked his watch. 'We must be close. Three o'clock was a fair arrival time.'

Kathleen came awake with a groan and sat up. 'Jesus, I feel awful. What time is it?' Ryan told her and she swung her legs to the floor. 'I'll have to go to the toilet again.'

'All right. Give me a minute.' He called Tully.

'What do you want?' Tully replied.

'My niece needs the toilet. We'll handle it the same as last time.'

'That's OK,' Tully replied then shaking with excitement he got the two guns from the chart-table drawer and passed one to Muller. 'When the right moment comes, put the wheel on the chain lock.'

'In this weather?' the German asked.

'It'll only be for a moment.' Tully whistled down the voice pipe and when Grant answered said, 'Jock, we're in business. Get your gun and wait at the top of the engine-room companionway. The girl's going to the toilet.'

'I'll be there,' Grant answered.

Tully punched the chart table with one fist. 'It'll work, it bloody well has to.'

Dolan went down the companionway and stood sullenly under the threat of Keogh's AK. 'I shan't be long,' Kathleen said.

Fox, hearing the voices, had moved into the shower, pulling the curtain closed. She went into the toilet cubicle and he waited, pouncing when she came out, twisting her left wrist behind her back and ramming the muzzle of his pistol into her neck.

'Now then, you bitch, get that door open.'

She cried out, 'Martin, watch yourself!' and Fox released her wrist, got the door open and pushed her out between Keogh and Dolan, his pistol still against her neck.

'Give that rifle to Dolan,' he ordered. 'Go on, do it!'

Kathleen screamed, 'Shoot them, Martin, the both of them. Don't mind me.'

'I'll kill her, I swear it!' Fox cried.

'No need. Just cool it.' Keogh handed the AK, butt first, to Dolan, who stepped back covering him with it, a look of unholy pleasure on his face.

'Now then, you bastard.'

The door to the engine-room companionway opened at the end of the passage and Grant stepped out, a revolver in his hand. 'I'm here, boys,' he called.

Fox lowered his pistol and turned to look at him and everything happened at once. Kathleen half-turned, her hand slipping inside her denim jacket. She found the Colt .25, pulled it out, rammed the muzzle in Fox's stomach and pulled the trigger twice. Keogh hitched his right trouser leg revealing the Walther in the ankle holster, dropped to his left knee, pulling the gun out in one fluid motion, his first bullet catching Dolan in the left shoulder. He dropped the AK, spinning round, and Keogh's second smashed his spine. Grant got off one wild shot. Keogh fired back, creasing his shoulder, and the Scotsman disappeared fast.

Keogh picked up the AK and put a hand on the girl's arm. 'Are you all right?'

'Fine.' She laughed shakily. 'I did what you told me and you were right. Hold it against them and you can't miss.'

'So let's get out of here.'

He got the door of the companionway open and called across to the truck. 'Michael, they tried to jump us.'

'Are you all right?' Ryan called, opening his door and sheltering behind it.

'Fine. Cover us. We're coming through.' He pushed Kathleen out. 'Keep behind my back, girl,' and he turned, looking up at the wheelhouse and fired a quick burst into the air when he saw a movement up there at the window.

Kathleen reached her uncle in safety. 'Get back into the rear cabin. You'll be safe there.' She did as she was told and he called to Keogh who was sheltering behind the passenger door. 'What happened?'

Keogh told him. 'So you were right after all.'

'I usually am. A bad habit.'

In the wheelhouse it was several minutes before Grant reached the bridge by a circuitous route involving the engine-room hatch. He was very

124

pale, eyes wild, blood staining his left shoulder. He pulled off his jacket, found a piece of engine-room rag and tried to bandage his shoulder.

'That little bitch shot Fox. She had a gun, then Keogh killed Dolan and had a go at me. What do we do now?'

'I don't damn well know, do I?' Tully answered.

He went to the stern window, killed the wheel-house light then opened the window, keeping in the shadows, and peered down. He saw the truck doors standing open like wings and realized Ryan and Keogh must be standing behind them. He took careful aim at Keogh's side, aiming below the door in the hope that he might get lucky and catch feet or ankles. He emptied his revolver, firing six times. The response was terrible, as both Ryan and Keogh fired a long burst back, dissolving the wheelhouse windows into a snowstorm of flying glass.

Tully and Grant went down on the floor fast, but Muller wasn't so lucky, several rounds catching him in the back. He fell, the wheel started to spin and Tully crawled to it and, half-crouching, pulled it round then secured the wheel with the chain lock.

'That'll hold for a while.'

'But how long for and what do we bloody do?' Grant asked.

'I don't know, do I?'

* * *

125

It was ten minutes later that the radio crackled and Ryan said, 'You there, Tully?'

'Yes, there's still three of us,' Tully lied. 'Muller, Grant and me.'

'Are you going to be sensible?'

'Why should I be? You need me more than I need you, Ryan.' The *Irish Rose* rolled heavily as the wind howled in. 'Unless you can handle a ship, and I don't think so, especially not in weather like this.'

'So what do you suggest?'

'I don't know. Only one thing's certain. You can't touch us up here if we keep our heads down and we can't get at you. I'd call that stalemate.'

'So, what do you suggest?'

'I don't know. I'll think about it.'

'He's right,' Keogh called across to him. 'No way of storming the wheelhouse. They'd have every advantage.'

'And even if we did and by some miracle succeeded in knocking them off, where would be the advantage?' Ryan said. 'Could we sail this thing on our own, you and me, Martin? I doubt it.'

'Keep pointing it at Ireland is about the best you could do as long as the engines kept going.'

'With no one to handle them?' Ryan shook his head. 'I don't think so.'

* * *

Nothing happened for some fifteen minutes and then Tully's voice crackled over the radio.

'Ryan, are you there?'

'What do you want?'

'We're three miles off the Down coast.'

'Still aiming for Kilalla? You could still land us there, take the other fifty thousand and go your way and no harm done.'

'I don't believe you. You'd shoot me like a dog after what's happened. It's not on and Kilalla is miles away north of here anyway.'

'So what do you suggest?'

'I can turn this tub round and put out to sea again any time I want.'

'And we sail on forever like *The Flying Dutchman*, you up there in the wheelhouse and us down here?' Ryan said. 'And where would that get us?'

'Nowhere, from your point of view.' Tully went off the air again.

'It's no good,' Keogh said. 'I'll have to try and rush the ladder and you can give me covering fire.'

'Covering fire? Are you mad or what?' Ryan said. 'You wouldn't stand a chance and you know it.'

Crouched down in the wheelhouse Tully said to Grant, 'How's the arm?'

'It hurts like hell but it was only a crease. I'll survive.'

'With you in the engine room and me up here we could still sail back to England, couldn't we?'

'I suppose so. What are you suggesting?'

'I'm going to try him with an offer one last time.'

Tully's voice sounded over the radio. 'Ryan?'

'What do you want?'

'I could turn out to sea like I said, we could go round in circles till the diesel oil runs out then we'd just drift until someone called the Coastguard and they came to investigate and then the fat would be in the fire for all of us.'

'True enough,' Ryan said. 'So what do you suggest?'

'Why not cut your losses? There's the big yellow inflatable behind you in the stern with a good outboard motor. We're only two miles off the coast now, as far as I know. You could make it easily now that the wind's dropping.'

'And leave the gold to you?' Ryan demanded. 'So what do we get out of this?'

'Your lives,' Tully said.

'And you trying to pick us off as we get in the inflatable.'

'I can't even see it from the wheelhouse. The truck's

in front of it. Think about it. I'll give you five minutes and then I'll turn this thing around.'

He went off the air and Kathleen said angrily, 'We can't do it, Uncle Michael, not after all we've been through.'

'I know, girl, I know.' He turned to Keogh. 'What do you think, Martin?'

'I don't think we have much choice.'

'So it's live to fight another day?' And then Ryan smiled that unholy smile of his. 'Of course, there is another possibility, which is to make sure Tully doesn't get the gold either.'

Kathleen gasped and Keogh said, 'And how would you do that?'

So Ryan told them.

A minute later he called Tully. 'All right, you're on. Give me a few moments while Keogh checks that you really can't see that inflatable because of the truck and I'll come back to you.'

In the wheelhouse Tully laughed hoarsely and turned to Grant. 'It's worked. The bastard's going to go. We've won.'

'If he means it.'

'Of course he does. No other way out. Nothing for him here now.'

Ryan's voice sounded again. 'OK, Tully, everything checks. I'll see you in hell one of these days.'

The transmission ended and Tully laughed exultantly. 'I've beaten the bastard. Fifty million pounds and it's all mine.'

'All ours, you mean?' Grant said.

'Of course.' Tully smiled. 'We need each other so let's get this tub turned around.'

Sheltered by the truck, Keogh and Ryan slid the inflatable over the stern rail and tethered it by its line. Keogh went over first and got to work on the outboard motor. It roared into life instantly with a strong heartbeat.

'Over you go, girl,' Ryan told Kathleen.

Keogh helped her in and the inflatable tossed this way and that in the choppy sea, the stern of the *Irish Rose* rising up and falling again just above them.

'Come on, Michael, for God's sake,' Keogh called.

'Not before I leave Tully his going-away present.' Ryan held up a half-pound block of Semtex and a one-minute timing pencil. He pulled open the stern deck hatch, dropped the Semtex inside and closed the hatch again. He was over the rail on the instant, untied the line and Keogh gunned the motor.

They were perhaps fifty yards away when the stern of the *Irish Rose* exploded into the darkness in a vivid tongue of flame. The end was incredibly quick, the ship tilting, the prow rising dramatically, and it slid backwards under the surface, vanishing in seconds in a hiss of steam.

'And you can chew on that, you bastard!' Michael Ryan said and put an arm around his niece. 'All right, Martin, take us to some sort of shore.'

It was four o'clock in the morning, the sky lightening just a little, when they coasted into a wide beach, the land rising on the other side cloaked with trees. Keogh killed the outboard motor, jumped over with the line and waded out of the water. Ryan helped Kathleen over the side and followed her.

'What do we do with the inflatable?' Keogh asked.

Ryan was inspecting it in the light of a small torch. 'No name on it as far as I can see. Shoot a couple of holes in it, Martin.'

Keogh waded in again and pushed the inflatable out to sea again. It drifted for a while, then an eddy took it out some distance. He took careful aim with his silenced Walther and fired twice. After a while the inflatable went down.

'And where do you think we'd be, Uncle Michael?' Kathleen asked.

'God knows, girl, but it hardly matters. We're home.' He turned to Keogh. What now, Martin?'

'I think it best we part company,' Keogh told him. 'You go your way, Michael Ryan, and I'll go mine.'

'Martin?' Kathleen sounded distressed. 'Can't we stay together?'

'I don't think so, Kate. Your uncle will have his plans and the Army Council and Reid to consider. One trip back home to dear old Ireland has been exciting enough for me. I'll say goodbye, Michael.' He shook Ryan's hand.

The girl grasped his arm, reached up and kissed his cheek. 'God bless you, Martin, and thanks for all you've done.'

'I didn't have the chance to pay you,' Ryan said. 'I'm sorry.'

'Not to worry.' Keogh smiled. 'It was a great ploy.'

He started to walk away and Ryan called, 'Who are you, Martin, who are you really?'

'God save us, there are days in the week when I don't know that myself,' and Keogh turned into the trees.

He disappeared and Ryan said, 'Off we go, girl. We'll find a road, follow it and see where we are.'

He led the way up through the trees, a ghostly

passage as dawn came, so that it was comparatively easy to see the way. They came to a narrow country road in a few minutes. There was a turning opposite and a signpost.

'You stay here in shelter and I'll see where we are.'

He walked through the rain to the signpost, examined it and came back, standing beside her in the shelter of the trees to light a cigarette.

'Drumdonald three miles to the left. Scotstown five miles the other way. We might as well go for the shorter walk.'

They stayed there for a moment and she said, 'All for nothing. We don't even know where the *Irish Rose* went down.'

'Don't we?' He laughed and took another black instrument from his pocket that looked rather like the Howler. 'Another gadget that young electronic genius at Queen's University found for me. It's called a Master Navigator. I gave him Marsh End and Kilalla and he programmed in their positions. This thing has given a constant reading of course and position all the way across. I know exactly where the *Irish Rose* went down.'

'My God,' she said, 'and you never told me.'

'There are things I keep close to myself.'

'So what do we do now? Reid will be looking for us and that swine Scully.'

'And the Army Council,' Ryan said. 'No, time

to take a trip, I think. They say America's grand at this time of the year. We'll get to the safe house at Bundoran. False passports there. You know how careful I am. They're always in stock.'

'But money, Uncle Michael, what about that?'

'Oh, I wasn't exactly honest with Martin. I still have the second fifty thousand pounds I was to pay Tully in an envelope in my breast pocket.'

'My God, what a man you are.'

'It should keep us going for a while. When it runs out I'll think of something.'

'Such as?'

'I've robbed banks in Ulster and got away with it. No reason I can't do the same in America.'

'Sometimes I think you're a raving madman.'

'And sometimes I am, but let's get going.' He took her arm and they started along the road to Drumdonald.

There was silence, only the rain, and then Keogh stepped out of the trees where he had sheltered while listening to the conversation.

'You bloody old fox,' he said softly and there was a kind of admiration there.

He turned and started to walk the opposite way towards Scotstown.

It was six o'clock in the morning and in Dublin Jack Barry was half-awake, lying in the big bed beside his wife, when the portable phone he'd placed at the side of the bed sounded. He slid out of bed, picked it up and went into the bathroom.

'Yes.'

'A reverse charge call for you from a Mr Keogh. Will you take it?'

'Of course,' Barry said.

A moment later Keogh's voice sounded in his ear. 'That you, Jack?'

'Where are you?'

'A public telephone box in a village called Scotstown on the Down coast.'

'What's going on? I have twenty men from the County Down Brigade waiting at Kilalla.'

'Send them home, Jack, the *Irish Rose* won't be coming.'

'Tell me,' Barry ordered.

Which Keogh did. When he was finished Barry said, 'Christ, what a ploy and to end like that.'

'I know. Quite a fella, Michael Ryan.'

'I was thinking,' Barry said. 'Standing in the trees listening to him talk to his niece you could have shot the bugger and taken that Master Navigator thing. We'd have known the location of the damn boat then.'

'A major salvage operation to get that gold up, Jack.'

'That sounds like an excuse. Have you gone soft on me?'

'I liked him, Jack, and I liked the wee girl. The bullion didn't reach its destination, the Loyalists won't be able to arm for a civil war. Let it end there.'

Barry laughed harshly. 'Damn you, right as usual. Scotstown, you say? There's a pub there called The Loyalist, but don't believe it. The landlord, Kevin Stringer, is one of our own. I'll phone him now and tell him to expect you. I'll send a car for you later.'

'Sounds good to me.'

'Watch your back.'

Keogh came out of the phone box and stood there for a moment in the rain thinking of Michael Ryan and his niece, aware with some surprise that he wished the enemy well, then he lit a cigarette and went down the village street in search of the pub.

NEW YORK STATE
IRELAND
LONDON
WASHINGTON
IRELAND

1995

7

Green Rapids Detention Centre in Upper New York State was the pride of the penal system, totally secure yet civilized and liberal in its regime. It had within its boundaries a hospital system second to none and specialized in particular with prisoners who were serving terms up to and including life who also had serious medical problems. Many were transferees from the infamous Sing-Sing on the Hudson River, some with heart conditions, others with various forms of cancer.

The outer perimeter, with every electronic security system possible, was so secure that prisoners were allowed considerable freedom on the inside, which applied not only to the various work-shops but also to the park area where visitors, either family or lawyers, were allowed to walk freely with prisoners.

*　*　*

Paolo Salamone walked across the grass with his lawyer, Marco Sollazo. In spite of the Sicilian names, they were both good Americans born and bred. There the similarity ended.

Salamone was off the streets of New York's Little Italy and he'd followed the usual Mafia route. First as one of the boys, the *Piccioti*, gaining advancement, gaining respect. He'd acted as an executioner three times which had gained him entry into the family of Don Antonio Russo as a *Sicario*, a specialist assassin. He'd been to prison twice on comparatively minor matters including drug dealing. His downfall had been two years earlier when, on taking out one of Don Antonio's rivals, a street policeman had unexpectedly arrived on the scene. Salamone in a gun battle had received a bullet in the leg which had put him down. Unfortunately his own bullet had killed the police officer who just happened to be a woman. His sentence of twenty-five years instead of life reflected the skill of his lawyer, Don Antonio's nephew, Marco Sollazo.

The only reason Salamone had been transferred to Green Rapids from Sing-Sing was because he had taken a full nursing course and was therefore thought of more use in the Green Rapids medical facility.

Marco Sollazo was thirty-five, a saturnine, rather handsome man in an Armani striped suit and college tie, dark hair swept back. A product of Groton and Harvard Law School, carefully nurtured by his uncle, he was Don Antonio's pride and joy.

'Marco, you told me there was a chance you'd get me a re-hearing. Involuntary manslaughter. Now you tell me I could be here another twenty-three years.'

'I'm doing my best,' Marco said. 'It's difficult.'

'Yeah, well I'm doing my best. I know plenty about the family, but I don't speak out.'

'Paolo, I don't think Don Antonio would be pleased to hear you speak like that. It would distress him.'

Paolo said hastily, 'Hey, don't get me wrong, I'd never betray my Godfather. It's just like I could do with some help here.'

'I know, I know.' Marco sounded sympathetic. 'I'll explore every avenue. I mean, the Don has much influence. Who knows?'

Salamone plucked at his arm. 'What if I give you something good? Something real good?'

'And what would that be?'

There were prisoners and their visitors wandering everywhere on the grass and Salamone pulled Sollazo over to a bench and sat down. He pointed across to a man who was in his mid sixties with grey hair. The young dark-haired woman with him seemed about twenty-five.

'Liam Kelly, he calls himself. The woman is his niece, Jean Kelly. She's a theatre nurse down at Green Rapids General Hospital.'

'So?'

'He's doing twenty-five for shooting a policeman in Pleasantville ten years ago when he was robbing the bank. I met him in Sing-Sing then he had an angina attack and they moved him down here because of the hospital. I followed a few months later to join the staff. You see, we've got a good facility here, but Green Rapids is very special. Any problem and we send the patient straight down there.'

'So where is this leading?'

'The other month he had an attack. I should tell you they're Irish, but not the usual kind. That funny accent they have in the north of Ireland. Anyway, he's not in good health and he got a fever. They had him on a drip in a private room. I was night nurse at the time and had to check him out.'

'So?'

'When he was delirious he said all sorts of crazy things. Kept going on about some ship called the *Irish Rose* and then he would say he was the only one who knew where it had gone down, the only one who knew where the gold was.'

There was a long pause. Sollazo sat there frowning. 'The only one who knew where the gold was? He said that?'

'That's right.'

'So what did you make of it?'

Salamone was enjoying himself. 'I went to the prison library. We've got a great computer service here. I tapped in the *Irish Rose* name and hey presto.'

'Go on,' Sollazo told him.

'There was an item in the *New York Times* in the autumn of nineteen eighty-five. It seems a truck carrying fifty million pounds in gold bullion was knocked off up in the north-west of England on the coast. It said police enquiries indicated that it had put to sea on a ferry called the *Irish Rose*.'

'Then what?'

'The ship disappeared, but lifebelts and what was left of a lifeboat were washed up on the Irish coast. End of story.'

'And it said nothing about who was behind it?'

'Not a word.'

'Interesting,' Sollazo said. 'Let's take a walk.'

They strolled, across the grass and passed the bench where Kelly and his niece were sitting, heads together. She glanced up casually and Salamone said, 'Hi, Liam.'

'How's yourself, Paolo?' was the reply.

Sollazo and Salamone passed on and Kathleen Ryan said, 'Who was that one, Uncle Michael?'

'Paolo Salamone. He's a nurse in the hospital. We've something in common. We're both doing twenty-five years for shooting a policeman, only

in his case it was for shooting a policewoman.
Anyway, how are you?'

'I'm fine. They keep me busy at the hospital.'

'Still no man in your life?'

'Too much bother.' She smiled. 'Lucky I
managed the job at Green Rapids. At least I can
see you regularly.'

'And for how long, another fifteen years?' He
shook his head. 'You can't waste your life like this,
Kathleen.' He was angry now and stood up. 'God,
how could I have been so stupid? A small town
bank, I said. A piece of cake and then that policeman
came round the corner.'

'It was just one of those things.'

'Well thank God you managed to drive off and
get the hell out of it.'

He took out a pack of cigarettes and lit one.
She said, 'You know you shouldn't smoke.'

'So I can extend my life a year or two here in
good old Green Rapids Detention Centre?' He
grinned wryly and dropped the cigarette to the
ground. 'All right, I'll be good. Come on, I'll walk
you to the gate.'

There were a number of people going in the
same direction and she noticed Salamone and
Sollazo. They reached the security exit and paused.
Ryan kissed her on the cheek. 'Thanks for coming.'

'I'll see you Friday.'

She went through security and approached

her car. As she unlocked her door she saw Sollazo walking towards a silver Porsche. He glanced at her casually then looked away. For some reason it made her feel uncomfortable and she got in her car quickly and drove off.

Sollazo watched her go and reached for his mobile phone and called his office. When his secretary answered he said, 'Rosa, check the files for a report in the *New York Times* of a robbery in the north of England connected with a ship called the *Irish Rose*, which apparently went down at sea.'

'Very well, sir, anything else?'

'Yes, get our people in London to check for any newspaper stories there. They'll probably be in more detail. I want this like yesterday.'

'I'll get right on to it.'

'I'm having dinner early with Don Antonio.'

'At the Long Island house?'

'No, the Trump Tower apartment. As soon as you get that stuff from England fax it to me there.'

'I will.'

Sollazo drove away thinking about it and particularly the fact that, the way gold prices had climbed, fifty million pounds in bullion in nineteen eighty-five was now worth double.

In her room at Green Rapids General Hospital Kathleen Ryan undressed and went to the shower.

She was due on the evening shift in an hour, on call for emergency surgery until six in the morning, not that she minded for she loved her work, was good at it.

It had been her uncle who had insisted that she find a life for herself after his trial and sentencing and she'd put in five hard years of training. Sing-Sing had been the bad time. She hadn't been able to see him much while he was at that grim fortress. In a way his heart problem had been a blessing. The less restrictive regime at Green Rapids allowed a great deal of visiting and getting a post at the town hospital had made all the difference.

But it hurt her to see him there, a shadow of the man he had been in those great days back in Ireland when they'd taken on the might of the IRA, even on occasion the British Army, and won. At that memory, a thrill passed through her that was almost sexual.

She towelled off, dried her cropped hair and put on her uniform. She combed her hair, checking herself in the mirror, strong face, dark eyes, not pretty, but striking, this girl who had at the age of fourteen killed two members of the IRA with a hand grenade, who at the age of sixteen had shot dead at close quarters a man named Bert Fox.

It all came back. The Lake District, that lonely road and the taking of the transporter and Martin

Keogh and the final brutal confrontation on the *Irish Rose*. And at the memory, the old excitement surged through her.

'There's got to be more than this,' she said aloud. 'He can't rot in there for another fifteen years.'

Despair flooded over her and she sat down, opened a bottom drawer in her desk and took out a briefcase. Inside was a large envelope containing fifty thousand dollars in cash, money she had painstakingly saved, mad money against the day they would have to move fast, she and Uncle Michael, for from the time he had been moved from Sing-Sing to the easier regime of Green Rapids she had entertained the wild hope that he might be able to escape. She had even approached a forger in New York, an old cell mate of her uncle in Sing-Sing, who had provided her with two false Irish passports at a thousand dollars each, a special price as a favour.

She found them now and examined them. Daniel Forbes, that was her uncle, and she was Nancy Forbes. A waste, the whole thing, for as she soon discovered, in spite of its liberal regime, security at Green Rapids was stringent.

She looked at the photos in the false passport and somehow it was a stranger. 'Whatever happened to Kathleen Ryan?' she asked softly.

At that moment the door opened and another nurse looked in. 'Ready, Jean?'

'On my way,' Kathleen told her. 'I'll be right with you.'

She closed the briefcase, put it back in the drawer and went out.

Don Antonio Russo was seventy years of age and of ample proportions, his loose cream linen suit accentuating his bulk. His hair was long and grey, swept back from his fleshy, arrogant face. A man who had always been used to having his own way. He got up, leaning on his cane as Sollazo entered the sumptuous living room of the Trump Tower apartment.

'Marco, good to see you.' They embraced. 'A glass of champagne?' Don Antonio snapped his fingers at a manservant. 'Oh, by the way, there are some faxes for you. Can't your office give you a night off?'

'Sorry, Uncle, this is important. May I?'

'Of course.'

Sollazo went into the office, found the faxes and read them quickly. He returned to the living room, accepted his glass of champagne and sat opposite Russo.

'Can we talk business?'

'Always.'

'Good.' Sollazo told him in detail of his conversation with Salamone.

When he was finished the Don said, 'More than interesting. And the faxes?'

'They confirm the mention in the *New York Times*, but in more detail. Naturally, as usual with newspapers, the accounts differ, but broadly speaking they agree as to general details. A truck carrying fifty million pounds in gold bullion was knocked off on a country road in the English Lake District. A young boy told the police he'd been chased away from a ferry called the *Irish Rose* at an old disused jetty not far from the scene of the action. He also said he'd seen a truck of the right description turn off the main road towards the ferry later in the day.'

'So?'

'Obviously the bullion truck put to sea on the ferry.'

'And what happened?'

'Over the next few days a smashed up ship's boat, lifebelts and so on, all bearing the name *Irish Rose*, were washed up on the coast of County Down.'

'I see.' Don Antonio sat there frowning. 'And Salamone said that, in a fever, this man Kelly spoke of being the only one who knew where the boat went down?'

'That's right.'

'And you said bullion of the order of fifty million pounds?'

'Yes, but that was ten years ago. Gold prices

have greatly increased. I'd say at least one hundred million pounds in present terms.'

'Now, that kind of money is always interesting.'

'I was thinking,' Sollazo said, 'with the right kind of salvage boat these recovery jobs are quite easy these days, as long as you know where the ship is, which the authorities don't.'

'So they tell me.' Don Antonio sat there thinking about it. Finally he nodded. 'I wonder who this man Kelly was working for. Was it just business or the IRA or something like that?'

'It's a thought,' Sollazo said.

'You know a few years ago I had dealings with the IRA. We used to provide arms through a Sicilian connection. Their Chief of Staff was a man called Barry – Jack Barry.'

Sollazo said, 'It's all peace talk with the IRA these days. Gerry Adams at the White House speaking for their Sinn Fein party.'

'So what?' the Don said. 'Barry is an old fox. If anyone will know anything of this affair it will be he. His private number in Dublin will be in my special address book in the top right hand drawer of my desk. See if you can get him.'

In Dublin Jack Barry was sitting by the fire, bored out of his mind and reading a newspaper, rain brushing the window when the phone went.

'Barry here.'

'Mr Jack Barry? Is that you? An old friend, I hope. Don Antonio Russo.'

'Dear God,' Barry said, 'and what can I do for you?'

'More what can we do for each other, Mr Barry. I'm talking serious business here. Does the name *Irish Rose* mean anything to you?'

Barry swallowed hard. 'Should it?'

'What would you say if I told you that I know the whereabouts of a man who calls himself Kelly, but in a fever speaks of being the only one who knows where the ship has gone down, the only one who knows where the gold is?'

'I'd be more than interested.'

'Fine. It seems to me we might have a mutual interest here that could profit both of us. My nephew, Marco Sollazo, who is also my lawyer, will be with you tomorrow.'

'I look forward to meeting him.'

Don Antonio put the phone down. 'We have a good source at Green Rapids Detention Centre?'

'An excellent one.'

'Phone now. We need a copy of Kelly's photo as quickly as possible then get in touch with the airport and tell them to have the Gulfstream ready to go. Let's say midnight. They're four hours ahead in Ireland so you'll be able to see Barry late morning.'

'Of course, Uncle.'

'And then dinner.' Don Antonio smiled. 'Suddenly I have quite an appetite.'

In Dublin on the following morning it was just coming up to noon when Barry answered the sound of the bell at his front door and found Marco Sollazo standing there.

'Mr Barry?'

'And you'd be Mr Sollazo?'

'That's right.'

'Come in for a moment while I get my coat. You'll have to excuse the mess, I'm on my own these days. My wife died last year.'

Marco Sollazo waited in the small parlour. There was a sofa, two easy chairs, a fireplace, faded family photos of children at various stages of their development. It all fitted with the image of the pleasant-faced sixty-year-old man in the cardigan whom he had just met and yet this man had been for several crucial years Chief of Staff of the Provisional IRA.

Barry came in wearing a raincoat and cloth cap. 'We'll take a walk in the park and then have a drink and a bite to eat at Cohan's Bar.'

'Anything you like.'

Barry took an umbrella down from a hatpeg in the hall. 'Just in case,' he said. 'This is Ireland, remember.'

They crossed the road to where the park waited behind green-painted railings. Sollazo said, 'Your home, is it unsafe to talk there? Do they have you wired for sound?'

'Hell, no. Oh, they tried it back in the old days, the British Secret Intelligence Service, Irish Intelligence, Dublin Special Branch. I had my own experts who used to come round once a week and sweep the house. I expect your uncle had to take the same precautions.'

'And still does.'

'Well I'm not Chief of Staff for the IRA any more.' He smiled. 'A time for peace, Mr Sollazo, that's what they tell me.'

'So no more IRA?'

Barry laughed out loud. 'If you believe that you'll believe anything. There's another Chief of Staff in my place, our command structure intact throughout the country and, as your President and the British Prime Minister have found to their cost, we don't intend to give up our arms.'

'Yes, I understand from the newspapers that the refusal of your people to comply in the matter of arms is a main talking point when the President visits London on Friday.'

'They can talk until they're blue in the face, it won't make any difference. We'll hang on to our arms come what may.'

'You don't think this peace will last?'

153

'It never has before.' They turned through the park gates and it started to rain and Barry raised the umbrella. 'I told you it would. Anyway, let's get down to business.'

Sollazo took the photo his contact at Green Rapids had provided the previous night. 'Do you know this man?'

'I certainly do,' Barry nodded. 'His name is Michael Ryan, once a notorious gunman for the Loyalist cause, a black Orangeman from Belfast.'

'Would it surprise you to know that he's been in prison in America for the past ten years?'

Barry smiled. 'Now there's a wonder. He dropped out of sight in nineteen eighty-five, but totally, and I could never figure that out. What did he do?'

'He shot a policeman while robbing a bank. They gave him twenty-five years.'

'Poor sod.' Barry whistled. 'He must be sixty-five now. I don't suppose he's got much chance of seeing the light of day.'

'Not really. He can apply for probation after fifteen years but he'd be around seventy by then and not much chance of probation anyway. He shot a policeman, remember.'

'What name is he using?'

'Liam Kelly. He has a history of heart trouble so they moved him from Sing-Sing to Green Rapids Detention Centre. The medical facilities are good and the general hospital in the town is exceptional. He's visited regularly by his niece who is a nurse at the hospital. She calls herself Jean Kelly. I've seen her. Small and rather ugly in a peasant kind of way. Dark hair, around twenty-five or six.'

'That would be Kathleen Ryan – she *is* his niece. Well, now, fancy that, and after all these years.' The rain increased in a sudden rush and he took Sollazo by the arm. 'Let's make for the shelter over there. I'd like to hear what you've got to say about the *Irish Rose*.'

When Sollazo had finished talking, Barry sat there, frowning slightly. Finally he spoke. 'Tell me something, why have you come to me?'

'Business,' Sollazo told him, 'strictly business. That bullion would be worth one hundred million pounds at today's prices.'

'And you'd like to get your hands on it?'

'Let me be explicit. My uncle feels that a joint venture would be the way to tackle this affair between ourselves and you of the IRA. A half share each. What could be fairer? If peace fails, fifty million in gold would buy you a great many arms, my friend.'

'Indeed it would and your uncle with his usual instinct for doing the right thing has sent you to entirely the right place and not for the reason you think.'

'I think you should explain.'

'You see, I know as much as anyone about the *Irish Rose* affair, as much as Ryan himself.'

'But how could you?'

'I knew Ryan was up to something, the usual whispers, even a hint that it was gold, so I infiltrated one of my own men into his organization, a man we'll call Martin Keogh.'

'Not his real name?'

'That's right. One of my very best operators. He actually was with Ryan every step of the way and took part in the robbery. He was on the *Irish Rose* when it went down.'

'Tell me,' Sollazo said. 'Tell me everything.'

Later, sitting in a corner booth at Cohan's Bar drinking Guinness and eating ham sandwiches, Sollazo said, 'A remarkable story; and this man Keogh? Is he still around?'

'In a manner of speaking. He left the IRA some years ago and worked as a freelance or mercenary, call it what you like. He's worked for just about everybody in his time, the old KGB, the PLO, even the Israelis.'

'And where is he now?'

'With British Intelligence.'

'That seems rather surprising.'

'The Brits set up a highly secret outfit to combat

terrorism and handle the really dirty jobs back in nineteen seventy-two. Since then it's been headed by a man called Brigadier Charles Ferguson and he isn't responsible to the Director of the Security Services. He's responsible only to the Prime Minister. That's why it's known in the trade as the Prime Minister's Private Army.'

'And the man you call Keogh works for this Ferguson?'

'Indeed he does. He's Ferguson's trouble shooter. The old fox blackmailed him into joining him some three years ago. Offered to wipe his slate clean. No repercussions as to his IRA past. He needed someone like that on his team. Set a thief to catch a thief, you get the idea.'

'I do indeed. And what is this Keogh's real name?'

'Dillon – Sean Dillon, in his day the most feared enforcer I had.'

They walked back through the park. Sollazo said, 'Quite a man this Dillon, but hardly likely to give us any assistance.'

'We don't need him. He told me everything there was to know about the whole affair and now I've told you.'

'The man Reid, the one who killed the man in London. Is he still around?'

'Serving a sentence for murder. He's in prison in Ulster.'

'One thing. This Loyalist Army Council you mentioned? I'm right in assuming they would dearly like to get their hands on the bullion?'

'They certainly would. The Loyalist side are heavily dissatisfied with the way the peace process is going. They think of themselves as being sold out. The militant elements envisage civil war eventually. That gold would be more than useful. It would help them to obtain the kind of weaponry they would need.'

'And you wouldn't like that so may I take it that you will join us on this venture?'

'Not officially, not at the moment. Let me explain. People are desperate for peace here. You can't trust anybody and that includes Sinn Fein and the IRA itself. If I approach the present Chief of Staff he'd have to discuss it with members of the Army Council and the whole thing would leak in no time.'

'I see. So what do you suggest?'

'We keep it between ourselves for the moment.' Barry smiled wryly. 'And don't think I'm after it for myself. Money means nothing to me, but my cause does. You get the position of the *Irish Rose* out of Ryan, then a quiet sort of expedition is all we need to start with. Small boat, a diver to go down and make sure it's there.'

'And afterwards?'

'That would be up to you. I'm sure you can arrange some sort of phoney marine expedition. A suitable front while the real business of raising the gold goes on.' He grinned. 'I've every faith in you.'

There was a black limousine parked at the kerb by the house, a hard-looking man with a broken nose leaning against it. He wore a dark blue chauffeur's uniform.

'My driver.'

'And bodyguard from the look of him.'

'Giovanni Mori.' Sollazo took Barry's hand. 'A real pleasure. I like meeting legends, Mr Barry, one so seldom gets the chance. I'll be in touch.'

He got into the passenger seat and Mori went round and slid behind the wheel. 'Did it go well, *signore?*' he asked as he drove away.

'Very well,' Sollazo told him. 'To the airport, Giovanni. We return to New York,' and he leaned back, closed his eyes and went over everything Barry had told him.

It was nine o'clock in the evening in New York when he presented himself once again at the Trump Tower apartment. Don Antonio sat there, hands clasped over the silver handle of his cane and listened as Sollazo told him everything he had learned from Barry.

When he was finished the old Don nodded. 'An amazing story.'

'So we proceed?'

'Of course. A very lucrative venture. The essential first step is to obtain the location of the *Irish Rose* from this man Ryan.'

'I agree. On the other hand why should he deal with me at all when there is nothing in it for him?'

'Do you think you could accomplish his release from prison?'

'I doubt it. It was a policeman he killed, remember.'

The Don nodded. 'There are more ways than one of skinning a cat. I'm sure you will come up with something and you do have Salamone at the prison. He could prove invaluable. I leave this in your capable hands.' He smiled. 'Now, a glass of wine. I see the President is visiting London, by the way?'

8

Don Antonio was right, for in London the most important matter on the Prime Minister's agenda was his meeting with the President of the United States at the end of the week. It was also at that point Brigadier Charles Ferguson's sole concern. He was agitated and showed it as his Daimler languished in heavy traffic.

'Sometimes I think this whole damned city has ground to a halt.'

'Sure and sometimes it has,' Sean Dillon said sitting on the jump seat opposite.

He was a small man, no more than five feet five, with hair so fair that it was almost white, handsome enough with a slight perpetual smile on his mouth as if mocking the world he saw about him. He wore an easy fitting blue flannel suit, the jacket single-breasted and a dark blue silk polo.

'I'd like to remind you that my appointment is with the Prime Minister, Dillon, I can hardly be late for that.'

'He's a decent enough stick,' Dillon said. 'He'll see you right.'

The woman sitting next to Ferguson wore a fawn Armani trouser suit and black horn-rimmed glasses that contrasted with her red hair. She was in her late twenties and attractive enough to be worth a page or two in *Vogue*. She was in fact Detective Chief Inspector Hannah Bernstein from Special Branch at Scotland Yard, on loan to Ferguson as his assistant.

'You're hopeless, Dillon,' she said. 'No respect for anyone, you Irish.'

'It's all that rain, girl dear,' he said.

'Don't waste your time on him,' Ferguson told her. 'A hopeless case.'

The Daimler was admitted through the security gates at the end of Downing Street and drew up at the door of Number Ten. 'I shan't be more than twenty minutes,' Ferguson told them.

'Will that old bowser Simon Carter be there?' Dillon asked.

'That is no way to refer to the Deputy Director of Security Services,' Ferguson said.

'Yes, well don't forget to tell him I think his security plans for the American President's visit stink.'

'Hardly appropriate, Dillon. Try and possess yourself in patience until I return.'

He crossed the pavement, the policeman on duty saluted, the door opened and he went in.

'The grand gentleman that he is. Sure and the Empire is in safe hands.' Dillon took a cigarette from his old silver case and lit it.

'We don't have an Empire any longer, Dillon,' she said.

'Is that a fact and does the Government know that?'

She shook her head. 'Hopeless, Dillon, that's what you are and you'll kill yourself if you keep on smoking those things.'

'True, but then I always knew I'd come to a bad end.'

When Ferguson was shown into the Prime Minister's study Simon Carter was already seated. A small man in his early fifties with snow white hair, he had once been a Professor of History. Never an agent in the field himself, he was one of the faceless men who controlled Britain's security system. He disliked Ferguson, had done for years, and resented the Brigadier's privileged position and the fact that he was answerable to the Prime Minister only.

'Sorry I'm late, Prime Minister.'

He made no excuses and the Prime Minister smiled. 'That's all right.' He picked up a file. 'The security plans the Deputy Director and his people have planned for the President's visit. You've read this?'

'Naturally.'

'I'm particularly anxious that his visit to the House of Commons goes well on Friday morning. Refreshments on the Terrace at ten-thirty.'

'No problems there, Prime Minister,' Carter said. 'The one place during his whole trip which will provide no security problem at all is the House of Commons.' He turned to the Brigadier, the usual arrogant look on his face. 'Don't you agree, Ferguson?'

Ferguson would have let it go, but Carter's look made him angry.

'Well, do you, Brigadier?' the Prime Minister asked.

'Seems all right on the surface of things, but, to be frank, Prime Minister, Dillon doesn't think much of it at all. He believes general security at the House of Commons to be very poor indeed.'

'Dillon?' Carter's eyes bulged. 'That damned scoundrel. I really must protest, Prime Minister, that Brigadier Ferguson continues to employ a man once an IRA gunman, a man with a record in the general field of European terrorism that can only be described as infamous.'

'I protest in my turn,' Ferguson said. 'Dillon has been of considerable service to the Crown as you well know, Prime Minister, not least to the Royal Family itself.'

'Yes, I'm well aware of that.' The Prime Minister frowned. 'But this is too important for personal bickering, gentlemen. My decision.' He sat back and said to Carter, 'I'd like you to meet with the Brigadier and Dillon at the House of Commons. I'd like you to hear what he has to say.'

Carter controlled his anger with difficulty. 'If you say so, Prime Minister.'

'Yes, I'm afraid I do. And now you must excuse me. I have a Cabinet meeting.'

Everyone stands in line to get into the House of Commons, not only tourists, but constituents waiting to see Members of Parliament. Ferguson, Dillon and Hannah Bernstein waited their turn, Ferguson with some impatience.

'The grand place this,' Dillon said. 'They tell me they have twenty-six restaurants and bars and the food and drink subsidized by the taxpayer. A fine job being an MP.'

'Yes, well at least they don't have to queue to get in the damn place,' Ferguson told him.

A very large police sergeant watching the line intently saw Hannah, stiffened to attention and came forward. 'Chief Inspector Bernstein. Nice to see you, ma'am. Here, let me pass you through. You won't remember me.'

'Oh, but I recall you very well. Sergeant Hall, isn't it?'

'Yes, ma'am. I was first on the scene when you shot that bastard who held up the supermarket. You were on your way to the American Embassy.'

'Your wicked past catches up,' Dillon murmured.

'This is a colleague, Mr Dillon, and my boss, Brigadier Ferguson,' she said.

Sergeant Hall became very military. 'Let me pass you all through, Brigadier.'

'That's very kind, Sergeant.'

'My pleasure, sir.'

He led them through the barrier and saluted and they walked on towards the Central Lobby. 'How fortunate you were here, Chief Inspector,' Ferguson told her. 'We could have stood in that wretched queue forever.'

'Humiliating, isn't it?' Dillon said.

They moved on through various corridors, and finally went out on to the Terrace overlooking the Thames, Westminster Bridge to the left and the Embankment on the far side of the river. A row of tall Victorian lamps ran along the parapet. There was quite a crowd, visitors as well as MPs enjoying a drink from the Terrace Bar.

Dillon hailed a passing waiter. 'Half a bottle of Krug non-vintage and three glasses.' He smiled. 'On me, Brigadier.'

'How generous,' Ferguson said. 'Though remembering how you made six hundred thousand pounds out of that Michael Aroun affair in ninety-one, Dillon, I'd say you can afford it.'

'True, Brigadier, true.' Dillon leaned over the parapet and looked down at the waters of the Thames flowing by. He said to Hannah, 'You notice the rather synthetic carpet we're standing on is green?'

'Yes.'

'Notice where it changes to red? That's the House of Lords end, you see, just there where the scaffolding goes down into the water.'

'I see.'

'Great on tradition, you Brits.'

'I'm Jewish, Dillon, as you well know.'

'Oh, I do. Grandad a Rabbi, your father a Professor of Surgery and you an MA from Cambridge University. Now what could be more British?'

At that moment Carter appeared and approached them impatiently. 'Right, Ferguson, please don't waste my time. What have you got to say?'

'Dillon?' Ferguson said.

'I think your security is shot full of holes,' Dillon told Carter. 'Too many people, twenty-six restaurants and bars, scores of entrances and exits not only for MPs, but staff and workmen.'

'Come now, everyone has a security pass, everyone is checked.'

'Then there's the river.'

'The river? What nonsense. It's tidal, Dillon, and the current is lethal. Never less than three knots and sometimes five.'

'Is that so? Then I'm sorry.'

'I should think you would be.' Carter turned to Ferguson. 'May I go?'

Ferguson looked at Dillon and the Irishman smiled wearily. 'The great conceit of yourself you have, Mr Carter. A little bet with the man, Brigadier. I'll turn up on the Terrace on Friday morning when the President and the Prime Minister are here, and all quite illegal. Mr Carter gets five hundred pounds if I fail and a five-pound note if I succeed.'

'You're on, damn you,' Carter told him and held out his hand to Ferguson. 'Shake on it.' He started to laugh. 'What an amusing little chap you are, Dillon,' and he walked away.

'Do you know what you're doing, Dillon?' Ferguson demanded.

Dillon leaned over the parapet and looked at the water swirling fifteen feet below. 'Oh, yes, I think so, especially if the Chief Inspector here can come up with the right information.'

Ferguson's suite of offices was on the third floor of the Ministry of Defence overlooking Horse Guards Avenue and it was an hour later that Dillon and Hannah Bernstein went into her office.

She sat down at her desk. 'All right, what do you want?'

'The biggest expert on the Thames river. Now who would that be? Someone in Customs & Excise or maybe the River Police.'

'I'll try them both,' she said.

'Good. I'll go and make the tea while you're doing it.'

He went into the outer office whistling and put the kettle on. When it had boiled he made the tea, arranged the cups and a milk jug on a tray and took it in. Hannah was on the phone.

'Thank you, Inspector.' She put the phone down and sat back as Dillon poured the tea. 'How domesticated. That was the River Police telling me who the greatest expert on the River Thames is.' She turned to her computer and tapped the keys. 'Subject coming up, Dillon. Not River Police, not Customs but a London gangster.'

Dillon started to laugh.

The information rolled on the screen. 'Harry Salter, aged sixty-five, did seven years for bank robbery in his twenties, no prison time since,' Hannah said. 'But look at his record from Criminal Intelligence. Owns pleasure boats on the river, the Dark Man pub at Wapping, a warehouse development worth more than one million pounds.'

'The cunning one him,' Dillon said.

'A smuggler, Dillon, every racket on the river. Cigarettes, booze, diamonds from Holland. Anything.'

'Not quite,' Dillon told her. 'Look what it says. No drug connection, no prostitution, no strip clubs.' He sat back. 'What we've got here is an old-fashioned gangster. He probably objects to men who swear in front of women.'

'He's still a gangster, Dillon, suspected of killing other gangsters.'

'And where's the harm in that if they leave the civilians alone? Let's see his picture.'

It rolled around and Dillon studied the fleshy face intently. 'Just as I expected. Fair enough.'

'Well he looks like Bill Sykes to me,' Hannah said.

'Known associates?'

'Billy Salter, age twenty-five, his nephew.' The information came up on the screen again. 'Six months for assault, another six months for assault, twelve months for affray.'

'A hot-tempered lad.'

'And these two, Joe Baxter and Sam Hall; more of the same, Dillon. A very unsavoury bunch.'

'Who might just suit my purposes.'

'Except for one thing.'

'And what would that be?'

'The River Police had a tip-off. Salter and his gang will be downriver tonight at nine in one of his pleasure boats, the *River Queen*. There's a Dutch boat coming in called the *Amsterdam*. The *River Queen* will be at anchor off Harley Dock. As the Amsterdam goes past one of the stewards throws a package across. Uncut diamonds. Two hundred thousand pounds.'

'And the River Police waiting to pounce?'

'Not at all. They'll be waiting for the *River Queen* to berth at Cable Wharfe by Salter's pub, the Dark Man, at Wapping. They'll pick him up there.'

'What a shame. It could have been such a lovely relationship.'

'Anything else I can do for you?' Hannah Bernstein demanded.

'Not really. I can see you've shafted me pretty

thoroughly and taken pleasure in it. I'll just go
away and think again.'

At eight-thirty, Dillon was waiting on Harley Dock
in an ancient and inconspicuous Toyota van he
had borrowed from the vehicle pool at the
Ministry of Defence. He was already wearing a
black diving suit, the cowl up over his head.
Occasionally a boat passed on the river and he
sat behind the wheel of the Toyota and watched
through a pair of infra-red night glasses as the
River Queen arrived and anchored. There was
movement on deck; two men and two more on
the upper-deck wheelhouse.

He waited and then there was a noise of engines
downriver and the *Amsterdam* appeared, a medium-
sized freighter. With his night glasses, he could
actually see the man at the rail and the bundle he
hurled. It landed on the pleasure boat's canopy.

The freighter moved on and Dillon was already
clamping a tank to his inflatable. He picked up
his fins, moved to the edge of the dock and pulled
them on. Then he pulled on his mask, reached for
his mouthpiece and jumped.

He surfaced by the anchor line, pulled off his inflatable and the tank, then his fins and fastened them

to the line. He waited for a moment then went up hand-over-hand.

He went in through the anchor-chain port and crouched on deck, listening. There was the sound of laughter coming from the deck cabin and he went forward, stood and peered through a port hole. Salter was there, his nephew Billy, Baxter and Hall. Salter was cutting open a yellow life jacket at the table. He took out the cloth bundle.

'Two hundred grand.'

Dillon unzipped his diving suit and took out the silenced Walther. He went to the door, paused, then threw it open and stepped inside.

'God bless all here.'

There was silence, the four of them grouped around the table like some tableau, Harry Salter and his nephew seated, Baxter and Hall standing, beer glasses in their hands.

Salter said. 'And what's your game then?'

'Open the bundle.'

'I'm fucked if I will, I don't think you've got the bottle to use that thing.'

Dillon fired on the instant, shattering the whisky glass on the table at Salter's right hand, doing the same thing to the beer glass Baxter was holding. Billy Salter cried out sharply as a jagged splinter of glass cut his right cheek.

There was silence and then Dillon said, 'More?'

'OK, you made your point,' Salter said. 'What do you want?'

'The diamonds – show me.'

'Tell him to get stuffed,' Billy said, a hand to his cheek where blood flowed.

'Then what?' Salter asked him.

He unfastened the cloth bundle. Inside was a yellow oilskin pouch with a zip fastener. 'Open it,' Dillon ordered.

Salter did as he was told and tossed the pouch across where it fell at Dillon's feet. He picked it up, unzipped the front of his diving suit and stowed it away. He half turned and took the key out of the door.

Salter said. 'I'll find you. Nobody does this to Harry Salter and gets away with it.'

'And didn't I hear James Cagney saying that in an old gangster film on the *Midnight Movie* show on television last week?' Dillon grinned. 'I know it doesn't look it right now, but I've actually done you a good turn. Maybe you can do me one sometime.'

He slipped out and closed the door. Hall and Baxter rushed it, but too late as Dillon turned the key in the lock. He vaulted over the stern down into the water, retrieved his inflatable jack, air tank and fins and pulled them on. Then he went under the surface and swam back to Harley Dock.

On board the *River Queen* in the saloon Baxter

stood on the table and unclipped the deck hatch above his head. When it was open Harry Salter and Hall gave him a push up. A few moments later and he was outside the saloon door and opening it.

'Here, how's my face?' Billy asked his uncle.

Salter inspected it. 'You'll live. It's only a scratch. There's sticking plaster in the medical kit in the wheelhouse.'

'So what are we going to do?' Billy demanded.

'Find out who shopped us,' Salter said. 'Let's face it, only a limited range of people knew about this job. So, the sooner I run that bastard to earth, the sooner I'll find our friend.' He turned to Baxter and Hall. 'Haul up the anchor and let's get out of here and back to Wapping.'

Dillon had stripped his diving suit, dressed in shirt, jeans and his old reefer, and was already making his way to Wapping. It was ten-thirty as he drove along streets that were deserted and lined by decaying warehouses of what had once been the greatest port in the world. Eventually he cut through a part of the city that was considerably more busy and then passed the Tower of London and reached Wapping High Street.

He parked the Toyota at the kerb and proceeded on foot to Cable Wharfe. He had already checked out Salter's pub, the Dark Man, earlier. It was almost eleven o'clock and closing time. A drink would give him an excuse to be in the area so he walked along the wharf openly and went into the saloon bar. There were two old women at a marble-topped table drinking stout and three men at the end of the bar with beer in front of them who looked as if they might be seamen, but only just.

The barmaid was in her forties, blonde hair swept back from a face that was heavily made up. 'What's your pleasure, sunshine?' she asked Dillon.

Dillon smiled that special smile of his, nothing but warmth and immense charm. 'Well, if it's only drink we're talking about, let's make it Bushmills.'

'Sorry, but you'll have to drink up fast,' she told him as she gave him the Bushmills. 'Closing time and I've got to think of my licence with coppers around.'

'And where would they be?'

'The three at the end of the bar. They're no more seamen than my arse.'

'So what are they up to?'

'God knows.'

'Then I'll get out of it.' Dillon swallowed his Bushmills. 'I'll say goodnight to you.'

The two old women were leaving and Dillon followed them along the wharf, aware of a police van parked in a courtyard to the left, a police car across the road.

'A trifle conspicuous,' he said softly, reached Wapping High Street and doubled back. He found what he wanted, another disused warehouse, carefully negotiated stairs leading to the first floor and crouched on one of the old loading platforms beneath a crane. He had a perfect view of the river, the wharf and the Dark Man. He took out his infrared night glasses, focused them, and the *River Queen* came into view.

As the *River Queen* docked all hell broke loose. The police van and car that Dillon had noticed earlier drove on to the wharf and at the same time two River Police patrol boats moved out of the shadows where they had been waiting and pulled alongside. As uniformed police came over the rail they found Hall and Baxter tying up. Salter and Billy came out of the saloon and looked up at the half dozen policemen on the wharf. The line parted and a tall man in his fifties in the uniform of a superintendent came forward.

'Why it's Superintendent Brown, our old friend, Billy,' Salter said. 'And how are you, Tony?'

Brown smiled. 'Permission to come aboard, Harry,' and he climbed down followed by the other police officers.

'So what's all this?' Salter demanded.

'Well, Harry, I know there wouldn't be anything

in the pub. You're too smart for that and we've turned you over often enough. However, I've reason to believe you're carrying an illegal shipment of diamonds on this vessel to the amount of two hundred thousand pounds. Very silly, Harry, to slip like that after all these years.' Brown turned to the sergeant at his elbow. 'Read him his rights and, the rest of you, start looking.'

'Diamonds on the *River Queen*,' Salter laughed out loud. 'Tony, my old son, you really have got it wrong this time.'

It was almost one o'clock in the morning when they finished. Salter and his crew were sitting at the table in the saloon playing Gin Rummy when the Superintendent looked in.

'A word, Harry.'

The police had finished their fruitless task and were getting into the van. The two patrol boats started up and moved away. It was raining now and Salter and Brown stood under the canopy on deck.

'So what gives?' Salter asked.

'Harry, I don't know what happened tonight, but I had what seemed like the hottest tip in my life.'

'Well, whoever your snout was, I hope you didn't pay the bastard.'

Brown shook his head. 'You're getting old, Harry, too old to do ten years in Parkhurst. Think about it.'

'I will, Tony.'

Brown clambered up on to the wharf and turned. 'We've known each other a long time, Harry, so I'll do you a favour. I'd be very careful in future about the Dutch end of things.' He got in the police car beside his driver and they moved away.

'Jesus,' Billy said. 'We could all have gone down the steps for a long time. That bastard back there when he took the stones, what was it he said? That he'd done you a good turn.'

'That's right, quite a coincidence,' Salter said. 'Only I don't believe in them. Anyway, let's go up to the pub and get a drink.'

Dillon waited until all was quiet, then went back down the stairs of the old warehouse and walked to the pub. There was a light on in the saloon and when he looked in he saw Salter sitting on a stool at the end of the bar. Billy, sticking plaster on his face, sat drinking at one of the tables with Baxter and Hall. Dillon moved on, turned up the side alley and looked in the kitchen. The barmaid was drinking a cup of tea and reading a newspaper.

He opened the kitchen door. She looked up in alarm. 'I see the peelers have gone,' Dillon said.

'Christ, who are you?'

'Old friend of Harry's. If he's as bright as I think he is he might even be expecting me. I'll go through to the bar.'

Harry Salter drank his Scotch and waited, looking at his reflection in the old Victorian mirror behind the bar. A small wind touched his cheek as the door opened, there was a sliding sound as the yellow oilskin bag slid along the bar and stopped in front of him.

'There you go,' Dillon said.

The other three stopped talking and Salter lifted the bag in one hand, then turned to look at Dillon standing there at the end of the bar in his old reefer coat. Dillon took out a cigarette and lit it and Salter, a crook from the age of fifteen, knew trouble when he saw it.

'And what's your game, my old son?' he asked.

'It's him,' Billy cried. 'The fucking bastard.'

'Leave off, Billy,' Salter told him.

'After what he did? Look at my bleeding face.' Billy picked up the lager bottle in front of him, smashed it on the edge of the table and hurled himself at Dillon, the broken bottled extended. Dillon swayed to one side, caught the wrist and hammered Billy's arm against the bar so that he howled with pain and dropped the bottle. Dillon held him face down on the bar, Billy's arm tight as an iron bar.

'God, Mr Salter, but he never learns, this nephew of yours.'

'Don't be a silly boy, Billy,' Salter said. 'If he hadn't nicked the stones downriver we'd be booking in at Tower Bridge Division Police Station with the prospect of going down the steps for ten years. All I want to know is the reason for all this.' He smiled at Dillon. 'You've got a name, my old son?'

'Dillon – Sean Dillon.'

Salter went behind the bar and Dillon released Billy who stood there massaging his arm then went and sat down with Baxter and Hall, his face sullen.

Salter said, 'You're no copper, I can smell one of those a mile off.'

'God save us,' Dillon said, 'I've had enough trouble with those bowsers to last me a lifetime. Let's put it this way, Mr Salter. I work for one of those Government organizations that isn't supposed to exist.'

Salter stood there looking at him for a long moment then said, 'What's your pleasure?'

'Bushmills whiskey if you don't have Krug champagne.'

Salter laughed out loud. 'I like it, I really do. Bushmills I can manage right now. Krug I'll supply next time.' He took a bottle down from the shelf and poured a generous measure. 'So what's it about?'

'Cheers.' Dillon toasted him. 'Well, the thing is I wanted to meet the greatest expert on the Thames River and when I accessed the police computer it turned out to be you. The trouble was that no sooner did I find you than I discovered I was going to lose you. Someone I work with, very big at Special Branch, found out the River Police were going to stiff you.'

'Very inconvenient,' Salter said.

'Well it would have been so I decided to do something about it.' Dillon smiled. 'The rest you know.'

Salter poured himself another drink. 'You want something from me, that's it, isn't it? Some sort of kick back?'

'Your expertise, Mr Salter, your knowledge of the river.'

'What for?'

'You may have read in the papers that the President of the United States and the Prime Minister are to meet on the Terrace at the House of Commons on Friday morning.'

'So what?'

'I think the security stinks and I have to prove it so sometime after midnight on Friday morning I want you to help me float in to the Terrace. I'll hide out in one of the store rooms behind the

Terrace Bar and give them a nice surprise at the appropriate moment.'

Salter stared at him in amazement. 'You must be raving bloody mad. Are you a lunatic or something?'

'It's been suggested before.'

Salter turned to the other three. 'Did you hear that? We've got a bleeding loony here.' He turned back to Dillon. 'But I like you. Not only will I do it, you can call me Harry.'

'Terrific,' Dillon said. 'Could I have another Bushmills?'

'I can do better, much better.' Salter opened the fridge at the back of the bar, took out a bottle and turned. 'Krug champagne, my old son. How does that suit you?'

9

The following day was Thursday and when Dillon went into Hannah Bernstein's office on the third floor at the Ministry of Defence it was just before noon.

'My God, Dillon, what time do you call this? He's been asking for you.'

'The hard night I had, girl dear. In fact I only came in to ask you to have a delicious light luncheon with me.'

'You're quite mad.' She pressed her intercom. 'He's here, Brigadier.'

'Send him in.' There was a pause. 'And you, Chief Inspector.'

She led the way, opening the door for Dillon who advanced to the desk where Ferguson was working at a pile of papers. He didn't look up.

'God save the good work,' Dillon said and waited. Ferguson ignored him and the Irishman laughed. 'God save you kindly is the correct answer to that, Brigadier.'

Ferguson sat back. 'I am well aware that as a boy you went to the Royal Academy of Dramatic Art, Dillon. I am well aware that you actually acted with the National Theatre.'

'Lyngstrand in *The Lady from the Sea*. Ibsen that was,' Dillon reminded him.

'Until you decided to take up the theatre of the street for the IRA. As my mother, God rest her, was Irish, I do my best to understand you, but your constant role of the stage Irishman proves wearisome.'

'God save us, your honour, but I'll try to mend my ways.'

'For God's sake, be serious. You're leaving me with egg on my face because of this ridiculous bet with Carter. You know how much the Intelligence Service hates our very existence. They'd like nothing better than to make me look a fool in front of the Prime Minister.'

'Don't I know that?' Dillon said. 'That's why I thought I'd make Carter look the fool.'

Ferguson frowned. 'Are you seriously telling me you think you can?'

'Of course.'

The Brigadier frowned. 'Where have you been? It's almost noon.'

'I had a hard night preparing the way, so to speak.'

'Tell me.'

'You wouldn't want to know,' Dillon said. 'But one thing I'll promise you. The next time you'll see me will be at ten-thirty tomorrow morning on the Terrace together with the President of the United States and the Prime Minister.'

Ferguson sat back staring at him. 'My God, Sean, you actually think you can do it.'

'I know I can, Brigadier and watch yourself. You just called me Sean.'

'Are you going to tell me how?'

'Aspects of it are so illegal that it's better you shouldn't know. I'll discuss it with this good-looking woman here if I can take her to lunch.'

Ferguson laughed in spite of himself. 'Oh, go on, you rogue. Get out of here; but if it costs me five hundred pounds it comes out of your salary.'

They returned to Hannah's office. She said, 'You really think you can pull it off?'

'Nothing is impossible to the great Dillon. A magician, that's what British Intelligence called me in the great days in Ulster. They never laid hands on me once, Hannah, your lot. The master of disguise. Did I tell you about the time I dressed as a woman?'

'I don't want to know this, Dillon, because if I do, I have to consider how many you killed.'

'Fighting a war, Hannah, that's what I was doing, but that was then and this is now. Get your coat and we'll away. I am right about Jewish people? No seafood but you can eat smoked salmon?'

'Of course. Why?'

'Good. Krug champagne, scrambled eggs and smoked salmon, the best in town.'

'But where?'

He held her coat for her. 'Jesus, girl, but will you stop asking all these questions?'

He took her to the Piano Bar at the Dorchester, the best in London, with its magnificent mirrored ceiling, was greeted by the manager as an old friend and led to a booth. Dillon ordered his usual, Krug champagne non-vintage and scrambled eggs, smoked salmon and a salad for both of them.

'God, but you live well, Dillon,' she said. 'That's an Armani suit you're wearing and you can afford these prices.'

'I'm still trying to spend some of that six hundred thousand pounds I got out of Michael Aroun for failing to blow up the Prime Minister and the War Cabinet at Number Ten during the Gulf War.'

'You've no shame, have you? None at all?'

'Why pretend? It's what I was and it's what I am. The same man, Hannah my love, and times you've been glad of it.'

The champagne came, was opened and poured.

He toasted her. 'To the best-looking policewoman in London.'

'That kind of flattery gets you nowhere. Now tell me what's going on.'

When he was finished she gazed at him in horror. 'You used me, you used privileged police intelligence to get a notorious gangster and his men off the hook?'

'He's not such a bad old stick.' Dillon sipped some champagne. 'And I needed him.'

'How could you do such a thing?'

'Come off it, Hannah, Ferguson does things to suit himself all the time. What about that Lithuanian bastard, Platoff, the other month? If ever a man deserved to be shot it was him, but he was more useful to us than the other people so Ferguson did a deal and, as I remember, you brokered it.'

She glared at him. 'Damn you, Dillon.'

'Sure and you look lovely when you're angry.' The waiter approached at that moment with their food. 'Eat up like a good girl.'

'Dillon, you are a sexist pig.'

'And you are a nice Jewish girl who should be having babies and making her husband's life miserable instead of shooting people on behalf of Scotland Yard.'

She laughed, in spite of herself. 'This is lovely. So tell me how you intend to do it.'

'The river. I'll swim in.'

'But the current there can be ferocious with the tide running. It's suicide, Dillon. You mustn't.'

'Yes, you're right. That's why the Terrace is a weak spot in the security system.'

'But how can you hope to get away with it?'

'Difficult, but not impossible,' and he explained.

The *River Queen* was still tied up at Cable Wharfe when Dillon turned up in the Toyota at eleven o'clock that evening. The pub was just closing and he sat there watching the last customers emerge and walk away towards Wapping High Street. The barmaid stood at the door talking to Billy. She closed the door and he crossed to the boat.

Dillon got out of the Toyota. 'Good man yourself, Billy, could you be giving me a hand?'

Billy looked at him, a kind of reluctant admiration on his face. 'You know you're mad, don't you? I mean my uncle's told me what you're up to. Crazy. For one thing you won't even get into the Terrace. The current's real murder out there.'

'If I don't get back you can sell the Toyota. My hand on it.'

He held it out and Billy shook it instinctively.

'Mad bastard. OK, what have we got here?' and he opened the rear door of the van.

In the saloon, Dillon laid out his gear watched by Harry Salter and the other three. There was his heavy nylon diving suit with hood, nylon socks and gloves.

'You're going to need that bleeding lot,' Salter told him. 'That water's bloody cold tonight.'

'I never thought it wouldn't be.'

Dillon laid out his fins and clipped the air tank he'd brought to the inflatable. He checked his weight belt, then opened a hang bag and took out a small Halogen lamp and a waterproof purse.

'You won't need that lamp,' Salter said. 'I've passed the Terrace regularly in the early hours and they leave that row of Victorian lamps on. Even if you get there, Dillon, you could get done. They must have security guards prowling. One glimpse and you've had it.'

'Yes, well, I know that.' Dillon opened the waterproof pouch and checked the contents.

'And what's that?'

'Picklocks. I need to get into one of the storerooms as I told you to spend the rest of the night.'

Salter shook his head. 'And you know how to use those things.' He shook his head. 'No, don't answer that. With that accent of yours are you sure you're not going to shoot the Prime Minister?'

'Perish the thought.' Dillon unzipped a waterproof bag and checked the contents.

'And what have you got there?' Salter asked.

'White shirt, bow tie, nice white jacket, black slacks and shoes.' Dillon smiled. 'After all, I *am* supposed to be a waiter.'

He zipped the bag up again and Billy fell about laughing. 'Dillon, I like you, I really do. You're crazy, you don't give a stuff, just like me.'

'I'll take that as a compliment.' Dillon stood up and looked down at his gear. 'That's it, then.' He turned. 'I'm in your hands now, Harry.'

'All right, my old son, let's go over it.'

There was a very large-scale map on the table and they all gathered round it. 'Here we go. House of Commons, Embankment opposite and there's Westminster Bridge. Now I'm telling you this is one of the worst times of the year. A very high tide, turning around three o'clock in the morning and, to float you in, I need the tide on the turn and driving downriver, but it's an abnormal speed. A good five knots. Maybe you should consider that.'

'I have,' Dillon told him.

'There's no way you can control that current

by swimming. It's too strong. But if you're hanging on the stern as I approach and I drop you at just the right moment you could have a chance.'

'Fine,' Dillon said. 'It'll do me.'

'Crazy.' Salter shook his head. 'Crazy.'

Dillon grinned, found a packet of cigarettes and went out on deck, standing under the canopy and looked at the rain. Salter joined him.

'I love this old river.' He leaned against the bulkhead. 'I was a river rat when I was a kid. My old man did a runner and my mum did bits of cleaning to keep body and soul together. Anything I could nick I did, fags, booze, anything.'

'And progressed from there.'

'I've never done drugs, never done women, that's filth as far as I'm concerned. Mind you, I've always been a hard bastard. I've killed in my time, but only some sod who was out to kill me.'

'I see.'

'And you?'

'Oh, I've been at war with the world for more than twenty years.'

'With that accent does that mean what I think it does?'

Dillon said, 'Not any longer, Harry; as I said, I do work for a rather shadowy branch of the Security Services. Let's leave it at that.'

'All right, my old son.' Salter grinned. 'But with what you've got ahead of you you're going to need food in your belly. We'll all go up to Wapping High Street. Best fish and chip shop in London there.'

Just before three the *River Queen* passed under Westminster Bridge and turned, fighting the surging tide. The deck lights were out, only a subdued light in the wheelhouse. Dillon's gear was laid out in the stern and Salter stood there with him.

'I'm going to take over from Billy at the wheel. When he comes down here he'll have a two-way radio. You hang off at the stern. You'll be OK as far as the propellers go. With the design of this boat they're well underneath.'

'Then what?'

'At what I consider the right moment I'll call Billy on the radio and, when he gives you the shout, you go. If I get it right, the current could bang you against the Terrace. If I don't, God help you.'

'Thanks, Harry,' Dillon grinned. 'You're a hell of a fella.'

'Get stuffed, you bloody lunatic,' Salter told him and walked away.

Dillon turned to Hall and Baxter who stood waiting. 'All right, lads, let's get this lot on.'

* * *

Ten minutes later, he hung on a line from the stern rail, his two equipment bags trailing from his belt, aware of Billy leaning over the rail above him. They were in the shadows, the water very turbulent, and Dillon was conscious of the fierceness of the current. And then Billy called down to him and he let go the line.

He went down five or six feet and the force of the current was incredible, like a great hand seizing him in a relentless grip. He was thrown to the surface, was aware of the *River Queen* disappearing into the dark, of the lights of the Victorian lamps on the Terrace and then he went under again. A moment later he banged against the stonework of the Terrace, surfaced and cannoned into the scaffolding that dropped down into the water at the division of the Lords and Commons.

He hung there for a long moment and then unbuckled his inflatable and air tank and let the current take them. He did the same with his fins and mask, paused then started to climb. He went over the parapet, trailing his two equipment bags, and crouched in the shadows.

A door opened further along the Terrace and a security guard appeared. He walked forward and stood at the parapet and lit a cigarette, the smoke pungent on the damp air. Dillon waited for five agonizing minutes until finally the man tossed the stub of his cigarette into the river, turned and went back inside.

Dillon unfastened the lines of his equipment bags then unzipped his diving suit and stood there naked except for swimming trunks. He dropped the diving suit into the river then picked up the equipment bags and went to the side of the Terrace Bar where there were storerooms. He opened the small equipment bag, took out the Halogen lamp and opened the purse containing the picklocks. He switched on the lamp and went to work. It took him less than five minutes and the door opened.

He made a quick exploration. There were stacks of towels and tablecloths, cartons of wine glasses. There were also two toilets and a washbasin in another room at the rear. He opened the larger equipment bag, took out the clothes it contained and a towel he had put in. He dried himself thoroughly, took off the swimming trunks and dressed in the waiter's clothes he had brought.

He checked his watch. It was now a quarter to four. Depending on what time the Terrace staff started, he had about four to five hours to kill. There was a sizeable stock cupboard with various kinds of linen inside. There was no key in the door so he locked it from the inside and arranged some piles of towels into a rough bed. It was surprising how cheerful he felt.

'Harry will be pleased,' he thought and fell almost instantly asleep.

He came awake with a start, aware of the door handle rattling. He glanced at his watch and saw it was almost nine o'clock. He heard a voice call, 'The bloody door's locked. I'll go and see if I can find a key.'

Footsteps retreated, the outer door opened and closed. Dillon opened the door in seconds, moved into one of the toilet stalls and locked it. He waited and, after a while, the outer door opened and someone entered. There were two of them because after the door was opened a man said, 'Right, take those tablecloths and get cracking.'

A woman said, 'All right, Mr Smith.'

The door banged and the man started whistling and moving around. After a while he moved into the next toilet stall and sat down and lit a cigarette. Dillon flushed the toilet and went out. The man's white jacket hung on a peg by the basin, a plastic identity card on the jacket. Dillon unpinned it and fastened it to his own jacket so that it was half obscured by his lapel.

When he went outside, the Terrace was already a scene of activity, waiters everywhere at work in the bar and making up tables. Dillon picked up a napkin from a table, draped it over one arm and reached for a tray. He went straight out past two security guards and up the steps.

For an hour he went walkabout, visiting restaurants, not only in the Commons, but the House of Lords, keeping constantly on the move, his tray at the ready. Not once was he challenged. God knows what Ferguson would make of that. As for Carter . . .

It was just after ten that he made his way back to the Terrace. It was a hive of activity. He went in past the security guards and paused. A grey-haired man in black coat and striped trousers was ordering waiters here and there, telling them what to do. He didn't even give Dillon a second glance when he spoke to him.

'You – canapés from the rear table.'

'Yes, sir,' Dillon said.

He stood against the wall with other waiters and a few moments later, Members of Parliament started to flood in. It was amazing how quickly the Terrace filled up and the waiters got to work and served refreshments. Dillon did his bit, taking a tray of canapés around and then he caught sight of Ferguson, Hannah Bernstein and Carter entering.

Dillon turned away, but stood close enough to hear Carter say, 'Sorry for you, Ferguson, that little bastard's left you with egg on your face.'

'If you say so,' Ferguson said.

A moment later, an announcement sounded over the Tannoy. 'Ladies and gentlemen, the Prime Minister and the President of the United States.'

They came through the entrance and stood there and the crowd broke into spontaneous applause. Dillon crossed to the table, picked up a canapé dish with a lid, hovered over it for a moment then turned. The President and the Prime Minister were moving through the crowd, pausing to speak to people. They reached Simon Carter, Ferguson and Hannah Bernstein and stopped.

Dillon heard the President say, 'Brigadier Ferguson. Good to see you again.' He greeted Carter, then Hannah.

Dillon walked forward. 'Excuse me, gentlemen.'

He was aware of the look of amazement on Hannah's face, of Ferguson's incredulous frown and on Carter's face nothing but shock. Dillon lifted the lid of the canapé dish, disclosing a five pound note nestling on top.

'Your fiver, sir.'

Carter was incandescent with rage, but the most interesting reaction was from President Clinton. 'Why, Mr Dillon, is that you?' he said.

It was the middle of the afternoon and they were together in Ferguson's office, the three of them.

There was a look of unholy joy on Ferguson's face. 'You cunning Irish bastard.'

'And you a half one.'

'The look on Carter's face. Delicious. I had to explain to the President and the Prime Minister, of course, which didn't help Carter. The President thought it was fantastic. I must tell you that after our previous help to him with the peace process in Ireland last year he had a high opinion of you, Dillon. It's now even higher. So, how did you do it?'

'From the river, Brigadier, but I'd rather not get into details.'

Ferguson turned to Hannah Bernstein. 'Do you know, Chief Inspector?'

'I'm afraid I do, sir.'

'As bad as that, is it?'

'Let's put it this way: the background to it is so criminal that if I were still working for Special Branch at Scotland Yard I'd have no other choice but to read Dillon his rights and arrest him. However, under the peculiar circumstances of my employment with you such considerations do not apply.'

'Good God.' Ferguson shook his head. 'Still, I knew what I was taking on when I recruited you, Dillon; only myself to blame. Go about your business, the both of you,' and he opened a file in front of him.

* * *

At the same time at Green Rapids Detention Centre Kathleen Ryan and her uncle walked through the park. There were as usual, thanks to the Warden's liberal visitation policy, a large number of visitors. Paolo Salamone walked some little distance behind. He had received a phone call from Sollazo as his lawyer just after breakfast.

It had been brief and to the point. 'Regarding the matter we discussed the other day and the individual concerned, any further information would certainly help your case.'

Salamone hadn't known such excitement in a long time. There was a real chance now, with Sollazo and the Don on his side, that he might get some review of his sentence and anything was worth that, which was why he kept an eye out for the Kelly girl. He knew from talking to her uncle that she mainly worked the night shift at the hospital which allowed her to visit three, sometimes four times a week.

They didn't seem to be talking much and he saw them stroll towards one of the small rustic shelters beside the lake. Salamone hurried through a small plantation of trees behind the hut and stood at the back. He could hear them talking quite plainly.

'You seem depressed today, girl.'

'And why shouldn't I be, you in here like a caged animal.'

'Little I can do about that, little anyone can do.'

'You know, when they transferred you here I was full of hope. That's why I saw that fella Cassidy you shared a cell with once at Sing-Sing and got the forged passports. I thought there would be a chance of making a break,' Kathleen said.

'Not from here. You know why the regime here is so liberal. Because the security is so tight. Every modern electronic marvel on these walls, cameras scrutinizing every move. I'm going to die here, Kathleen, and that's the truth of it. Time we talked about your future, time you moved on and, when you decide to go, I've things to say.'

'Such as?'

'It can wait.'

'Then don't talk rubbish. How's your health?'

'Not bad. I take the pills, do as I'm told. They'll be taking me down to Green Rapids General Hospital on Tuesday morning for another heart scan.'

'I'm on the night shift, but I'll go in and look out for you. I'll see you again tomorrow anyway, I've got the time in the morning. Around eleven.'

'That's nice.'

They got up and walked away and Salamone went back up through the trees.

As they approached the security gates Kathleen said, 'Are you still on the same pills?'

'No, a new one.' He took a plastic bottle from his shirt pocket. 'There you go.'

She checked it. 'Dazane? That's a new one on me. I'll check it out at the hospital.' She gave the bottle back to him and kissed his cheek. 'I'll be seeing you.'

Salamone phoned through to Sollazo's office using one of the prisoners' call boxes. The secretary was dubious. Mr Sollazo was busy, but she finally gave in to Salamone's persistence and put him through.

'What have you got?' Sollazo asked. 'It better be good.'

'I overheard Kelly and his niece talking. She talked about how she'd hoped he'd be able to make a break when he transferred from Sing-Sing to Green Rapids. Some chance. Nobody's crashed out of here since it opened.'

'So why should this interest me?'

'She was talking about false passports she'd got from some forger called Cassidy who used to share a cell with Kelly at Sing-Sing.'

'Now that is interesting,' Sollazo said. 'Anything else?'

'Not really. Oh, yes, he's going to Green Rapids General Hospital on Tuesday morning to have a heart scan. As I said, he suffers from angina. By the way, she said she was going to see him again in the morning at eleven.'

'You've done well, Paolo, keep up the good work. Just one thing I didn't tell you. Liam Kelly is actually Michael Ryan, once a big activist in Irish politics on the Protestant side. He's killed more men than he can remember.'

'Jesus!' Salamone said.

'His niece is Kathleen Ryan. She, too, has killed in her time. These aren't ordinary crooks, Paolo, they are revolutionaries and, as we know, such people are like wild dogs, a little touched in the head. Never take them for granted.'

'I won't, Mr Sollazo, and you'll do what you can for me?'

'That goes without saying.'

Sollazo put down the phone, sat there thinking about it then buzzed his secretary. 'Find Mori for me, he should be somewhere about.'

He went back to the legal brief in front of him, smiling slightly as he saw the fatal flaw in the District Attorney's case. There was a knock at the door and Mori entered.

'Yes, *signore*,' he said in Sicilian.

Sollazo sat back. 'I've heard from Salamone, more information on Ryan and his niece. It seems she got false passports from a forger called Cassidy who shared a cell with Ryan in Sing-Sing. Find him and bring him to me. Somebody will know him.'

'No problem,' Mori told him. 'I'll make a few calls,' and he went out.

It was only one-and-a-half hours later that he parked his limousine outside the small photo and print shop in a Bronx side street and entered. A black youth was attending a machine that churned out holiday snaps.

He paused and came to the counter. 'Yes, sir?'

'Mr Cassidy. Tell him he's wanted.'

'He's in the back, I'll get him.'

'No need, kid, I'll handle it myself.'

Mori went behind the counter and opened the door. Cassidy, a small balding man with wire spectacles, was working on what to Mori looked like a share certificate.

Mori said, 'Up to your old tricks?'

Cassidy, who knew trouble when he saw it, stood up. 'What is this?' he blustered.

'I represent the Russo family and Don Antonio's nephew and lawyer, Mr Marco Sollazo, would appreciate your help in a small matter.'

Cassidy went very pale and removed his spectacles with a shaking hand. 'Anything I can do.'

'I thought you'd feel like that. You do a nice line in false passports and I take it you're the careful kind of guy who keeps records. Am I right?'

Cassidy licked his lips nervously. 'That's right. Who are we talking about?'

'A guy you shared a cell with at Sing-Sing, Liam Kelly. His niece came to see you some time ago.'

'Sure,' Cassidy said. 'I've got all the details.'

'Then stick them in a file and let's go. Mr Sollazo doesn't like to be kept waiting.'

'Irish passports, you say?' Sollazo said to Cassidy who stood before his desk.

'Sure, Mr Sollazo, in the names of Daniel and Nancy Forbes. There was no problem getting a current photo of Kelly. They have one of those photo machines at the prison. They're always needing pictures for various security tags the cons use up there.'

'When was this?'

'Eighteen months ago. They're current passports of the European Community variety with brown covers. Kelly's supposed to be an artist. I thought that was good because he paints in his cell.'

'And the girl?'

'Nurse, which is what she is.'

'I know,' Sollazo said. 'And this was first class work?'

'Oh, sure, entry and exit stamps for everywhere from Hong Kong to the UK. I even gave them visas for Egypt. Good work, I swear on my life, Mr Sollazo.'

'I'm sure you're telling the truth.' Sollazo turned to Mori. 'If he proves false, Giovanni, you have my permission to break both his legs and arms.'

'A pleasure.' Mori didn't even smile.

Cassidy was sweating. 'Please, Mr Sollazo, I'm an honest guy.'

Sollazo burst out laughing. 'Get out of here.'

Mori saw him through the door then returned. 'Anything else, *signore*?'

'Yes, I want you to go and see Salamone. It seems Ryan is being taken to Green Rapids General Hospital on Tuesday morning for a heart scan. Find out all you can, how the system works when they take one of the inmates for that kind of check.'

'Does the *signore* mean what I think he means?'

'Perhaps. Afterwards, check out the hospital. I don't need to tell you to be discreet. You always are.'

'Thank you, *signore*,' Mori said, face impassive as he went out, and Sollazo went back to work.

Salamone was desperately afraid of Mori, but then most people were for he was the Russo family's most feared enforcer, so he received him with some trepidation. They walked over the grass towards the lake and Mori told him why he had come.

Salamone, eager to please, was more than helpful. 'They use a special security ambulance to take guys down to the hospital. I've gone myself when they've had a stretcher case needing a nurse.'

'How many guards?'

'The driver and a guy riding shotgun beside him. Usually another two in the back with the cons. It depends how many, but I can tell you Tuesday morning is light, just Kelly or Ryan or whatever they call him and a guy called Bryant who's going to have a keyhole op on his prostate. I've seen the schedule.'

'Fine,' Mori said. 'So where would they take Ryan?'

'Third floor. There's a clinic there called General Heart Surgery.'

'So a guard takes him up there, or two maybe?'

'Usually one. I mean the guy has a heart condition. He's handcuffed, of course.'

'At all times?'

'Not while he's having treatment.'

'Good,' Mori said. 'That's all I need to know. You know the old saying from Sicily? Keep the tongue in the mouth or it gets cut out.'

'Jesus, Giovanni.' Paolo sounded shocked. 'I mean, I love my Don.'

'Sure you do.' Mori patted his face and walked away.

* * *

208

The hospital car park was full, but someone pulled out as Mori arrived so Mori took the space which he noted was reserved for the Chief of Surgery. He went in through the main entrance. It was very modern, lots of tiling and high technology, staff everywhere, nurses in uniform, doctors in white coats and many people who were presumably visitors.

He strode confidently through the concourse and took a lift to the fourth floor quite deliberately. The corridor he stepped out into was very quiet. A door opposite said storeroom, then there was a lift with very wide doors, obviously designed to carry stretchers and trolleys. Next to it a door said Staff Rest Room. Mori opened it without hesitation and went in.

There were washbasins and toilet cubicles and a row of pegs, some of them occupied by overalls and white coats, one of which had a plastic security card pinned to it in the name of a Doctor Lynn, Radiology. Mori put it on and went out.

He took the lift down to the third floor, exited and strolled confidently along, looking for the clinic Salamone had described, and there it was: General Heart Surgery. He opened the swing door and went in.

There were two or three patients on the benches, a young black nurse at reception. She looked up and smiled and Mori put his hands in his pockets so that the white coat parted, just in case she knew the name on the identity card.

'Can I help you, Doctor?'

'I'm new, I'm afraid; Radiology. I've got to see a patient up here on Tuesday morning, an inmate from Green Rapids Detention Centre. I was just checking. You know, getting my bearings. A heart patient.'

'Oh sure, Mr Kelly. He's been here on several occasions. Yes, you're in the right place. Clinic Three right down the hall, that's where he's treated.'

'Well thank you,' Mori told her and went down the hall. He glanced through the round window in the door of Clinic Three, saw a patient on a trolley, a nurse bending over him.

He passed on to a door marked Fire Exit, opened it and found himself in a quiet corridor. The doors opposite were marked Freight Elevator. He called it up and, when it arrived, punched the basement button. When he stepped out, he found doors standing wide to an underground car park, walked through and found himself in the car park where he had left his limousine. He stood there smiling then went and opened the driver's door, took off the white coat and threw it in the back, then he got behind the wheel.

When Kathleen Ryan entered the Pharmacology Department of the hospital the young doctor on duty was Indian, a Doctor Sieed. She wore a sari. She knew Kathleen and liked her.

'What can I do for you, nurse?'

'My uncle is an angina patient. I was just talking to him and he told me he was on new pills, something I'm not familiar with. Dazane.'

Doctor Sieed nodded. 'A recent addition. It has an excellent record but the dosage is critical. One, three times a day.'

'Yes, I noticed that.'

'Overdose can be a problem. Three at the same time would actually promote a severe angina attack.'

'Of a critical nature?'

'Probably not, but it would give the patient a bad shock for a couple of days. Tell him to be careful.'

'Thank you.'

Kathleen went along to the staff room, got her coat and shoulder bag and left by the main entrance. As she walked across the car park Giovanni Mori drove past her in the limousine and turned into the main road.

10

The Don was in an expansive mood when Sollazo went to see him. 'You look pleased with yourself, Marco.'

'I think I have a solution.'

'Good, but family business first. Anything for me to sign?'

'A couple of property deeds, a transfer. I have them here.' Sollazo opened his briefcase and took out various papers.

'Let's get on with it.' He produced a pen and did what was necessary. 'Good. Now a couple of my very special Vodka Martinis.

'The best in the world.'

'Of course.' Russo went behind the bar and mixed the drinks and Sollazo sat on a bar stool. The Martini was excellent and he savoured it with pleasure. The old man toasted him. 'The Ryan business. Tell me.'

Which Sollazo did in finest detail. When he was

finished the Don said, 'You really think Mori could manage this on his own?'

'Absolutely and so simple. No one else involved.'

'It would require Ryan's co-operation.'

'But of course.'

'And he'll want his niece with him.'

'Naturally.'

'So how will you persuade him?'

'To quote your favourite film, I'll make him an offer he can't refuse.'

The old man nodded. 'There must be no link between you and Ryan, no link with the family. In the event of success we don't want the police tying us in.'

'No problem there. When I go to Green Rapids it's to see Salamone, all perfectly legitimate, but the regime there is so ridiculously liberal, prisoners walking around the park area with their families or attorneys, that it's possible to talk to anyone. Salamone tells me the girl visits her uncle again tomorrow at eleven. I'll see him then and take the opportunity of speaking to Ryan.'

The Don sipped his Martini thoughtfully. 'Tell me, Salamone's expectations of some sort of move-ment as regards reducing his sentence – have you any hopes there?'

'None at all, but I try to keep his hopes up for other reasons. He knows a great deal about family business.'

'Too much. There is an old Sicilian saying, "Better to lop the branch than lose the tree."' The Don nodded gravely. 'And there would be the point that he is the only link between us and this Ryan affair.'

'He's entirely disposable,' Sollazo said calmly. 'So he has an accident one day. We have friends in there happy to oblige.'

'Good. I'll let you get on with it then.'

It was a fine bright morning just before eleven when Sollazo strolled through the park with Salamone.

'You've done well for us,' the lawyer said. 'The Don is pleased.'

'Great.' Salamone nodded eagerly. 'And how's my case going?'

'I'm working on it, Paolo; these things take time.'

At that moment he saw Michael Ryan and Kathleen move down towards the lake and sit down in one of the rustic shelters.

Kathleen was saying, 'Dazane, that new heart pill you're on. You have to be careful to stick to the right dosage.'

'Sure and I know that. One three times a day.'

'I checked with Doctor Sieed. If you took three at the same time it would actually promote an angina attack.'

'And that would be curtains?'

'Let's say you wouldn't feel too good for a while.'

At that moment Marco Sollazo appeared before them, elegant in his dark suit and long Armani raincoat.

'Good morning, Mr Ryan.' He smiled at Kathleen. 'Miss Ryan.'

Ryan went very still. 'You've got the wrong names, mister, you must have made a mistake.'

'I don't think so.'

Kathleen said, 'Leave off, Uncle Michael.' She looked at Sollazo grimly. 'What's it about?'

'To start with, I know all about you. Michael and Kathleen Ryan, still wanted in Ulster for a number of terrorist activities on behalf of the Loyalist cause. I suppose the British could apply for your extradition if they knew where you were, Miss Ryan.'

'Damn you,' she said. 'What is it you want?'

'The gold bullion that went down ten years ago on the *Irish Rose* off the coast of County Down, and please don't say you don't know what I'm talking about.'

They both sat there staring at him. Finally Ryan said, 'You seem to know a great deal.'

'I know everything.'

'Right then,' Ryan told him. 'Then you must know that the *Irish Rose* sank in the darkness with a bad sea running. We were off course. I don't know where it went down.'

'Yes, you do. You had a gadget called a Master Navigator in your pocket, a sort of mini computer that perfectly calculated your course and position.'

Ryan, for once, looked amazed. 'But how could you know such a thing? Only myself knew that and Kathleen when I told her.'

'Someone was standing behind a tree listening when you told her. A man you knew as Martin Keogh.'

It was Kathleen who spoke now, her face solemn. 'You speak as if he was someone else?'

'Oh, he was. Did you ever meet the IRA Chief of Staff at that time, Mr Ryan, Jack Barry?'

'Not face-to-face.'

'He knew your original plan had been turned down by your Army Council, heard a whisper that you intended to go ahead privately so he ordered his best man to infiltrate you.'

Kathleen's face was very pale. 'Who was he?'

'A man called Sean Dillon. You've heard of him?'

'Oh, yes.' Ryan nodded. 'A legend. The man of a thousand faces, they used to say. He was once an actor. Foiled the Army and the RUC for a year.' He shook his head. 'Never got lifted once. So he was Martin.'

'The bastard.' Kathleen said.

'He could have killed you on the road that morning and taken the Master Navigator. Barry was annoyed with him for not doing so. He told Barry he liked you.' He smiled at the girl. 'And you.'

'Fuck him.' There were hot tears in her eyes. 'I hope he rots in hell.'

'Actually he's working for a highly secret branch of British Intelligence these days.'

'God save us.' Ryan laughed out loud. 'And wouldn't that be the Martin we knew and loved.'

'I know who you are now,' Ryan said. 'You're the Mafia attorney who looks after Paolo Salamone. You work for the Russo family.'

'Does that matter? Look, to business. I know everything right down to the fact that you, Miss Ryan, are in possession of false Irish passports in the names of Daniel and Nancy Forbes. I know that you're a nurse at Green Rapids General Hospital.'

'You know a lot, mister, but where is this leading?'

'To me arranging the escape of your uncle from hospital when he goes for his heart scan on Tuesday morning.'

There was a total silence and a kind of awe on Ryan's face. 'Dear God and you actually mean it.'

'Certainly.'

'Just a minute,' Kathleen put in and her face was hard. 'What would he have to do in exchange for that?'

'Disclose the position of the *Irish Rose*,' Sollazo said calmly. 'We've done a deal with Jack Barry. I saw him the other day in Dublin. He's no longer Chief of Staff, but he's willing to co-operate on behalf of his movement. A preliminary survey to locate the ship first then my organization will lay on some suitable salvage operation as a front.'

'You're working with the fucking IRA?' Kathleen said.

'Yes, on a fifty-fifty basis.'

'And they get the fruits of my uncle's labours? What's in it for him?'

'I could say one million pounds, but let's be fair. I'll make it two million.'

'Jesus, son, you've got your nerve,' Ryan said.

'You do have an alternative,' Sollazo told him. 'You could sit here for another fifteen years.'

Ryan's face was pale. 'But to work with Barry and the bloody IRA.'

Kathleen put a hand on his arm. 'We've got to be practical.' She turned to Sollazo. 'I'm included.'

'Of course. Once he's out, you join in. You'll be taken to a safe retreat to start with.'

'And leaving the country will be no problem?'

'Absolutely not. We'll fly to Ireland, probably in a Gulfstream. I'll be with you.'

'So that's it?'

'No. I'd like the location of the *Irish Rose*, the bearings indicated on that Master Navigator. Don't tell me the figures aren't burned into your brain.'

Kathleen put a hand on her uncle's arm. 'Oh, no, mister. You get that when we're safe out of here and in Ireland and not before.'

Sollazo smiled. 'Of course, Miss Ryan, I accept your terms. Now, let me explain exactly what I expect to happen.'

It was raining when the prison ambulance turned into the car park on Tuesday morning and pulled into a special parking spot close to the main entrance. Kathleen Ryan sat in her own car watching and saw her uncle and another man get out of the ambulance each handcuffed to a guard. Another guard and the driver got out and lit cigarettes as the prisoners were led inside.

She got out of the car, picked up the suitcase and walked round to the underground car park, doing exactly as she had been told, seeking a green-panel truck that carried the sign HENLEY LAUNDRY. She found it easily enough, Giovanni Mori sitting behind the wheel smoking a cigarette.

'I'm Kathleen Ryan. You're Mori.'

'That's right.' He got out, reached back inside and produced the white doctor's coat he'd stolen. As he pulled it on he said. 'So they've gone up?'

'Just now.'

'Sit in the passenger seat. I won't be long.' He reached inside the truck, took out another white coat and draped it across his arm.

'You've never met my uncle.'

'I've seen his picture,' he said calmly, went to the freight elevator and punched the button for the third floor.

He paused in the corridor then opened the fire door and entered the hallway of the General Heart Surgery Department. He glanced through the round window of the door marked Clinic Three. Ryan was lying on a table and a young doctor was busy attaching various wires to him. Mori walked down the hall and looked through the window of the swing door leading to the reception area. There was a duty nurse behind the desk, a couple of patients and the uniformed prison guard sitting on the benches reading magazines. Mori went back to Clinic Three, opened the door and went in.

The young doctor looked up, continuing to fasten the wires. 'Hello, doctor, what can I do for you?'

The leather sap Mori took from his pocket was filled with leadshot. It swung once and the doctor went down with a groan. Ryan was already swinging his legs to the floor, pulling the wires and connectors from his body.

Mori threw the white coat to him. 'Put it on.'

He opened the door leading into the toilet and shower room and hauled the doctor inside, closed the door and turned.

'Out we go, turn left and through the fire door.'

A moment later, they were descending in the freight elevator. They emerged into the underground car park and crossed to the laundry truck, Kathleen watching, her face pale with excitement.

Mori opened the rear door. 'In you get. You'll find what clothes you need in there. Get out of the prison uniform and make it fast. We haven't got long.'

He took off his white coat, tossed it into a nearby trash can, got behind the wheel and drove away, passing the prison ambulance at the main entrance, the two guards lounging beside it, and turned out into the highway.

By unfortunate chance it was a good fifteen minutes before a nurse went into Clinic Three and was surprised to find it unoccupied. She went down to Reception and spoke to the duty nurse there.

'What happened to Doctor Jessup and the patient?'

'They should still be there. Treatment takes an hour.'

'Well they aren't.'

'I'll come and see.'

The prison guard was still reading his magazine, when the door swung violently and the two nurses, having found the doctor's unconscious body in the toilet, rushed in.

At that precise moment, the laundry van turned into the crowded car park of a large supermarket fifteen miles down the highway and Mori pulled in beside a dark sedan.

'This is where we change,' he told Kathleen, went round to the rear and opened the door. 'Out you get.'

Ryan clambered out wearing a brown tweed suit and a raincoat. Kathleen kissed him impulsively. 'You made it, Uncle Michael.'

Mori unlocked the sedan. 'In you get.'

Ryan and his niece got in the rear, Mori slid behind the wheel and put on a chauffeur's cap that perfectly matched his navy blue suit then drove away.

Ryan said. 'Where are we going? They must have put the alarm out by now. There'll be cops everywhere.'

'Long Island.'

'But that's a hell of a way from here,' Kathleen said. 'They'll have roadblocks on the highway and at the toll bridges.'

'None of which will do them the slightest good. Trust me and just sit tight.'

About ten minutes later there was the sound of sirens and three Patrol cars passed on the other lane of the highway. Ryan said, 'Christ, we could be in trouble here.'

Mori shrugged. 'Keep the faith. We're nearly there.'

A few moments later he took a slip road and then a left turn. A signpost said Jackson Aero Club and they came to it a few minutes later. There was a car park with a few vehicles, a single storey administration block, two hangars and an airstrip and twenty or so single and twin-engined aeroplanes parked. There was also a Swallow helicopter standing on the edge of the airstrip.

Mori parked the sedan. 'This is it,' he said and got out. He reached for Kathleen's suitcase. 'I'll take that. Come on, let's get moving.'

The pilot, a hard-looking young man in black sunglasses, started the engine as they approached. Mori opened the rear door. 'Go on, in you get. Let's move it.'

Ryan and Kathleen scrambled in and Mori followed. He closed and locked the door, then belted up, turned to Ryan and smiled for the first time.

'Long Island next stop. See what I mean? Easy when you know how.'

They landed at Westhampton Airport on Long Island. A limousine with a driver drove straight out to the helicopter to pick them up.

As they drove away Kathleen said, 'Do I get time to catch my breath? Where to now?'

'The Russo residence at Quogue. Don Antonio wants to meet you,' Mori told her.

'Does he,' she said belligerently. 'And he always gets what he wants, does he?'

'Absolutely.' Mori turned and smiled for the second time. 'I'd remember that, if I were you, sweetness.'

The word of the escape spread like lightning at Green Rapids Detention Centre. Salamone, on duty in the prison hospital, received the word from a man on laundry detail called Chomsky. He paused as he was pushing a trolley full of soiled linen out of the ward.

'Hey, Paolo, you heard the good word? That guy, Kelly, the Irish guy?'

'What about him?'

'Escaped when he was down at the General Hospital for treatment. I got it from Grimes up in the Warden's Office. All hell broken out. It's this joint's first escape.'

'Well all I can say is I wish him luck,' Paolo said.

He thought about it for the next half-hour until his meal break. When it came, he went to one of the inmates' phone boxes and used his card to ring Sollazo who was just about to leave for Long Island when his secretary offered him the call.

'Yes, Paolo?'

'Hell, we did good, didn't we? I did good.'

'Only what I expected.'

'So I can look for some sugar? You promised you'd get me out. I've made my bones on this one. I've earned it. I mean, you wouldn't let me down?'

There was urgency in his voice, but more. The hint of a threat and Sollazo recognized it at once.

'My dear Paolo, have no fear. I'm really going to take care of you and much sooner than you think. Be patient.'

He sat there thinking about it then picked up the phone and dialled a number. It was picked up instantly. Sollazo didn't need to identify himself.

'In the matter of Salamone, we need a solution. Get in touch with your man at Green Rapids and tell him you want a result and I do mean now.'

'Consider it done.'

Sollazzo put down the phone, got his raincoat and briefcase and left.

The great sitting room in Russo's magnificent house at Quogue seemed to stretch to infinity, glass sliding doors opening on to a kind of boardwalk plat-form above the water. In the dim light of early evening, Ryan and Kathleen sat at a table by the rail.

'I can't believe this,' she said.

'I know. I keep thinking I'll wake up and find it's morning and I'm in my cell.'

Sollazzo stepped out from the sitting room. 'Ah, there you are. Allow me to introduce my uncle, Don Antonio Russo.'

The Don walked out behind him, leaning on his cane, a cigar in his mouth. He extended a hand. 'Mr Ryan, a pleasure and Miss Ryan.' He turned to Sollazzo. 'A celebration is in order, I think.'

'Taken care of, Uncle.'

Mori came in with a bottle of champagne in a bucket and glasses on a tray.

'Ah, the hero of the hour. You did well, Giovanni.'

Mori managed to look modest. He opened the champagne and charged the glasses. The Don said, 'Go and get another glass. We won't drink without you.' Mori did as he was told. When he returned

227

and filled his own glass the Don said, 'A toast. To you, Mr Ryan, and your return to the land of the living and to our joint enterprise, the *Irish Rose*.'

At Green Rapids Salamone was just finishing his nursing shift at the prison hospital. He went into the men's room to wash his face and hands and one of the porters followed him in. When he looked up he saw it was Chomsky, who leaned against the wall and lit a cigarette.

'You heard anything else on Ryan?'

'Not a word,' Salamone said.

'Boy, but the joint is really humming.' Salamone dried his hands and moved out and Chomsky followed. 'What worries me is that they could kill some of our privileges, know what I mean?'

'I sure do.'

They reached the end of the hallway. There was a mirror, flowers on a stand in front of it at the side of the elevator. Salamone pushed the button for the ground floor and then saw Chomsky's face in the mirror and knew he was in trouble. The elevator doors opened and there was no elevator, only the shaft, and he slewed to one side as the other man rushed him, arms stiff and went in head-first. There was a strangled cry and then a thud as he landed six floors down.

Salamone didn't hesitate. He went straight to

the fire exit at the end of the hall, opened it and went down the stairs two at a time. He didn't go to the ground floor, there would already be a fuss there, so he stopped on second and went to the nurse's rest room, got himself some very black coffee and sat there, sucking on a cigarette.

He was in deep shit, he knew that, and there was only one direction it could be coming from, the only one that made sense. Chomsky had worked for the family on too many occasions for there to be any other explanation. There was one other disturbing fact to consider. It wouldn't be left there. There were other guys like Chomsky only too willing to do the Russo family a favour.

'I've got to get out of here,' he said aloud. 'But where? I mean, what in the hell do I do?'

He got up and paced up and down, pausing suddenly, an intent look on his face. 'Johnson – Blake Johnson. Christ, if anyone can do anything he could.'

Ten minutes later he was ushered into Deputy Warden Cook's office. Cook, sitting behind his desk, looked up. 'What is it, Paolo? You told my secretary life or death.'

'Mr Cook, I got a dynamite story. I want to see an FBI agent called Blake Johnson.'

'You do, do you, just like that?'

'Listen, Mr Cook, if I stay here I'm dead. You want that?'

Cook frowned and he sat back. 'That bad?' He nodded slower. 'And that important?'

'It's big, OK. It could even give you a few answers on Kelly and how he bust out.'

Cook was immediately on the alert. 'You know something?'

'Only for Blake Johnson.'

'All right. Wait outside. I'll check with the FBI.'

It was perhaps half an hour later that he opened his door and called Salamone in. 'Mr Johnson is no longer with the FBI. He works with some Presidential Security unit in Washington. I'm going to phone him now and I'll let you talk to him.'

'That's fine by me.'

Blake Johnson was forty-six, a tall, handsome man who wore a suit well. His hair was so black that it took ten years off his age. A marine in Vietnam at nineteen, he'd emerged with two Purple Hearts, a Vietnamese Cross of Valour and a Silver Star. A law degree had followed at Georgia State on the Marines. Afterwards the FBI, and with such resounding success that he had been appointed to his present position. For a year he had headed what was known at the White House as the Basement, the President's private hit squad as some termed it, totally separate from the CIA or the FBI, responsible to the President alone.

When the phone rang in his office he found Cook on the line. The Deputy Warden explained the problem and ended by saying, 'You do know this man?'

'Oh, sure,' Johnson said. 'I put him away for bank robbery once. I'll talk to him. Give him privacy. He might find it difficult if he thinks anyone else is listening.'

Ten minutes later after speaking to Salamone Johnson was talking to the Deputy Warden again. 'First of all, to establish my credentials, I work directly for the President. I'm in charge of his special security and intelligence unit.'

'I see,' Cook said, suitably impressed.

'I can assure you that what Salamone had to tell me is way beyond any normal criminal matter. It's no exaggeration to tell you that grave matters of national security are involved.'

'Good God!' Cook said.

'This is what you do. You place Salamone in a secure cell under guard. I take it you have a heli-copter landing pad there.'

'Of course.'

'Good. I'll have a helicopter down to you within a couple of hours. The Federal Marshal who takes him in charge will have a Presidential warrant for him. That clears you.'

'One thing. We had a prisoner called Kelly escape today,' Cook said, 'while he was undergoing treatment at the local hospital. Salamone indicated that he might know something about that.'

Johnson, who had told Salamone to keep his mouth shut, lied smoothly, 'Hell, no, he was worried you wouldn't get in touch with me so he said what he did to get you interested.'

'The bastard,' Cook said.

'His kind usually are, but he's of crucial importance to us. The President will be more than grateful for your assistance in this matter.'

'I'm only too happy to oblige, that goes without saying.'

'My thanks on his behalf.'

In his office in the White House basement, Johnson sat back and thought about it then he pressed an old-fashioned buzzer. The door opened almost instantly and a grey-haired woman of fifty, Alice Quarbey, his secretary, entered, a pad in her hand.

'Mr Johnson?'

'Make out a general warrant in the name of Paolo Salamone. He's a prisoner at Green Rapids

Detention Centre. Get it over to the Federal Marshal's office. I want him picked up by helicopter as soon as possible. They can bring him back to Washington and hold him at the Hurley Street Secure Unit.'

'Anything else.'

'Better start writing. Get on that computer and dig up everything there is on an Irish terrorist, Protestant variety, called Michael Ryan, also his niece, a Kathleen Ryan. Couple that with any information about a gold bullion heist in the English Lake District in the Autumn of nineteen eighty-five.'

She was writing busily. 'Sounds intriguing.'

'It gets even better. Check out any information on a ship called the *Irish Rose* that sank off the coast of County Down in Ulster at the same time.' He grinned. 'That's it. Naturally I expect all this yesterday.'

'I take your point.'

She went out and Johnson sat there going over all of it in his mind. His office had direct access to both FBI and CIA computers and had friendly links with the British. There would surely be some really solid information on this. He needed that before speaking to the President.

He opened a silver box on his desk, sighed and took out a cigarette, put it in his mouth and reached for a lighter. He'd actually stopped a year before and yet, whenever his gut feeling told him he was on to something, he reached for a smoke. Ah, well, just one wouldn't do any harm.

At the house at Quogue they enjoyed an excellent dinner at six o'clock. Roast duck, potatoes, green salad, all washed down with more champagne.

'I haven't eaten like this in years,' Ryan said.

'I shouldn't imagine you have,' the Don told him drily, 'but the best is yet to come.' He rang a little silver bell and the maid apeared with a chafing dish. 'Cannolo, Sicily's favourite sweet. Very simple. Flour, eggs, cream.'

'Marvellous,' Kathleen said as the maid served them.

'Enjoy them. Later over the coffee we talk business.'

Darkness was falling as they sat on the boardwalk and the maid served coffee. When she was finished he waved her away.

'What happens now?' Kathleen asked.

'Marco will take you to a small beach cottage not far from here. You'll be safe there. Mori will keep an eye on you.'

'And then?'

'McArthur Airport is not far away. I keep a

Gulfstream there. You'll fly to Dublin with my nephew and Mori.' He smiled. 'Unless the circumstances change.'

There was a certain menace to that smile and Kathleen shivered. Ryan said, 'What are we getting at here?'

'Your niece told my nephew that he could only have the position of the *Irish Rose,* the bearings and so forth, when you are safe in Ireland.'

'That's right.'

'I require them now, an act of faith, if you like.' He smiled again.

Kathleen shook her head and said stubbornly. 'Oh, no, mister, you wait until we're in Ireland.'

'Then that too must wait,' he said. 'At least for you, *signorina.*' He turned to Ryan. 'You go, she stays here and takes her chances.'

Ryan exploded. 'You can't do that.'

'I can do anything, my friend. I learned from my father many years ago to always look for a man's weakness. Yours is your niece, Mr Ryan.' He stood up. 'Think about it. Come, Marco, give them time.'

When they had gone Kathleen said, 'The bastards. I'd like to shoot the lot of them.'

'Well you can't and we don't have a choice. We've got to get out of America as soon as possible. I couldn't face going back inside, but I also couldn't face leaving you here.'

'So you'll do it? What if they dump us? What if you give him the position and that bugger Mori shoots us?'

'I don't think so. I'm too useful to them for a number of reasons and if they intend to shoot us at some stage, they can just as easily do it in Ireland.' He smiled bleakly. 'No, I'll give him what he wants.'

'Then give him a false position,' she said.

'You're not thinking straight. At some point in time we'll be in a boat with these bowsers and a diver going down and if the *Irish Rose* isn't there then that bastard Mori will give us a bullet in the head and over the side.' Ryan shook his head. 'No, we must get out of here and safely to Ireland. You see there's another reason. The truth is, I haven't been strictly honest with you.'

She gazed at him searchingly, 'Tell me.'

So he did.

Afterwards she sat there holding his hand. 'All these years and you never told me.'

'I always did say I never trusted anyone in my life, not even you.'

'Well you do now and you're right. We must get to Ireland. Once we're there we'll think of something.' She raised her voice. 'Don Antonio?'

He appeared with Sollazo. 'You've thought it over?'

'Yes and we agree.'

'Excellent.' Sollazo took his diary from his breast pocket and a pen. Don Antonio Russo smiled. 'I knew you were a practical young woman, *signorina,* the moment I clapped eyes on you.'

11

In the Oval Office the President sat and listened as Blake Johnson told him the worst.

'I've seen the man Salamone at the Hurley Street Secure Unit since he got in and I've grilled him thoroughly. Everything he knows he's told me. You've read the file I sent up with all the relevant facts as to Ryan's background. As you can see, British Intelligence had a report on Ryan's involvement with the truck heist. It came from the Protestant terrorist Reid when he was arrested for murdering two soldiers and was trying to do a deal. He speaks of Ryan and his niece being responsible and a man named Martin Keogh. He, it seems, was a total mystery. No details available.'

'A wild one, this Ryan,' the President said. 'And this young woman.' He shook his head. 'I sometimes despair of human beings.' He straightened,

'So, where are we? What happens with these Russo people?'

'In my opinion, we'll get nowhere in that direction. Marco Sollazo is one of the most celebrated attorneys in Manhattan. If approached on this matter he would express shock and dismay, disavow any suggestion that he even knew Ryan. The new liberality of institutions like Green Rapids, the way visitors and prisoners are allowed to wander, facilitated Sollazo's ability to contact Ryan, but it's also a situation in which he would be able to deny all contact. Yes, he was at Green Rapids, but only to see Salamone and in Salamone we have only the word of a convicted felon, a bank robber who murdered a policewoman.' He shook his head. 'The District Attorney wouldn't waste five minutes on it.'

'And Don Antonio Russo?'

'Besides his nephew, the finest legal brains in New York are on his pay roll. He's never spent a day in a cell in his entire life.'

'But do you believe Slamone?'

'I'm afraid so.'

'So what do you think is happening?'

'I think Sollazo and his uncle took Ryan from gaol to get their hands on the bullion. They'll do some sort of a deal obviously. Let's say fifty-fifty. That bullion is worth one hundred and fifty million dollars now. Remember Ryan is a fanatic, totally dedicated to the Protestant cause.'

'Such a vast sum of money devoted to arms for that cause?' The President shook his head. 'Peace right out of the window. It is a prospect too bitter to contemplate. All my work and the work of Mr John Major to go for nothing.'

'Exactly, Mr President, so it seems to me that putting Don Antonio Russo or his nephew in a cell is of secondary significance. The only important thing would be to prevent that gold or part of it falling into Loyalist hands. Quite frankly, it would enable them to tool up for a civil war.'

'No, we can't have that. What's your best guess as to the next step?'

'They'll take Ryan and the girl to Ireland. Then, they'll try to locate the ship. Probably a relatively simple operation at first, a boat, a diver. Once located, some sort of salvage operation.'

'I want this stopped at all costs.' The President frowned and then suddenly smiled. 'I think this could be a job for Dillon.'

'Dillon, Mr President?'

'You remember what happened when I met Prime Minister John Major on the Terrace at the House of Commons the other week? The bogus waiter? Sean Dillon, originally the most feared enforcer the IRA had, now trouble shooter for Brigadier Charles Ferguson, your British counterpart, Blake.'

'Of course, Mr President.'

'Fine. So, to start with, get me the Prime Minister on the secure line.'

In his study at Number Ten Downing Street, John Major listened. When the President had finished he said, 'I totally agree, Mr President, we can't allow this to happen. I'll empower Brigadier Ferguson to intervene at once and I'm sure Dillon will play his usual part. Leave it with me.'

He put the phone down, sat there thinking about it then lifted the phone again and spoke to his aide. 'Brigadier Charles Ferguson. I want him here at the earliest moment.'

He sat back frowning. *Ireland, God Dammit.* It never went away, in spite of everything he'd done, even to the extent of putting his political career on the line.

Charles Ferguson sat quietly, a grave expression on his face, as the Prime Minister gave him the facts on the matter. When he was finished, he said, 'I want this stopped, Brigadier. There's no way I want to see such huge funds going to either of the two sides in Ireland. We've had enough bloodshed. We can't afford a civil war.'

'I couldn't agree more, Prime Minister.'

'I want Dillon on this, Brigadier,' John Major said.

'All right, I do not approve of his IRA and terrorist background which is why I distance myself, but there is no doubt of the man's extraordinary capabilities. He saved the Royal Family considerable anxiety over the Windsor affair the other year. All that nonsense over the Nazis. Then the attack on the Peace Process by the terrorist group January 30. He saved the life of Senator Patrick Keogh when he had the courage to address Sinn Fein and the IRA in Ireland and beg for peace. No, I know that Dillon is a totally ruthless man, but he's what we need for this business.'

'I agree, Prime Minister.'

John Major looked up at him as Ferguson stood. 'They call your people the Prime Minister's Private Army, so it gives you extraordinary powers. Use them, Brigadier, use them.'

When Hannah Bernstein and Sean Dillon were summoned to Ferguson's office, they found him standing by the window. He turned, very serious.

'Absolutely top priority. Everything else stops. I have direct orders from the Prime Minister to expedite a current problem to the utmost. There is a file there on my desk marked IRISH ROSE. Take it to your office, Chief Inspector. Read it, the both of you, then come back.'

*   *   *

Hannah Bernstein worked her way through the file, reading the old news clippings, the details of Ryan's activities, then Salamone's account of what had happened at Green Rapids. Dillon leaned over her shoulder and read it too.

She said, 'All right, we have a very nasty Prod activist, Michael Ryan, and his vicious little niece, Kathleen. What do we know? The gold bullion heist in the Lake District, the *Irish Rose* seen, according to the police, by a young boy and his dog out fishing at Marsh End. So we presume the truck went on board – *presume*. Next fact. Lifebelts and bits from *Irish Rose* wash up on the Down coast.

'Then we have Salamone. For Ryan read Kelly, who robs a bank in New York State, kills a copper and gets twenty-five years. In the sweat of his fever he discloses that he's the only one who knows where *Irish Rose* is. The rest we know.

'So Ryan and the girl are on the loose aided by the Russo family. So what? We know nothing, Dillon.'

'Except that logically, all roads lead to Ireland, girl dear, and there's more. I've a terrible confession to make. Let's go in and see the man and I'll tell you both at the same time.'

*   *   *

Ferguson sat behind the desk, Hannah Bernstein facing him. Dillon lounged by the window, hands in his pockets.

'Well, what do you think?' Ferguson said. 'Putting all things together including informer's tittle-tattle and rumours plus information from the swine Reid, back in nineteen eighty-five, one hell of a slick job was pulled by Michael Ryan, his niece Kathleen and some mystery man called Martin Keogh. That is confirmed in an obscure Royal Ulster Constabulary report of a raid they made on Ryan's pub in Belfast, the Orange Drum. Some wretched one-armed barman named Ivor-somebody remembers the girl being saved from gang rape by some Catholic youths, saved by this Keogh. This was only a day or two before he saw them for the last time. He said they left together in a taxi for the airport and he understood they were going to London.'

'That's right, Brigadier,' Hannah said. 'Reid mentioned their contact, a Protestant organizer called Hugh Bell who ran a pub in Kilburn called the William and Mary. Killed in a road accident.'

'Was he bollocks. Too convenient that,' Dillon said. 'He was seen off by Reid and his minder, a bastard called Scully.'

They both stared at him. 'But that isn't in the file. How would you know?'

'Because I was Martin Keogh,' Dillon said and

turned to Ferguson. 'I'll just help myself to your whiskey, Brigadier, and then I'll reveal all.'

Ferguson said, 'Dear God, Dillon, you never cease to amaze me.'

'I had a past, Brigadier, you knew that when you took me on.'

'Yes, a past is one way of describing it. An IRA activist for something like twenty years.'

'British paratroopers killed my father, Brigadier; I was trying to make someone pay. When you're nineteen you look at things that way.'

'And the PLO. Was that for political belief or money?'

'A man has to earn a living, Brigadier.' Dillon smiled. 'I'd remind you I worked for the Israelis too.'

'But now you work here,' Hannah said. 'Don't you feel any duty of disclosure as to your past activities?'

'If that means selling out old friends in the IRA, no. I was Jack Barry's right hand for years, then let's say I got disenchanted with the glorious cause and left and don't forget how I came to be here. It was either a Serb firing squad or an agreement to work for his highness here and, don't kid yourself, he was willing to leave me to the firing squad. Don't let's be hypocritical, the pot calling the kettle black.' He shrugged. 'How clean are your hands, girl dear, after working for this office?'

And that hurt. 'Damn you, Dillon!'

Ferguson said, 'Cut it out. You've got work to do. Go through this thing with a fine tooth comb. Everything. Access all intelligence information computers, not only MI5 and 6 but Scotland Yard, the RUC in Ulster and the Garda in Dublin. I want a result so get on with it.'

They went out to Hannah's office. Dillon said, 'Still friends?'

She glared at him then suddenly smiled grudgingly. 'I've said it before. You're an absolute bastard, Dillon, but I like you.'

Standing in his shirtsleeves with a cup of tea in the computer room Dillon watched as Hannah scanned the screen then sat back with an angry sigh.

'Not a thing on the RUC computer from Ulster, only Ryan's previous history and that stops ten years ago.'

'Well, it would, wouldn't it, he's been in the Nick since then. Nothing special when I tried Scotland Yard Intelligence records and nothing with Carter's bunch,' Dillon said.

'My eyes are falling out from looking at that

damn screen,' she told him. 'I'm going to take a break and make some coffee. How about you?'

'I'll make a start on Garda Intelligence from Dublin.'

As she got up he frowned and shook his head. 'I've gone over it again and again. The truck heist, the Farm at Folly's End, Marsh End, the voyage and then the sinking and that early morning in County Down. Michael and Kathleen taking the road to Drumdonald and me turning for Scotstown.'

'What is it?' she asked.

'I'm missing something. I've gone through my own memories and re-read all the newspaper clippings and there's something I'm missing.'

'That happens sometimes.'

'Not to the great Dillon.'

He sat at the computer and she paused in the doorway. 'You could have killed Ryan on the road that morning and taken that Master Navigator. You would have had the position of the ship to give Barry.'

'I know.' He grinned. 'Aren't I the complicated one?'

She went out and he started to tap into Garda files.

At that precise moment the Gulfstream was half-way across the Atlantic. Sollazo was up front and appeared to be sleeping. Mori was on the other side of the aisle from him. Ryan and Kathleen sat on either side of the aisle at the back. He'd discovered the small bar and had poured himself a large whisky.

'Dublin's fair city next stop. Old Ireland.' He shook his head. 'A long time to be away and it's all changed, so they tell me. Nothing but talk of peace.'

'Bloody nonsense,' she said. 'Put Sinn Fein in the saddle and they'll drive every Protestant in the land into the sea. It will be worse than Bosnia.'

'The fierce one, you are.'

'And good reason to be as no one knows better than you.'

He reached over and patted her hand. 'Just one thing. We'll have to box clever in Dublin so hold your tongue and don't vex Jack Barry when you meet him. Just bide your time till we see a chance to run for it.' He reached to the bar and got another whisky miniature. 'Money, that's what we need.'

'Well, in that respect I've not been honest with you! I've saved for years, always putting money on one side against that mad hope that you would break free. So, I cleared my account.'

'Jesus, girl, how much?'

'Fifty thousand, give or take a dollar.' She picked up her shoulder bag. 'There's a false bottom in here. It's in there. Half hundred dollar bills, the rest five hundreds.'

His face was pale with excitement. 'God, but this is great.' He sat there thinking about it. 'Money buys everything in this life. In the old days when I was on Army Council jobs I used to use that fella Tony McGuire and his air taxi firm and that was in Down, just outside Ladytown. It was the quick way to England if I wanted to avoid security at Aldergrove Airport.'

'Would he still be in business?'

'I don't see why not. If not him, someone else. It would be a good way out if we did manage to do a bunk and the hounds hot on our heels.'

'What about approaching the Army Council in Belfast?'

'I don't know. It's been ten years, Kathleen; ten long years and everyone strong for peace so they tell me. I wonder where it leaves people like Reid and Scully.'

'Long gone now with any luck,' she said.

'So, how do we slip the leash?'

'I've had a thought.' She looked troubled. 'But I'm not sure you should risk it.'

'Christ, girl, I'll try anything. Tell me?'

When she had finished he sat there thinking about it. 'Clever, I'll say that.'

'And maybe it won't be necessary. Maybe there'll be another way?'

'Who knows.' He grinned. 'What the hell, I think I'll have another whisky.'

It was perhaps three hours later that Dillon, sitting at the computer screen, shouted, 'Bingo! Give the man a cigar.'

Hannah rushed in. 'What on earth is it?'

'The Great Dillon does it again. Worked my way through all the information the Garda have on Loyalists and drew a blank. Not a word on *Irish Rose* beyond the facts we had before I opened my big mouth.'

'So?'

'Then I tried the Sinn Fein and Provo connection.' He laughed. 'Then I thought, why not go back to the Dinosaurs, the hard men from the old days, and that brought me to Jack Barry, once Chief of Staff, now retired.'

'And?'

'Peace being so fragile, the Garda still keep an eye on all the main players and they pay for inside information. It's an old Irish custom, what we call informing, touts all over the place.'

'Touts?'

'Informers who do it for money. That's what we've got here.' He gestured to the screen.

'Tell me.'

'No, go and get the Brigadier and let's all enjoy it.'

Ferguson stood to one side as Dillon tapped the keys again, Hannah sitting beside him. He sat back. 'Right, here it is. Last week some tout called O'Leary was in Cohan's Bar which is not far from Jack Barry's house. He said Barry came in with a very well dressed man, an American because O'Leary caught a word or two. They sat in a booth, had a snack lunch and a drink. He said they had their heads together the whole time.'

'So where does this get us?' Ferguson demanded.

'They left and took to the park. Barry's house is on the other side. O'Leary drove round there and saw a limousine with a driver parked outside. He waited until the American left in the limousine and followed it to Dublin Airport.'

'And then?'

'The American left in a private plane, a Gulfstream. Its flight plan was to McArthur Field in Long Island.' Dillon laughed. 'No prizes for guessing who owns that plane.'

'I'll get on to Johnson straight away,' Ferguson said, turned and hurried into his office.

* * *

At his desk, Blake Johnson was working his way through a file when Alice Quarbey came in with her pad.

Johnson sat back. 'All right, tell me.'

'The details on the Gulfstream Brigadier Ferguson got from the Garda were easily checked. It's owned by the Russo Corporation and is usually based at McArthur Airport in Long Island. According to airport records it logged out with two passengers last week. Marco Sollazo and Giovanni Mori.'

'God, that's great,' Johnson said. 'We're getting somewhere.'

'Now comes the hard part. The same Gulfstream left McArthur nine hours ago. Passengers as before with the addition of two Irish citizens, a Daniel and Nancy Forbes.'

'Damn!' Johnson said. 'I must contact Ferguson.'

'A waste of time if you want to do anything,' Alice told him. 'I've just checked. They landed at Dublin two hours ago.'

Johnson shook his head. 'You know something, Alice, I think it's time for another cigarette and get me Brigadier Ferguson anyway.'

Ferguson sat with the phone in his hand and Dillon and Hannah waited. The Brigadier nodded. 'Thank you, Superintendent.' He put the phone down.

'That was Costello of Garda Special Branch. The Gulfstream landed, disgorged four passengers, re-fuelled and left.'

'Anything else?'

'Yes, one bit of luck. An airport security officer, a retired Detective Sergeant in Special Branch, noticed them at the main entrance getting into a large shooting brake. He noticed them because Jack Barry was at the wheel and he recognized him.'

'So we know where we are,' Dillon said. 'The Russos in cahoots with the Provisional IRA. I wonder how Michael Ryan likes that?'

'Not much, I suspect,' Hannah Bernstein said. 'On the other hand it's totally obvious that the Russo family got him out and now he has to pay.'

'One thing is certain,' Dillon said. 'No point in raiding Barry's home or rubbish like that. He'll have a safe house somewhere.'

They sat there thinking about it and suddenly Charles Ferguson laughed. 'I know who we need, the greatest expert on the IRA in existence – Liam Devlin.'

He opened a drawer in his desk, took out a small black book and leafed through it. Hannah Bernstein said, 'Liam Devlin?'

'Scholar, poet, once a professor at Trinity College, gunman for the IRA who probably killed more men than I did. Living legend of the IRA,' Dillon told her.

Ferguson was talking. 'Is that you, Devlin, you old rogue?'

In the parlour of his cottage in the village of Kilrea outside Dublin, Liam Devlin listened as Ferguson talked. When he was finished Devlin laughed.

'Jesus, but you've got a ton of trouble on this one, Brigadier.'

'It's important, Devlin, you must see that.'

'Oh, I do. I mean we're all big for the cause of peace. Send Dillon and that Chief Inspector of yours to see me, only tell him not to try and shoot me this time.'

Ferguson put down the phone. 'He'll see you two and, believe me, if anyone can help, it's Devlin. He knows more about the IRA than anyone so order the Lear jet, pack your bags and get moving.'

'Sir.' Hannah moved to the door and Dillon went after her.

Ferguson called, 'And, Dillon . . .'

'Brigadier.'

'He'd be obliged if you wouldn't try to shoot him this time.'

Hannah looked shocked, but Dillon smiled. 'Now, do I look like the sort of fella that would do a thing like that, Brigadier?'

12

The Lear jet lifted off at Gatwick and climbed to thirty thousand feet. Dillon sat across the aisle from Hannah Bernstein.

'Devlin – Liam Devlin,' Hannah said. 'I always thought it was just a fairy story, the German attempt to kidnap Winston Churchill.'

'True enough. November nineteen forty-three. A strange one, Liam. He was born in Ulster. His father was executed by the English during the Anglo-Irish War in nineteen twenty-one. A brilliant scholar. He took first class honours in English Literature at Trinity College. He carried a gun for the IRA during the thirties, went to the Spanish Civil War and served with the International Brigade. The Italians took him prisoner and gave him to German Intelligence, what was called the *Abwehr*. They did what they could with him, but the trouble was he was very anti-fascist.'

'What happened?'

'After an abortive trip by parachute to liaise with the IRA in Ireland he managed to get back to Germany and spent his time lecturing in English at Berlin University.'

'Then what?'

'Oh, the ultimate commando job. A crack force of German paratroopers dropped into Norfolk in November nineteen forty-three to kidnap Winston Churchill. Devlin went on ahead as a kind of middle man.'

'But I thought you said he was anti-fascist?'

'Well, they paid him well – funds for the IRA and I suspect that if someone on the Allied side had asked him to snatch Hitler out of Berchtesgaden he'd have tried that too.'

'I see.'

'He told me once that the greatest question in life is to ask am I playing the game or is the game playing me.' He smiled ruefully. 'I know what he means.'

'And you tried to kill him?'

'And he me.'

'I assumed you must have been friends.'

'We were. He taught me a great deal.' He shrugged. 'I went through the purity-of-violence phase, the kind of Marxist revolutionary who'd kill the Pope if he'd thought it would further the cause. Liam was more old-fashioned. He wanted to meet his enemy face-to-face like a soldier of the revolution. We didn't agree to differ. Shots were exchanged and we parted, both of us the worse for wear.'

'And you regret that?'

'Oh, yes, the greatest man I ever knew in my life.'

'He must be pretty old by now.'

'Eighty-five next birthday.'

'Good God!' she said blankly.

Barry had owned the old farmhouse just outside the village of Ballyburn, fifteen miles north of Dublin, for years. He rented the land to a local farmer, a Sinn Fein sympathizer, and used the house itself only for the occasional weekend since the death of his wife.

When he unlocked the front door and led the way in there was a smell of damp. Kathleen Ryan shivered. 'God, you could catch your death here.'

'The fire's laid in the sitting room and in the kitchen stove. I'll light them up and we'll be fine in no time.' He had a carrier bag in his hand and he went into the stone-flagged kitchen and put the bag on the table. 'Fresh bread, milk, eggs and bacon. You could make us a fry-up, girl.'

'You can make your own bloody fry-up.'

He smiled 'The hot one, Kathleen Ryan, aren't you? Suit yourself.'

He opened the stove and put a match to it and turned. Michael Ryan was leaning against the wall, hands in pockets, an intent look on his face.

'Sure and you'd like to shoot me, wouldn't you, Michael?'

'Nothing would suit me better.'

Barry laughed and turned to the girl. 'Well at least you could make us a nice cup of tea.'

He went out into the hall and found Sollazo hanging up his raincoat. Mori was in the sitting room putting a match to the log fire. It was pleasant enough, a few rugs scattered on the flagged floor. There was a dining table with six chairs, a sofa and large wing-backed chairs on either side of the fire and the ceiling was beamed. There was a statue of the Virgin Mary on the mantelpiece and a picture on the wall.

'I didn't know you were a religious man, Mr Barry?'

'That was my wife, God rest her. Mass on most mornings when she could manage it. She worried about me, Mr Sollazo. All those wild years in the Movement.' He shook his head. 'The hard time I gave her.'

'And where are our friends?'

'In the kitchen. Don't worry. The back door is locked and I've got the keys of the brake.' He raised his voice. 'Where's that tea?'

* * *

Kathleen, waiting for the kettle to boil on the stove, was talking quietly to her uncle. 'Have you had your pill?'

'Yes.'

'Then just take it slowly and don't upset yourself. The last thing we need at this moment in time is you on your back.'

'All right, girl,' he said, 'don't fuss.'

She made the tea and discovering a jar of instant coffee, spooned some into two mugs and added hot water. It was at that moment that Barry called. She put everything on a tray and they went through.

'Coffee for you two,' she told Sollazo. 'Only the instant variety, but you'll have to make do.'

Mori tasted it and made a face. 'Disgusting.'

Barry laughed. 'You can't have everything in this life, son, you should try the tea. Two things the Irish do extremely well, brew Guinness and make tea.'

Kathleen poured. 'There you go then.'

Barry took one of the cups and sipped his tea. 'And that's grand, the cup that cheers. I'll just finish it in peace and then we'll get down to business.'

Kathleen, her uncle and Sollazo leaned on the table and watched as Barry unfolded a large-scale map of the east coast of Ireland, including both the Republic and Ulster.

'Here we are at Ballyburn. Now up through Dundalk into County Down and you see Drumdonald and Scotstown. That's the area where you landed. Now all I need are the bearings for the position of *Irish Rose*.' He looked at Ryan. 'What was it again, Michael?'

Pale in the face and with great reluctance, Ryan told him. Barry had a ruler and pencil at hand. 'A cinch, this. As you can see the map is marked in degrees top and bottom.' He quickly drew two lines, one bisecting the other. 'There you are, three miles out I make it. Just off Rathlin Island. Did you know that, Michael?'

'It was dark.'

'Ah, well, let's have a look at the Admiralty chart for the area. I got one of those too.'

It was larger in scale and covered the Down coast, the Isle of Man and the north-west of England. He repeated the exercise. 'There you go.' He threw down the pencil. 'Fifteen to twenty fathoms she's lying in.'

'Between ninety and a hundred and twenty feet.' Sollazo nodded. 'No problem.'

Barry nodded. 'When your uncle phoned me last night to say you were taking off he told me that as far as the preliminary dive to establish the ship's position was concerned, you'd do it yourself. He said you were an expert Scuba diver.'

'I've been diving in the Caribbean for years, the

Virgins, St Lucia.' Sollazo shrugged. 'Mori dives with me. We can easily handle a dive like this.'

'Your uncle asked me to provide the equipment. I know the right man. Friendly to our cause, you might say. He has a place on a trading estate on the outskirts of Dublin. I thought you and I could take a run in this afternoon.'

'That's fine and Mori can baby-sit our friends here. He'll need to be armed. Can you see to that?'

'There's an arsenal here if you know where to look for it. I'll see to it.'

'Fuck you, mister,' Kathleen Ryan said and stormed out.

Kilrea College was next to a convent on the outskirts of the village. The garden was a joy, flowers and bushes of every description, and the College itself was Victorian with Gothic gables and leaded windows. Dillon gave the bell pull a tug and it echoed inside. A moment later the door opened and Liam Devlin stood there.

'So there you are, you young bastard,' he said to Dillon, in Irish.

'As ever was,' Dillon replied in the same language.

Devlin turned to Hannah. 'And you'll be that old sod Ferguson's good right hand, the famous Chief Detective Inspector Hannah Bernstein.'

He looked her over with approval. 'The lucky one he is and always was. Anyway, *cead mile falte* and that's Irish for a hundred thousand welcomes. Come away in.'

Hannah was totally astonished. She'd expected an old man of eighty-five and instead found someone full of energy and life, still with some colour in his hair, wearing a black silk shirt and Armani slacks cut in the latest fashion. The eyes were the bluest she had ever seen and he had the same ironic quirk to his mouth as did Dillon. It was as if they were laughing at a world too absurd to take seriously.

The sitting room was a delight, all very Victorian from the fire in the grate and the mahogany furniture to the Atkinson Grimshaw paintings. She was examining them when Devlin brought tea from the kitchen on a tray.

'Good God, these are the real thing?'

'Yes, I invested wisely a few years back. I've always had a thing for old Grimshaw. Love his night scenes. Whistler once said that to call him the master of the nocturne was false. That anything he knew he'd learned from Grimshaw.'

He poured the tea and Hannah said, 'My grandfather has one. *The Thames Embankment at Night*.'

'Oh, a man of taste and discernment. What does he do?'

'He's a Rabbi.'

Devlin laughed out loud. 'Jesus, girl, and that's a show stopper if ever I heard one.'

Hannah felt suddenly breathless. *What an absolutely marvellous, marvellous man. One of the most extraordinary people she'd ever met.*

Devlin sat in a chair by the fire. 'So it's working for the Brits now, is it, Sean?'

'Sure and you know I am.'

'Does that give you a problem, Mr Devlin?' Hannah asked.

'Call me Liam, girl dear. No, whatever I am I'm no hypocrite. I once worked for Ferguson myself.'

'He didn't say,' Hannah frowned.

'Well he wouldn't. He wanted someone to break an American Irish lad called Martin Brosnan out of a French prison on Belle Island and me being a friend of Martin's found it difficult to say no.' He glanced at Dillon. 'And he no friend of yours, Sean. Told me he thought they'd done for you after you tried to blow up the British War Cabinet during the Gulf War.'

'Yes, well I was wearing a nylon and titanium waistcoat and it stopped the bullets,' Dillon said.

Devlin laughed. 'Nine lives this one and I taught him everything I know.' He shook his head and there was an edge to his voice. 'You know something, Sean, you're the dark side of me.'

'And you, Liam, are the good side of me,' Dillon said.

Devlin frowned for a moment and then laughed out loud. 'You always did have a way with the words.' He shook his head. 'Still, let's get down to business.'

They went through all the information available and Dillon once again gave a meticulous account of the robbery and the voyage to Down on the *Irish Rose*. When all this was finished, Devlin sat there frowning, a cigarette in one hand.

'All right. First of all, we don't want the Garda on this. Sure, they could arrest Ryan, hold him until the Americans asked for extradition. They could even hold Kathleen and this fella Sollazo and his bully boy as accessories, but none of that matters. The only thing that does is finding the *Irish Rose* and making sure that gold can't be used for the wrong purposes.'

'So what can we do?' Hannah asked. 'I mean if Barry and the Provisional IRA are in this . . .'

Devlin cut her off. 'I don't think so. Gerry Adams, Martin McGuinness and Sinn Fein have a big investment in the peace process. Sure there's still the problem of persuading the Provos to give up their arms, but nobody wants trouble at the moment, the politics are too finely balanced.' He shook his head. 'No, I'll bet you a fiver the Provisional IRA Army Council know nothing about this.'

'You mean Barry is in this for his own ends?' Hannah asked.

'Oh, no, a true patriot, Jack. My guess is he'll play it close to his chest because he knows damn well the Army Council don't want trouble at this stage of the political game.'

'So what do you suggest, Liam?' Dillon demanded.

'I'll go and see the Chief of Staff and sound him out. I know the Dublin pub where he has a bite to eat at lunchtime every day.'

'And he'll see you?' Hannah asked.

Devlin laughed out loud. 'They all see me, girl dear, I'm the living legend and that can be very useful, but not you and the lad here.' He turned to Dillon. 'A time for peace, but there are those who see you as an apostate working for the Brits. They'd like nothing better than putting a bullet in you.'

'And that's a fact.'

'Take the Chief Inspector to Casey's in the village. What the English call good pub grub.' He smiled at Hannah. 'I'll see you later.'

The pub on one of the quays on the Liffey was called the Irish Hussar, a haunt of Irish Republicans, and it was already half-full when Liam Devlin went in just after noon. Colum O'Brien, Chief of Staff of the Provisional IRA, was sitting in a booth at the far end, a pint of Guinness at one hand and a savoury looking dish before him. He tucked a napkin below his chin.

Devlin said, 'Shame on you, Colum, and you tucking into a Lancashire Hot Pot, an English dish.'

O'Brien looked up and smiled with genuine pleasure. 'Liam, you ould bastard. What are you doing here?'

'Oh, I was in town on business and a man has to eat.' A young woman came over and Devlin said, 'I'll have the same as your man here.'

'And give him a large Bushmills whiskey,' O'Brien said. 'Only the best for Liam Devlin.'

The young woman was truly shocked. 'You're Liam Devlin? I've heard of you since I was a child. I thought you were dead.'

'And that says it all.' Devlin laughed. 'Away with you, girl, and bring me the Bushmills.'

Devlin took his time raising politics only when they had eaten and were enjoying a pot of Barry's tea.

'So where are we with the peace process?' he finally asked.

'Still roadblocked,' O'Brien told him. 'It's the bloody British Government with their demands that we get rid of all our arms, Liam. That's too much. I mean, do they imagine the other side aren't stockpiling?'

'I suppose you see Gerry Adams and McGuinness regularly. What's the good word?'

'Hope, Liam, that's the good word. Anybody who thinks Gerry and Martin don't want this peace to last is crazy, but peace with honour.'

'And what about the Loyalist side of things?'

'Difficult that. They think the British Government have sold them out, or will do, and there's some truth in that, but they must face the fact that the day will come when they'll have to take their place in a united Ireland. That will take change.'

'From the Catholic side too,' Devlin said. 'Anyway, how do the old warhorses see it? What's Jack Barry up to these days?'

'Not much since he retired and not needed with the peace movement making changes. I see him now and then, but not often. You know his wife died?'

'Yes, I heard that. God rest her. Is he still in Abbey Road by the park?'

'As far as I know. I don't know how he fills his time.'

'Out to grass like me.' Devlin got up. 'Well, I've enjoyed the crack, Colum. We used to say our day will come. Let's hope it has.'

* * *

It was years since he'd visited Jack Barry's house in Abbey Road, but when he drove there and parked the car it all came back and he found the house easily enough. He tried the knocker on the front door and waited. He had no intention of confronting Barry about the *Irish Rose* affair. Just an old friend who happened to be passing, but in any event he was disappointed. He went round to the small garden at the back and peered through the kitchen window.

A voice said, 'Can I help you?' and he turned and found a young woman taking washing off the line next door.

Devlin gave her his best smile. 'I was looking for Jack Barry.'

'I saw him getting into the big station wagon early this morning. He parks it in the street. If it isn't there now he'll be away somewhere. Is it important?'

'Not at all. An old friend who happened to be in the neighbourhood, that's all. So, you've no idea where he might be?'

'He's here most of the time. A lovely man. Used to be a schoolteacher then his wife died. They used to go away to the country at weekends. They had a cottage or something like that.'

'Would you know where?'

'I'm afraid not.'

'Ah, well, if he turns up tell him Charlie Black

called,' Devlin lied cheerfully and went back to his car.

He was smiling as he drove away, wondering what she'd say if she knew that the nice man next door had once been Chief of Staff of the Provisional IRA.

The warehouse on the trading estate on the outskirts of Dublin was called Seahorse Supplies and the owner was a man called Tony Bradley, middle-aged and balding with a distinct beer belly. An IRA activist in his youth, a five year sentence in Portlaoise Prison fifty miles from Dublin had cooled his ardour. His sympathy and support were still with the Republican cause, however, and he had been a great fundraiser when he came home from the North Sea oilfields, where he had been a diver, and had set up Seahorse.

The warehouse was packed with diving equipment of every kind and Bradley stopped at a goods table and took out an order pad. 'Great to see you again, Jack. In fact a great honour.'

'Last time was in the pub at Ballyburn when I was spending a weekend at my farmhouse,' Barry said.

'And that was just a happy chance, me passing through. So what can I do?'

'My friend, Mr Sollazo, needs some diving equipment. You hire as well as sell, don't you?'

'Of course.' Bradley turned to Sollazo. 'Just tell me what you need.'

'Two of everything,' Sollazo told him. 'Masks, diving suits, one medium, one large, and with hoods, gloves, fins, weight belts with twelve pounds in each, regulators, buoyancy control devices and four air tanks. Oh, and a couple of Orca diving computers.' He turned to Barry. 'They tell you how deep you are, how long you've got, when you should come up.'

'Great,' Bradley said. 'I tell you what, Jack, I'll open the freight door and you bring your station wagon in and we'll load up right here.'

He bustled off, calling an assistant to help him, and Barry left Sollazo there and went and got the car.

He stood watching as Sollazo carefully checked each item. 'You take a lot of care,' he said.

Sollazo shrugged. 'I always take care, even though I've done two hundred fifteen dives. You wouldn't believe the number of people killed scuba diving each year and usually because of stupidity.' He smiled. 'You see, Mr Barry, we shouldn't be down there in the first place.'

Bradley and his man finished stowing the gear and he said, 'Anything else?'

'Underwater lights,' Sollazo said.

'No problems. I've got the very thing.' He went

to a stack, took down two cardboard boxes and brought them over. 'Halogen lamps like the Royal Navy use. Long-life batteries and a charger included.' He put them in the car and stood, hands on hips, frowning. 'Something missing.' And then he smiled. 'I know.' He darted away and came back with two diver's knives in sheaths with leg straps. 'Now I think that is it,' he said.

Barry said, 'Just one thing. There used to be an item called a Master Navigator.'

'Still is,' Bradley said. 'Just been updated.'

It was Sollazo who said, 'Could we see one?'

'Of course.' Bradley darted off again and was back in a few moments, a black box in his hand. He opened it and took out the Navigator. 'There you go.'

Sollazo examined it, the rows of buttons and the read-out panel. He glanced at Barry enquiringly and the Irishman said, 'What happens if I insert the. bearings for, let's say, a wreck at sea?'

'Well what happens is a triumph of modern technology,' Bradley said. 'There's an instruction book here and it's very simple.'

'No need,' Sollazo told him. 'I'll give you the figures, you feed them in and we'll watch.'

He took out his diary and dictated the position of the *Irish Rose* to Bradley who punched it in. The figures appeared on the read-out panel. 'Check that they're correct,' Bradley said.

Sollazo did so. 'Perfect.'

'Good.' Bradley pressed a blue button. 'Now it's on hold. You activate it by pressing the red button. You get a slow and monotonous pinging. When you reach the actual position, the pinging becomes frantic. You stop it by pressing the blue button again.'

'And that we'll definitely have.' Barry said. 'Send me a bill at Abbey Road, Tony, and you'll get my cheque.'

'Ah, sure, pay me when you return the gear, Jack.'

Bradley stood to one side as they drove away and waved.

'Good,' Sollazo said. 'The one thing you haven't mentioned so far is a boat.'

'It's being taken care of. I mentioned Drumdonald and Scotstown as being in the general area of the Down coast where Ryan, his niece and Sean Dillon landed. Scotstown is a small fishing village. There's a pub there called The Loyalist. It's not what it seems. Kevin Stringer, the landlord, is one of our own. It was to there that Dillon went for sanctuary after landing from *Irish Rose*. Anyway, I've spoken to Kevin and he's found us something he thinks could be suitable. I think you and I should drive up there tomorrow. We can take all the equipment with us. If the boat is OK Kevin can stow the equipment on board and we'll come back. I'll take some Semtex and pencil timers, by the way, in case we have to blast our way into the boat.'

'And then?'

'Return the following day, all of us, Ryan and the girl included, and we'll go out to Rathlin Island and find the damned boat.'

'You think we will?'

'I always travel hopefully,' Jack Barry said.

It was late in the afternoon when Devlin arrived back at Kilrea Cottage. Dillon was sprawled beside the fire, eyes closed and Hannah was reading a book when Devlin entered.

He looked tired and she got up, concerned. 'Let me get you a cup of tea.'

'That would be grand.'

He dropped into her chair and Dillon sat up. 'Any luck?'

'Well I saw Colum O'Brien, the present Chief of Staff, and satisfied myself that as far as he is concerned Jack Barry is not up to anything. As for the rest, I've made discreet enquiries of various sources, some of whom I have to check back with tomorrow.'

'So that's it?' Dillon said.

'For the moment.' Devlin sat up straight as

Hannah brought tea in. 'Girl, you're the wonder of the world.' He took the cup. 'When I've had this, I'll have a bath and then take you for dinner.'

When Sollazo and Barry went into the farmhouse they found Mori in the sitting room reading a book. He looked up. 'This is great stuff. *A History of the Saints of Ireland.* These guys make the Mafia look like kindergarten.'

'Where are they?' Sollazo asked.

'In the kitchen. She's cooking. I had to go and stand in the garden in the rain while her uncle dug up potatoes with a fork, also carrots. Then she got cucumbers and lettuce and tomatoes from the greenhouse. She could be a useful little broad.'

'Who's killed at least three men, to my knowledge,' Barry said.

'Exactly,' Sollazo told him.

Sollazo went into the kitchen. There was a good smell, Kathleen standing at the stove checking pans. Ryan was at the table mixing a salad.

'A woman of many parts, I see,' Sollazo said.

'You'd better believe it, mister,' she replied.

Seated at his desk, the phone in his hand, Ferguson said, 'I've spoken to Dillon. Our contact, Devlin, has feelers out, but no results of far.'

In his office in the basement at the White House Blake Johnson said, 'Too much to hope for an early result. As you know, the President is concerned in this matter. Do keep me posted, Brigadier.'

'Of course I will.'

Ferguson put down the phone and sat back. 'Come on, Dillon,' he said softly. 'Give me a result.'

Devlin, as a favoured customer at his local pub, was given the best booth in the corner of the restaurant. He insisted on ordering for all of them so they started with a Lentil and Potato soup to be followed by Irish ham in a white sauce with new potatoes and boiled cabbage.

Hannah said, 'I'm sorry, Liam, I'm Jewish; you've forgotten. Ham is out.'

He was immediately contrite. 'Would poached salmon be in?'

'That I could manage.'

'I should tell you as a serving police officer that the emphasis is on poached.'

'Oh, dear.'

He turned to Dillon. 'As for you, boy, forget your ideas about the Krug champagne. All they do is a house champagne here at twelve quid the bottle.'

'Irish champagne?' Hannah said.

'Well the name on the label is French.'

Dillon raised his hands. 'Order it, I surrender.'

The meal was delicious, the champagne almost acceptable and the conversation the most interesting Hannah Bernstein had heard in years.

'So your grandad's a Rabbi, your father a Professor of Surgery and you went to Cambridge University?' Devlin said. 'That's a terrible weight to bear and you a peeler? How did that come about?'

'I wanted to do something worthwhile. Money wasn't a consideration. I've got plenty of that.'

'God, you on the beat in a blue uniform must have been the grand sight.'

'Don't be sexist, Mr Devlin.'

'Liam. Do I have to tell you again? But a nice Jewish girl like you. I mean, didn't your Da want you to marry and have babies?'

'This nice Jewish girl shot dead Norah Bell,' Dillon said.

Devlin stopped smiling. 'Jesus, big for the Protestant cause, that one.'

'And I killed the boyfriend, Ahern,' Dillon said. 'They were in London to knock off the American President.'

Hannah looked strained and Devlin put a hand on hers. 'It is not on you, any of it, girl, it's the world we live in. Now, a Bushmills whiskey to put me to sleep and we'll go home.'

He shouted the order across to the barman, turned back with a smile then suddenly frowned. 'I've had a thought.'

'And what would that be?' Dillon asked.

'They've got to go looking for the site of the *Irish Rose*.'

'That's right. Somewhere off the Down coast. We landed in the general area of Drumdonald and Scotstown.'

'I'm not thinking of that, I'm thinking they have to go looking, which means chartering a boat, but more than that, wouldn't they need diving equipment?'

Dillon nodded. 'Of course.'

'And you, they tell me, are an expert in that field these days.'

'I've done my share. What are you getting at?'

'Well, they've got to get that equipment from somewhere and Dublin isn't exactly saturated with firms in that line of business.'

'No, it wouldn't be,' Dillon said.

'What if I told you there's a firm called Seahorse Supplies on the edge of Dublin that's owned by an old IRA hand called Tony Bradley? Served under Jack Barry, did five years in Portlaoise Prison. Now, if you were Jack Barry and you needed diving equipment where would you go?'

'Seahorse Supplies,' Hannah Bernstein said.

Devlin smiled and raised his glass in a toast. 'Exactly, which is where we'll go first thing in the morning. Everything comes to he who waits.'

13

It was eight-thirty the following morning when Tony Bradley turned his Land Rover into the car park outside the Seahorse Supplies warehouse. The staff didn't clock on until nine, but he always liked to get there early. There were a number of vehicles parked already, to do with other businesses nearby. He walked through them and paused to get out his keys. There was a small Judas gate in the great sliding doors for easy access. He unlocked it and there was a step behind him.

'Good man yourself, Tony.'

Bradley turned and found the three of them behind him but it was Devlin he recognized immediately. 'Dear God, Liam Devlin.'

'And another old friend. Surely you haven't forgotten Sean Dillon.'

Bradley knew fear then of the kind that made

his stomach contract. This had to be heavy, he knew that. 'Sean, it's been a long time.'

He glanced at Hannah nervously. 'And who might you be?'

'She's with us, that's who she is, so in you go,' Dillon told him and pushed him in through the Judas gate.

Bradley was very frightened now. 'I've done nothing. What is this?'

'Sit.' Dillon pushed him down on a packing case.

'A question or two then we'll let you go,' Devlin said. 'You had Jack Barry here.'

He deliberately made it a statement of fact and it worked. 'That's right,' Bradley said eagerly. 'Yesterday afternoon.'

'Buying diving equipment?'

'Yes, he was here with an American, a Mr Sollazo. He was the expert. Hired a load of diving gear. I thought it was something to do with the Organization with it being Jack.'

'I'm afraid not,' Devlin told him. 'Jack's been a bit naughty. Up to no good, you might say. Colum O'Brien and the Army Council would not be best pleased.'

'My God,' Bradley said, 'and how was I to know that?'

'Yes, you're in bad trouble, old son,' Devlin told him. 'So you'd better retrieve your position. Colum

O'Brien doesn't know of your part in this so maybe I can help.'

'Anything,' Bradley moaned.

Devlin turned to Dillon. 'You're the diving expert?'

Dillon lit a cigarette and said to Bradley, 'Tell me what they took?'

Bradley hurriedly went through the list as he remembered it. 'I think that's all.' He paused then added quickly, 'No, I was forgetting the Master Navigator. I gave them the new model.'

'And a demonstration?' Dillon asked.

'More than that. The American gave me some bearings and I punched it in for them. Those things are like a homing device. They take you straight to the place.'

'Which was where?' Hannah cut in.

'How would I know, it was just bloody numbers.' He was getting upset. 'I've told you all I know.'

'Except where they were going when they left,' Devlin said.

'Barry lives in Abbey Road, everyone knows that.'

'Only he isn't there,' Devlin said gently. 'Now where else might he be?'

'How would I know?' Bradley said wildly.

Dillon produced his Walther with the Carswell silencer. 'I'm wondering whether a bullet in your left kneecap might improve your memory.'

'For God's sake, Sean.' Bradley was terrified and

then he remembered. 'Just a minute. The last time I saw Jack Barry was in a pub in Ballyburn. I was driving down from Dundalk and I stopped for a drink and there he was in the corner of the bar.'

'And what happened?'

'We had a crack and he told me he had an old farmhouse just outside the village. He'd intended to walk back, but I gave him a lift. It was an old place, all a bit run down. He said he didn't use it much since his wife died.' He was desperately searching for more information and found it. 'There was a sign on the gate where I dropped him. Victoria Farm. I remember because he made a joke about it being a Brit Royal Family name.'

There was sweat on his face now. Devlin said, 'There, that wasn't too hard, was it?'

'The truth, the whole truth and nothing but the truth?' Dillon said softly. 'It better be, Tony boy, or I'll be back to take care of that left kneecap.'

He turned away and moved to the Judas gate, Hannah at his side. She murmured softly, 'You really are a bastard, Dillon.'

'Yes, well, it gets results, girl dear, and that's what counts.'

Devlin smiled and put an arm around Bradley.

'Cheer up, Tony, it may never happen, but if you try and get in touch with Barry or speak of this to anyone I'm afraid Dillon will be very annoyed indeed and you know what that means.'

'Not a word, I swear it.'

'Good man yourself,' Devlin said and left him there.

Dillon and Hannah were waiting beside Devlin's silver Toyota saloon. 'The game's afoot, as Sherlock used to say, so to Ballyburn and you can drive, Sean, I'm getting old.'

Dillon got behind the wheel and Devlin held the rear door open for Hannah. 'You don't look pleased. You didn't like it back there.'

'I never do when I see the way he operates.'

'Yes, well he always was the hard man, our Sean,' and he went round to the other side and joined her.

At Victoria Farm they all had breakfast in the kitchen. When it was finished, Kathleen cleared the table and stacked the plates and, strangely enough, it was Mori who helped her when her uncle, Barry and Sollazo went out. She half expected Mori to make a pass at her, was all ready for it. Instead, he filled the sink with hot water and put the dirty dishes in.

'Leave them to soak. Less work that way.'

'And what's got into you, you big lump?' she demanded.

He laughed. 'My father owned a restaurant in Palermo. When I was a kid I worked there all the time in the kitchen. Later I was a waiter for him.'

'Then you took to the gun.'

He shrugged and said calmly, 'It paid better.'

When she went into the sitting room the three of them were looking at the map. 'That's it, then,' Barry was saying. 'Up to Dundalk then across the border. No trouble there these days since the peace talks. You can drive straight through.'

'And then Scotstown,' Sollazo said.

'Exactly. We might make it in a couple of hours, two-and-a-half at the most.'

'And who is "we"?' Kathleen asked.

'Sollazo and me,' Barry told her. 'You can stay here in Mori's tender care.'

'You've got your bloody cheek.'

'Yes, well, I'm in charge. Mr Sollazo and I will drive up to Scotstown with the diving gear. Kevin Stringer at The Loyalist thinks he has a suitable boat. We'll check it out. If it's OK, Kevin can stow the gear and we'll return. We'll be back here by five.'

She glared at him then looked at her uncle. He shrugged. 'All for the best, Kathleen.'

'If everything is on course, we'll all drive up to Scotstown in the morning,' Barry said.

'Oh, do what the hell you like,' she said and stormed out.

The Toyota coasted down the hill outside Ballyburn. Dillon slowed and there it was, the opened five-barred gate, the sign Victoria Farm and the farmhouse beyond.

'Pull up in the layby,' Devlin said. 'I've got some glasses in the glove compartment. He rummaged inside and found a pair of Zeiss binoculars. 'Just let me take a look.'

He stood beside the Toyota and focused them on the station wagon in the farmyard and at that moment the house door opened and they all came out, Barry, Sollazo, Mori and the Ryans.

'Christ,' Devlin said. 'It's the whole damn bunch of them. Jack Barry for starters. Take a look, Sean.'

Dillon took the binoculars, focused them and nodded. 'Barry, Michael and sweet Kathleen.'

Hannah had got out of the Toyota and he passed the binoculars to her. She took a look. 'The other two are Sollazo and his minder, Giovanni Mori,' she murmured to Devlin. 'We had photos of them faxed from Blake Johnson.' She stiffened. 'Barry and Sollazo have got into the station wagon. The others are going inside.'

'Out of here, quick,' Devlin said to Dillon.

They scrambled in and Dillon drove away quickly and took a side turning. He stopped. 'Give them a couple of minutes to see if they come this way. If not, I'll reverse and try and catch them up.'

It was Hannah, a moment later, watching through the rear window who said, 'There they go.'

'And with luck, to where we all want to be,' Devlin said, 'so after them, Sean.'

Dillon stayed well back, Devlin acting as look-out, and the amount of traffic on the road gave them plenty of cover. Drogheda was twenty miles, Dundalk another twenty and they were just under the hour as they passed through the town.

'The border soon,' Devlin told Hannah, 'then we cross over to Warrenpoint. If it's the Down coast, as it must be, we'll go through Rostrevor and down to Kilkeel and take the coast road.'

'Which would bring us to Drumdonald and Scotstown, the area where we landed after the *Irish Rose* went down,' Dillon observed.

'What was the name of the pub you went to in Scotstown?' Hannah said.

'The Loyalist,' Dillon laughed. 'The wrong name entirely. Kevin Stringer who runs it worked for Barry for years.' He frowned and turned to Devlin. 'What do you think?'

'That it sounds promising. We'll see. Now I'll take a little nap and you young ones keep alert.'

After Warrenpoint, the traffic thinned out, but there were still vehicles on the road, private cars and the occasional truck, enough to give cover if

Dillon stayed well back. It started to rain, sweeping in from the Mourne Mountains.

'Sweeping down to the sea, as the song says,' Devlin commented. 'A grand sight.'

'It certainly is,' Hannah said.

There were two cars and a large farm truck ahead of them and the station wagon in front. Devlin said, 'One thing, if we are going to end up in Scotstown or some such place we have a problem. Fishing villages only on this coast, a jetty, a harbour a few boats. Strangers stick out like a sore thumb.'

'We'll have to go gently,' Dillon said. 'Wait and see.'

The rain increased to a solid downpour and Barry, at the wheel of the station wagon, swore softly. 'The curse of this country.'

'You can say that again,' Sollazo said.

'Kilkeel coming up. There's a grand café on the road just before we go through. I don't know about you, but a cup of tea and a bacon sandwich would go down fine.'

'Suits me,' Sollazo told him.

A few moments later, they came to the very place and Barry turned into the car park. There were several trucks, a few cars and he parked beside them. There was a filling station and garage with a sign that said Patrick Murphy & Son. The café was at the other end of the car park. They ran through the rain and went in.

Dillon pulled the Toyota in between two trucks and switched off the engine. Hannah said, 'I'll go and see what's happening, I need the toilet anyway.'

She got out and hurried away through the rain. 'A darling girl,' Devlin said.

'She saved my life once and took a bullet in the doing,' Dillon told him.

'Jesus,' Devlin said, 'a nice Jewish girl like that.'

'I remember what Ferguson told me she said once,' Dillon said. 'It was after she shot Norah Bell; the bitch had stabbed me in the back twice. She said I'm not a nice Jewish girl at all, I'm a very Old Testament Jewish girl.'

Devlin laughed. 'God save us, if I wasn't seventy-five years of age I'd fall in love with her.'

'Seventy-five?' Dillon said. 'It's the great liar you are.'

Hannah came back and leaned down. 'They look settled. I saw Barry give the waitress an order. Look, I'm thinking about what you said, Liam, about us standing out like a sore thumb whenever we get where we're going. That might apply to you more than me. I mean if it turns out to be Scotstown, for example, this Kevin Stringer would know you, Sean, even you, Liam.'

'He *could* recognize me,' Devlin said. 'I was well known in these parts, mainly because I was born in County Down.' He grimaced. 'Sometimes it's hell being a living legend.'

Hannah said, 'Not me. I'm just an English tourist, or I could be. That garage has a car hire sign. Pass me my shoulder bag and I'll go and see what I can get. If our friends leave before I'm ready, just go. I'll follow the coast road Drumdonald and Scotstown way. I'll find you.'

Devlin handed her the bag. 'On your way, girl.'

There was a mechanic working on a car in the garage, a small man in a tweed suit and cap sitting in a glass office. He got up and came out.

'Patrick Murphy,' he said. 'And what can I do for you, Miss?'

'I've been touring with some friends, but they're going back to Belfast. They dropped me here because someone in Warrenpoint said you hired cars.'

'I do indeed. How long would it be for?'

'Two or three days. I want to roam the Down coast. Just take time off. Can you help?'

'Well, it's not the fancy stuff I can manage, but I've a Renault saloon over here if you've nothing against the French.'

'Nothing at all.'

She followed him across the garage and had a look. 'Newly checked and the tank is full,' he told her.

'Wonderful.' She embellished her story a little. 'When I come back, I'll be wanting to return to Belfast.'

'No problem. I run a taxi service. We'll take you to Warrenpoint. You can catch the train. Now, if you'll give me your licence, we'll get on with it. How would you be paying by the way?'

She opened her purse, took out the licence and checked her cards. 'Would American Express be all right?'

He smiled. 'Well, as they say on the television, that will do nicely.'

She drove out of the garage as Barry and Sollazo walked towards the station wagon. She pulled in behind the Toyota and briefly punched the horn. Dillon turned, raised a hand and gestured her forward. She pulled out between the trucks as the station wagon turned into the road and followed it and the Toyota came on behind.

Scotstown was desolate in the rain, thirty or forty houses, the jetty, a dozen or so fishing boats in the harbour all enveloped in a damp clinging mist.

There was a wood at the top of the hill overlooking the village. Hannah pulled in at the side of the road, looking down, and saw the station wagon turn into the car park of the public house. The Toyota stopped behind her and Dillon and Devlin got out.

'A long time since I was here,' Dillon said, 'but I was right, though. That's The Loyalist down there and, if Kevin Stringer's still there, he's Jack Barry's man.'

'Let's take a look at the harbour.' Devlin raised the binoculars. 'Not much, just fishing boats. No, wait a minute. There's some sort of motor launch anchored out there. Thirty or forty-footer, painted grey. Looks like serious business to me. Take a look.'

Dillon peered through the binoculars. 'You could be right.'

'I've got to be.'

Hannah took the binoculars from Dillon and checked for herself. She nodded. 'I agree, Liam, but what this needs is a closer look. I'll go and play the tourist. I could do with a nice cup of tea and a sandwich anyway. I'll try The Loyalist.'

'While we starve?' Dillon said.

'That's just your bad luck, Dillon,' she told him, went to the Renault, got in and drove away.

*   *   *

In the back parlour of The Loyalist Kevin Stringer embraced Barry. 'Jack, I can't tell you how great it is to see you again.'

'And you, Kevin. This is my associate, Mr Sollazo from New York. You've found a boat?'

'Indeed I have. *Avenger,* a motor launch a friend of mine up the coast bought for the shark fishing, only the sharks went away.'

Sollazo laughed out loud. 'That I like.'

'How far would you be going?' Stringer asked.

'Rathlin Island,' Barry said. 'Does anyone live there these days?'

'Not in years.'

'How far?'

'Only three or four miles.'

'Good, we can take a look.'

'Fine,' Stringer said. 'But come and have a drink and something to eat.'

'So you're doing food these days?' Barry said.

'We all need to make a living, Jack, and times are changing with the peace process. Tourists flooding back, Americans like Mr Sollazo. I have seven rooms here. In the summer I was full most weeks. But come and eat. Best Irish stew in the country.'

There were a few regulars in the bar having a drink. Barry and Sollazo sat at the table in the bow window, ate rabbit pie and drank Guinness.

On the other side of the bar, Hannah Bernstein did a good nervous act to the barman.

'Could I just have sandwiches?'

Kevin Stringer moved in fast and smiled, at his most expansive. 'Anything you'd like.'

'Well, salad would be fine,' she said.

'No problem. Touring are you?'

'That's right.'

'And to drink?'

'A vodka and tonic would be nice.'

'Coming up. Just you sit yourself down.'

There were some newspapers on a stand by the door. She took one and sat at a table at the far end of the room from the window. Barry had his back to her so it was Sollazo who noticed. Very nice, he thought. It was a strange quirk, but he'd always liked women who wore glasses.

An hour later, Sollazo, Barry and Stringer went down to the harbour. Stringer led the way to the slipway and a green inflatable with an outboard motor.

'Here we go,' he said.

Sollazo and Barry climbed in, Stringer followed and cast off. He started the outboard and they moved away. Hannah, wandering down from the pub, watched them go.

* * *

From the hill, Devlin followed their progress through the binoculars. 'I was right,' he said with some satisfaction. 'They're closing on the boat that looked promising.' He nodded. 'Now they're boarding. Have a look.'

Dillon did, watching them board, then swung to the jetty and focused on Hannah Bernstein. 'Take care, girl dear, take care,' he said softly.

On board *Avenger*, Barry and Sollazo followed Stringer as he showed them around. 'One cabin, two bunks, the saloon with benches that allow for another two bunks, galley, toilet and that's it.' They ended up in the wheelhouse.

Sollazo said, 'It seems as if it's seen better days.'

'Top show isn't everything. It looks shabby, but the hull is steel and by Akerboon. Penta petrol engine, twin screws. Good for twenty-five knots. She's got a depth sounder, radar, automatic steering. Everything you need.'

Barry turned to Sollazo. 'Are you happy?'

'Sounds good to me.'

Barry nodded and said to Stringer. 'Fine, Kevin. We'll unload the station wagon in your garage. You put the stuff on board later. We'll return to Dublin. We'll be back before noon tomorrow to put to sea.'

'That's fine, Jack.'

They went to the rail and Sollazo dropped into the inflatable. Stringer said eagerly, 'It's important is it, Jack? I mean for the Movement? The great days back?'

'I know what you mean, Kevin,' Barry said. 'To hell with peace.'

Hannah pulled in beside the Toyota at the top of the hill and got out. 'They came back from the boat and went to the pub.'

Dillon had the binoculars raised. 'The station wagon's just leaving. No matter, only one road they can go. We'll catch them.'

'So, if they're leaving they'll be coming back,' Devlin said.

'And I think I should be here to receive them,' Hannah said. 'Have you got a bag of any description in your car, Liam?'

'As a matter of fact I do.' Devlin opened the boot of the Toyota and produced a large holdall. 'Empty, I'm afraid.'

'That doesn't matter. I'll book into The Loyalist and play the tourist. They'll be back.'

'And we with them,' Dillon said.

Devlin put his hands on her shoulders. 'Take care. We'd hate to lose you.'

'Don't worry.' She raised her shoulder bag. 'I'm carrying.'

'Hannah, you're the wonder of the world.' Dillon kissed her on both cheeks and then softly on the mouth.

Her eyes widened. 'Damn you, Dillon, that was a first,' and she got into the Renault and drove away.

Ten minutes later and a delighted Kevin Stringer was showing her a bedroom with a view of the harbour. 'And how long would you be staying?' he asked.

'Two nights, possibly three. I'm just touring. Down from Belfast.'

'A great city. We don't have *en suite* facilities, but the bathroom and the necessary is just next door.'

'Wonderful.'

'I'll see you later. Dinner at seven if you like,' and he went out.

Dillon caught up with the station wagon within fifteen minutes and settled back. 'What do you think they're up to?'

'This was just a preliminary sortie to check the boat. They've probably dropped off the diving equipment. It's back to Ballyburn now. They'll return, maybe tomorrow, with the others.'

'And up we come again and what then?' Dillon asked.

'That's up to you and that young woman back there. She has the police authority, Sean. Scotstown is in Ulster and that's part of the United Kingdom. It's up to you and Ferguson.' Devlin leaned back. 'Maybe a little gunplay, who knows, but not as far as I'm concerned. I'm getting too old, Sean. The trigger finger isn't what it was. I'd let you down.'

'Cobblers,' Dillon said.

'I've done my bit. Good luck and God bless you, but count me out.'

It was almost four o'clock and at Victoria Farm Kathleen was in the kitchen boiling the kettle. Ryan sat at the table and Mori was in the sitting room.

She glanced at her watch. 'They're due back in an hour. If we're going to do it it should be now.'

'If you think it will work,' Ryan said.

'Look, Uncle Michael.' She held up the pill bottle. 'Three Dazane pills will bring on your angina symptoms. The effect will really start showing by the time Barry and Sollazo are back. Jack Barry isn't going to just let you lie there and die, he's not the kind.'

'You mean you hope he isn't?'

'Look, even if they did nothing, Dr Sieed told

me the symptoms wear off in a couple of days. On the other hand, if Barry listens to me and takes you to a hospital, that'll be our chance.'

He sat there looking at her and then laughed. 'Oh, what the hell, what have we got to lose?' She opened the bottle, put three pills in her palm, got a glass of water and went back to him.

'There you go then, Uncle Michael.'

Ryan's symptoms first became apparent within half an hour. He stayed there at the kitchen table, head in his hands and then he started to sweat. Fifteen minutes later the trembling started.

Kathleen called, 'Mori, get in here.'

The Sicilian appeared on the instant. 'What is it?'

'He's having an angina attack. He's had them before. Get him into the sitting room on the sofa.'

Mori pulled Ryan up and got an arm round him. They went out of the kitchen together and along the hall to the sitting room. Kathleen followed with a glass of water. Ryan looked terrible, his face grey and for the first time she felt doubt.

'Uncle Michael, drink this.' She put the water to his lips and at that moment he started to shake terribly. This was more, much more than she had expected and at that moment Barry came in the room, Sollazo at his back.

'For God's sake, what is it?'

'He's having another angina attack,' she said. 'He needs a hospital.'

'Don't be stupid.' Sollazo turned to Barry. 'Hospital is out.'

Barry knelt down and put a hand on Ryan's forehead. 'He's in a bad way.' He stood up and said to Mori. 'Get him in the station wagon.' He turned to Sollazo. 'It's all right. There's a nursing home just outside Dublin we've been using for years. Decent doctors, good facilities. We'll take him there. Twenty-five minutes.'

Standing beside the Toyota observing the farm-house through the binoculars Devlin said, 'There's something up. Sollazo and the Mori fella have just brought Ryan out of the house. They're putting him into the station wagon. They looked as if they were supporting him.'

'Let me look.' Dillon took the binoculars. 'They're all getting in, Barry and Kathleen too. Let's get ready to move.'

He slid behind the wheel and Devlin got in on the other side. A few moments later the station wagon turned into the road and Dillon followed.

There was a telephone box in the village, but it was out of order. Hannah needed to speak to

Ferguson – had to take a chance. She returned to The Loyalist and went up to her room. There was the usual system where she punched nine to get an outside line and she dialled Ferguson's direct line at the Ministry of Defence.

It was bad luck that Kevin Stringer was sitting at his desk in the office doing accounts and was intrigued by the sound of the rather long series of numbers clicking through. He reached for the main switchboard phone and lifted it gently.

'Brigadier Ferguson, Chief Inspector Bernstein.'

A little later Stringer heard a voice say, 'Ferguson here. What's happening, Chief Inspector?'

'I'm staying at The Loyalist in Scotstown, sir, on the Down coast. We followed them up here, Barry and Sollazo. They have a boat in the harbour and brought a load of diving gear. They've gone back to Barry's place outside Dublin, that's where the Ryans are. Dillon and Devlin are in hot pursuit.'

'You expect them to return?'

'Probably tomorrow. I'm staying on as an English tourist, lone female variety.'

'Well, for God's sake watch yourself.'

'Don't I always?'

She put the phone down. In the office Stringer sat thinking about it then he rang Barry's phone number at Ballyburn. There was no reply. He sat there thinking about it some more and finally opened his desk drawer and took out a Browning automatic.

Hannah, sitting at the dressing table, was aware of a slight noise and turned to find the door open, Stringer standing there, the Browning in his hand.

'Chief Inspector, is it? So what's your game, lady?'

14

The sign at the entrance to the drive said, Roselea Nursing Home. The station wagon turned in through the gates and Dillon in the Toyota stopped on the other side of the road.

'What in the hell is going on?'

'I'm not sure,' Devlin said, 'but my impression is something nobody counted on.'

In the reception area, they sat waiting, Mori, Sollazo, Barry and Kathleen. She was in a bad way and Barry had an arm round her.

'Don't worry, it'll be fine. The guy who runs this place, Dr Ali Hassan, is a brilliant doctor.' He tried to make a joke. 'An Egyptian Irishman. He's patched up more bullet holes in more members of the IRA in the last twenty years than most doctors have had hot dinners.'

'It's my fault,' she said. 'You don't understand.'

'Don't be crazy, girl, your uncle has a history of heart trouble, you know that as well as I do.'

Hassan, a small brown-skinned Arab in a white coat, a stethoscope around his neck appeared.

'How is he?' Barry demanded.

'Not good, not good at all.' Hassan turned to Kathleen. 'Your uncle has a history of angina? That's what he told me?'

'Yes.'

'But this attack is most extreme. I don't understand. What is his medication?'

'Dazane.'

'Good God, there's no chance he has overdosed?' She stared at him, her face bone white. He said urgently. 'Could he have overdosed?'

She nodded slowly. 'He took three of the pills at four o'clock.'

'Oh, my God.' Hassan turned and ran along the corridor. Kathleen went after him and Barry and Sollazo followed, leaving Mori in reception.

Ryan lay twitching on the bed in intensive care while Hassan and a male nurse worked on him. Kathleen, Barry and Sollazo peered in through the window and Barry held the girl tight. Suddenly, Ryan gave a terrible gurgle and reared up on the bed and then he relaxed, all life draining out of him.

Hassan came out. 'I'm afraid he has gone.'

Kathleen struck out at him. 'He can't have. It's not possible.'

Barry restrained her. 'Hold on, girl, it's not your fault.'

'But it is,' she said. 'I'm a trained nurse, I'm supposed to know these things. I checked at my old hospital at Green Rapids. The doctor told me three Dazane would give him an angina attack, but not more than a couple of bad days. It was our way out, don't you see? You'd have to take him to hospital and we'd have a chance to get free.'

She broke down entirely. Barry handed her over to Sollazo. 'Take her to the station wagon. I'll handle things here.'

Sollazo took her out and Barry turned to Hassan. 'You've been a good friend to the IRA, Ali, and we appreciate it, so this is another special one.'

'I understand, Jack.'

'You get him up to the crematorium tonight and put him through the ovens. No name, no certificate.'

'Whatever you say.'

'Good man yourself,' Barry said, turned and went out.

Dillon and Devlin sitting in the Toyota watched the station wagon drive away. Dillon said, 'Only the three of them and the girl and no Ryan. What goes on?'

'I know this place,' Devlin told him. 'An IRA safe house. It's run by a damn good surgeon, an Egyptian named Ali Hassan. Maybe we should pay him a visit?'

Ali Hassan, sitting in his office, only a desk light on, was aware of the door opening and glanced up to see Devlin, Dillon behind him.

Devlin said. 'Remember me? Liam Devlin. You took a bullet out of me eighteen years ago.'

'Oh, my God, Mr Devlin,' Hassan said.

'And this is a friend of mine, Sean Dillon, who's done as much for the cause as I have.'

'Mr Dillon,' Hassan said uncertainly.

'A few people we know were in earlier propping up a Mr Ryan between them,' Dillon said. 'They left without him. Why would that be?'

'I think you must be mistaken,' Hassan said desperately.

Dillon produced his Walther. 'Well, this doesn't agree with you so think again.'

Which Ali Hassan did and told them all.

At Victoria Farm, Kathleen was in the bedroom, still weeping. Barry, Sollazo and Mori were in the sitting room drinking whiskey when the phone rang.

Stringer said, 'Thank God you're there, Jack. Something's come up.'

He started to talk. When he was finished Barry said, 'Hold her tight, Kevin, we're on our way. We'll leave now.'

'I will, Jack.'

Barry put down the phone and turned to Sollazo. 'Do you recall a woman in glasses having lunch in The Loyalist today?'

'Sure,' Sollazo said. 'Good-looking lady in an Armani trouser suit.'

'She's not only a Detective Chief Inspector, she also works for Brigadier Charles Ferguson, the Prime Minister's special intelligence expert and guess who his trouble shooter is – Sean Dillon.'

'Christ!' Sollazo said. 'What do we do?'

'We get the hell out of here now. Don't ask me what's going on because I don't know, but we leave now for Scotstown and we check *Irish Rose* out tomorrow morning.' Barry turned to Mori. 'Get the girl.'

Mori glanced at his boss and Sollazo nodded. 'Do as he says.'

Devlin and Dillon sitting in the Toyota watched the station wagon leave. 'There you go,' Devlin said, 'hot for Scotstown. I should imagine Ryan's unfortunate demise has brought things forward.'

'We'd better get going then,' Dillon said.

'No rush, Sean, we'll go to my cottage first. After all, you know where they're going.'

At Kilrea Cottage, Devlin sat by the fire with a Bushmills in his hand. Dillon bustled in, his Walther in one hand, his spare in the ankle holster in the other. He pulled up his trouser, put his foot on a chair and fastened the ankle holster. He slipped the other Walther in his waistband against the small of his back.

Devlin said, 'I always favoured a Walther myself, Sean, there's one in the desk drawer. Get it out.' Dillon did as he was told. 'Now put it in your pocket.'

'But why?' Dillon said.

'Sean, lad, I'm too old. I'd only be a hindrance if the bullets start flying, so you're on your own now. Only one thing I can do, which is offer sound advice. You've a gun in your pocket. In a search Barry would find that easy enough. Then he'd check your back because he knows you favour that position. He'll find the other Walther. That should satisfy him, give you a chance of getting away with the ankle gun.' Devlin smiled. 'I mean this is all supposition. Maybe Barry won't have the chance of turning you over, but who knows?'

'God bless you, Liam, you're the best,' Dillon said.

'Give them hell, Sean,' Liam Devlin said. 'Now get on with you. I'll phone Ferguson and bring him up to date.'

It was four o'clock in the morning and Hannah Bernstein was sleeping fitfully on the sofa in the small parlour at the back of The Loyalist. There were security bars on the window and Stringer had locked her in. She came awake to the sound of a vehicle drawing up in the yard. She sat up and listened to the sound of voices. After a while, the door opened and Stringer led the way in.

They were all there, Barry, Sollazo, Mori and Kathleen, who looked pale and subdued from much weeping.

Stringer took Hannah's Walther from his pocket and gave it to Barry. 'This was in her shoulder bag.'

Barry weighed it in his hand then put it in his pocket. 'So, Chief Inspector Hannah Bernstein and you work for that old dog, Charlie Ferguson?'

'If you say so.'

'Oh, but I do. Careless of you making a telephone call like that with a nosey one like Kevin in the office to listen in.'

'We all make mistakes.'

'You mentioned Devlin and Sean Dillon? We can expect them nosing around, can we?'

'Look, Mr Barry, it's over, can't you see that? American Intelligence is on to Mr Sollazo here and at a White House level.'

'That's a lie,' Sollazo said. 'They can't be.'

'They know everything. How do you think Brigadier Ferguson came into the picture?' She shook her head. 'There's no way either the White House or Downing Street will stand by and see that bullion fall into the wrong hands. You see, Mr Barry, Sollazo is in this for greed, but not you. With those kind of resources, the Provisional IRA could keep going for ever if it needed to.'

'Shoot the bitch,' Kathleen Ryan said dully.

'I can take care of it,' Mori said.

Barry shook his head. 'She could still be useful as some kind of hostage.' He shook his head. 'Fancy that old fox Liam Devlin making a fool of me, but why? Why Liam?'

'Peace, Mr Barry, it's very fashionable these days,' Hannah told him, 'and most people want it.'

'To hell with polite conversation,' Sollazo said. 'What happens now?'

'Maybe we should get the hell out of here while we can,' Mori said.

Barry shook his head. 'My hunch is that Ferguson sent the Chief Inspector here and Dillon on a fishing expedition with Devlin supplying the local expertise. No Garda, no RUC, not at this stage. All they wanted was to know where the *Irish Rose* is lying. Once Ferguson knows that then it would be a job for a Royal Navy salvage team.'

'We've had it anyway,' Sollazo said bitterly. 'They know where we are.'

'Yes, but they still don't know where the *Irish Rose* is. I say we go out at dawn and make the dive anyway. Dammit man, if that gold is reachable we could raise a few bars and be on our way. A million – two million for a morning's work.'

And suddenly Sollazo smiled. 'What the hell, why not? I've been taking chances all my life. Too late to stop now, but what about Dillon and this guy Devlin?'

'Liam Devlin was the best in the business once, but he's eighty-five years of age. Dillon's the hard man.'

'Not to me he isn't,' Mori said.

'Well, it would make an interesting encounter, but no need. The Chief Inspector makes a very satisfactory hostage if Dillon and Devlin turn up.' He turned to Stringer. 'Right, Kevin, an early breakfast and we'll leave at dawn. You'll hold the fort here?'

Ferguson on his secure line finished talking to Blake Johnson. The American said, 'What happens now that Ryan is dead? Would you say the location has died with him?'

'Definitely not otherwise why would they have returned to Scotstown? My Chief Inspector, as I told you, is there undercover, Dillon in hot pursuit. A man of infinite resource and guile. He'll sort it out, he always does. He'll find out where that damn boat is.'

'And then?'

'Job for the Royal Navy's salvage section. Something nice and discreet. Make it look like an exercise.' He laughed. 'One thing is certain. There's no way our friends can mount a proper salvage operation on that boat, not now.'

'The President will be pleased to hear that.'

'And so will the Prime Minister when I tell him in the morning. I'll keep you up to date on future developments, naturally.'

'I'd appreciate that, Brigadier.'

Ferguson, sitting by the fire at his flat, put the phone down and went to the drinks cabinet and poured a large whisky.

'Come on, Dillon,' he said softly, 'sort the buggers out.'

Dillon at that moment was on the hill outside the village, the Toyota parked in the shelter of the wood. He scanned the front of The Loyalist with his binoculars then had a look at the *Avenger* at anchor out there in the harbour.

'And where will you be, Hannah my love. Still in bed at this time in the morning, I shouldn't wonder,' he said softly.

Dawn was coming up fast now and the morning was grey and grim, the damp clinging mist shrouding everything and rain fell relentlessly. He lit a cigarette and wondered how he was going to play it and then the front door of The Loyalist opened and they all came out, Jack Barry, Kathleen, Sollazo and Mori with Hannah Bernstein between them. Stringer stood in the doorway talking to Barry then went inside.

'Sweet mother of God!' Dillon said and followed them with his binoculars as they walked down the slipway and got into the green inflatable and cast off. The outboard hammered into life and they moved away. Dillon got into the Toyota and started the engine.

Kevin Stringer, making another pot of tea in the kitchen, was aware of a slight creaking as the back door opened. He turned and Dillon smiled at him.

'Dear God, it's you, Sean,' and Stringer's throat went dry.

'A long time, Kevin. So what's been happening here?'

'What do you mean?'

Dillon took the Walther from his pocket. 'This thing makes hardly a sound and you know me. I'll put you on sticks, so tell me.'

'Please, Sean, I'm only a middle man on this. I listened in when the woman was on the phone. She identified herself as a Chief Inspector and spoke to a Brigadier Ferguson. Mentioned you and Liam Devlin.'

'So, as they say in bad movies, all is revealed.'

'Michael Ryan's dead,' Stringer said. 'A heart attack.'

'I know that,' Dillon said. 'I know everything. So they're going out to *Irish Rose*?'

'That's right.'

'And the Chief Inspector?'

'Jack said she'd be a useful hostage if you turned up. The Ryan girl wanted to kill her. So did that bastard Mori.'

'Is that a fact? Well we can't have that so let's get down to the jetty fast before they leave.'

On the *Avenger* Barry was at the wheel, the two women sitting on the bench beside him. Sollazo was on the stern deck with Mori and starting to raise the anchor when Stringer's voice boomed across the water.

'Jack, Dillon's here.'

'Jesus, Joseph and Mary!' Jack Barry said and switched off the engine.

He went out on deck and Sollazo and Mori joined him at the rail. 'Is that him?'

'As ever was.' He raised his voice. 'Is it yourself, Sean?'

'And who else?' Dillon called back. 'Let's talk.'

'I'll be over.' Barry turned to Mori. 'Pull the inflatable in.' He shook his head. 'The mad bastard.'

'You sound as if you like him,' Sollazo said.

'He was like a son to me. The great days we knew together in Derry in the old days leading British paratroopers a fine old dance.'

Mori shaded his eyes with a hand. 'He doesn't look much to me.'

Barry dropped into the inflatable and looked up. 'On his worst day and your best he'd put you away without even thinking about it.'

He cast off and started the outboard.

Dillon lit a cigarette as the inflatable coasted in. 'You're looking good, Jack, the years have been kind.'

'Kinder still on you, you young bastard. Where's Liam Devlin?'

'Back in Kilrea. Eighty-five is a little old for gunplay.'

'The best of men in his day.'

'So here we are,' Dillon said. 'And what's to be done? You've had it, Jack, no point to it any more.'

'Not quite true, Sean. If we find the wreck, which we will, and the gold bars waiting . . .' He shrugged. 'A hard morning's work could net one million, perhaps two. Not to be sniffed at.'

'Ah, you were always the practical man,' Dillon said. 'Is Hannah Bernstein well?'

'Oh, yes. I like that one, a lady of parts.'

'And then some. Let her go. Take me.'

'And why should I?'

'Oh, I've been honing my talents since the old days. I can fly a plane, Jack, but I'm also the best damn diver you ever saw. I even blew up PLO boats in Beirut harbour for the Israelis.'

'You little rascal.' Barry laughed. 'No, Sean, she's too valuable to hand over just yet, too useful.'

'God help us then I'll just have to come along for the ride.'

'A nice thought, but let's check you out first.' Barry prodded his Browning. 'Check his pockets, Kevin.' Stringer did as he was told and found the Walther.

'Satisfied?' Dillon asked.

'When was I ever?' Barry smiled. 'Under his jacket and against his back, Kevin, he always favoured that position.'

Stringer found the second Walther. 'You're right, Jack,' and he handed it over.

'I usually am,' Barry told him. 'You hold the fort, Kevin.' He smiled up at Dillon. 'In you get, Sean. I think I'll put you to work.'

Dillon went over the rail first and Barry handed the line to Mori and followed. The two women came out of the wheelhouse. Dillon said to Hannah, 'Are you all right, girl dear?'

'I'm fine.'

Dillon glanced at Mori. 'Christ, but he looks as if he just learned to walk erect this morning. If he gives you any trouble let me know and I'll select two items on his person and break them.'

Mori erupted, but Sollazo got in between. 'Leave it, Giovanni.' He turned to Barry. 'Have you checked him out?'

'A Walther in his pocket and another in the back of his pants. A good job I remembered that, but I've got good news for you. Sean here is a Master diver. I mean, he's made money out of blowing things up. Don't you think we should put him to work?'

Sollazo smiled. 'Why, that really makes my morning.'

'Good, then let's have the anchor up.'

Kathleen Ryan had stood there staring at him

and now she moved forward, a strange, dazed look on her face.

'Martin, it is you, isn't it?'

There was something strange here, something not right. Dillon said gently. 'As ever was, Kate, I'm sorry about Michael.'

'I killed him,' she said. 'I persuaded him to overdose on his pills. Dr Sieed said it would be all right, that he'd just have an angina attack.' She ran a hand over her face. 'He died, Martin, and I killed him. Isn't that the terrible thing?'

It was Hannah who put an arm round her. 'Come on, love, let's go down to the cabin,' and she led her away.

The engines rumbled into life as Barry took *Avenger* out to sea. Mori said. 'That's all we need, a crazy woman.'

Dillon said. 'Tell me, son, do you work at being a shite or does it just come naturally?' and he turned and went and joined Barry in the wheelhouse.

To get the Walther from his ankle holster and to kill Barry, Mori and Sollazo in seconds was not impossible, but it required the right moment and the fact that Hannah came up on deck didn't help. Dillon smiled out at her as she stood under the deck canopy shielded from the rain.

He said to Barry, 'The great pity we end up dealing with scum, Jack.'

'I know, son, but one thing hasn't changed. Anything I get out of this goes to the organization we both served for so many years. Money for arms.'

'Times have changed, Jack.'

'We can't be sure.'

Dillon sighed. 'All right, you'd better fill me in. Where are we going?'

'Just off Rathlin Island.'

'And the Master Navigator will home in on the position?'

Barry looked startled. 'Is there nothing you don't know?'

'We've really been on your case Jack, thanks to Liam. Anyway, how deep will she be?'

'Well, off Rathlin Island, according to Admiralty charts, anything between ninety and one hundred and twenty feet.'

'That's not bad, not if you allow for the size of the vessel. Mind you it's how she's lying that matters.'

Sollazzo joined them. 'How much further?'

'Half a mile,' Barry said. 'I'm turning the Navigator on now.'

He handed it to Sollazzo. There was a monotonous pinging at regular intervals. 'Hey, it's working,' Sollazzo said.

'The closer we get, the more urgent the sound

and when we reach the final position the pinging becomes continuous.'

'Let's keep our fingers crossed.' Sollazo gave it back to him and turned to Dillon. 'I was going to dive with Mori, but as you're supposed to be such hot stuff –' He shrugged. 'You'd better come and check the gear.'

'My pleasure,' Dillon said and followed him out.

Rathlin Island loomed out of the mist and Barry reduced power as they coasted onward through water which was extraordinarily calm. The pinging on the Master Navigator had increased in urgency and suddenly it changed into a long, single high-pitched shriek.

'That's it,' Barry called. 'Get the anchor over.'

Mori and Sollazo hurried to comply. Kathleen was at the port rail and for a moment Dillon was at Hannah's shoulder.

'I'm carrying,' he whispered. 'Barry found two, but Devlin, the old fox, gave me a third. Ankle holster.'

'Careful,' she said. 'Not now. It could be a blood bath.'

'Not to worry, girl dear, I'd like to go down and take a look at an old friend, so to speak.'

The anchor rattled down, the *Avenger* stopped dead. There was silence then Barry came out of the wheelhouse. 'There you go, so let's get on with it.'

Sollazo turned to Dillon. 'Let's get ready. I'll go first.' And he went down to the saloon.

When he came back on deck he was wearing one of the diving suits and a weight belt and buoyancy jacket. 'Your turn,' he said to Dillon.

Dillon went down the companionway to the saloon and undressed to his underpants, unstrapping the ankle holster. There was a cupboard marked Emergency Flares. He opened it and slipped the Walther inside. As he reached for the diving suit there was a step on the companionway and Sollazo looked in.

'Come on, let's get moving.'

Dillon dragged on the suit awkwardly and the cowl over his head. He pulled on the socks then picked up the other weight belt and fastened it around his waist with the velcro tabs. Then he reached for the diver's knife in the sheath.

Sollazo said, 'Leave it. You're the last man in the world I want to see with a lethal weapon.'

'Suit yourself.'

Dillon picked up his inflatable then took the other Orca computer and went up on deck to where the others waited, sheltering from the rain under the deck awning. Sollazo followed him.

'I've been thinking,' he said. 'We've got to husband ourselves. We can only spend so much time down there, you know that, even less it it's lying at a hundred and twenty. You go first, Dillon, and see what you find.'

It made sense and Dillon smiled. 'My pleasure.'

With a skill born of long practice he lifted the inflatable and tank over his head, inserted his arms and strapped the velcro tabs across his chest. He sat down to put his fins on and took the Halogen lamp Mori passed to him, looping its cord round his left wrist. He leaned over the rail to swill out his mask then pulled it down and turned, sitting on the rail.

He raised a thumb. 'We who are about to die salute you, and all that old Roman rubbish,' he said, put his mouthpiece in, checked that the air was flowing and went over backwards.

He passed under the keel, found the anchor line and started down, pausing at fifteen feet to equalize the pressure in his ears. The water was extraordinarily clear yet strangely dark and he pulled himself down the anchor line, checking his Orca computer. Thirty, forty then sixty feet and there it was looking out of the gloom, tilted to one side, quite visible even without the lamp being turned on.

He was at ninety feet and the ship lay on a

smooth sandy bottom that sloped downwards. Here and there great fronds of seaweed undulated backwards and forwards in the current.

Dillon closed in on the prow and switched on his Halogen lamp and there it was clearly visible in spite of being encrusted in barnacles, the ship's name, *Irish Rose*, and this was special because he'd been part of what had happened here.

He moved towards the stern, torn apart by the force of the explosion, and there was the truck to one side of the ship. Obviously the explosion had torn it free from the deck clamps and, incredibly, it had settled upright on all six wheels.

Dillon moved to the rear, raised the door clamp and pulled. It refused to budge. He tried again, but got the same result. No point in wasting precious time at that depth so he made for the surface.

He went up the small side ladder to the deck, pushed up his mask and spat out his mouthpiece. They all stood waiting.

'For Christ's sake, Sean, tell us the worst,' Barry pleaded.

'Oh, it's there,' Dillon said, 'and at ninety feet, which is useful. Gives more bottom time.'

'And the truck?' Sollazo demanded.

'That's there too. It obviously became detached

from the deck in the explosion and it's standing upright beside the ship.'

'Marvellous,' Sollazo said.

'Only one thing I don't understand. When we grabbed the truck we used an electronic device called a Howler that screwed up the security system so everything unlocked.'

'So?' Sollazo said.

'I couldn't open the rear door.'

'So the electronics got shook up in the explosion,' Sollazo told him, 'or maybe the door jammed. We've got Semtex and pencil timers. Go down and blow it.'

'Yes, o master,' Dillon said. 'Just get me the necessary.'

Barry crouched beside him with a Semtex block. 'Here you go, Sean, and a three-minute pencil timer.'

'Czechoslovakia's contribution to world culture,' Dillon said.

'Can you manage?'

'Can a fish swim?'

Hannah called, 'Take care, Sean.'

'Don't I always?' He pulled down his mask, sat on the rail and went over.

He hauled himself down the anchor line again, the quickest route, made for the truck and floated there, working the plastic block of Semtex around the door clamp. Then he broke the timer pencil. There was a gently fizzing and he turned and made for the surface. Barry reached a hand down to help him up the ladder. Dillon sat down and the others moved to the rail. After a while, the sea boiled, turning over angrily and a number of dead fish surfaced. Soon it was still again.

Dillon grinned up at Sollazo. 'Don't tell me, down I go again.'

The truck had moved to one side but was still upright and the rear doors had been blasted apart, one hanging on the hinges, the other lying some distance away where it had been thrown. Sand hovered in clouds. Dillon approached and switched on the Halogen light and experienced a considerable shock. The truck was empty.

He hung at the bottom of the ladder, took out his mouthpiece and looked up as they all leaned over the rail.

'You're not going to like this one little bit, Jack,' Dillon said, 'but there's nothing there.'

'What do you mean there's nothing there?' Barry demanded.

'I mean the truck's empty.'

'It can't be empty,' Barry said. 'You told me you looked in the back when you knocked it off on that road. It was there then.'

'Yes it was,' Dillon said. 'But it isn't now.'

Kathleen Ryan's face was burning, her eyes dark holes. 'Someone must have been here before.'

'Not possible,' Dillon said. 'The door was fast and no sign of blasting.'

'Mori, help me,' Sollazo said and reached for his inflatable and tank. 'You're going down again, Dillon, and I'm going with you. I think you're lying.'

'Suit yourself,' Dillon told him and went under again, starting down the anchor line.

He hovered beside the wreckage of the stern of the *Irish Rose*, hanging on to a rail, and Sollazo drifted down to join him. He poised there, then swam towards the truck. Dillon went after him.

Sollazo hung on the edge of the door and peered inside. He turned once to glance at Dillon, his face clear, then turned to the dark interior again. Dillon came up behind him, pulled the diver's knife from Sollazo's leg sheath, reached over and sliced open his air hose.

Bubbles spiralled at once, Sollazo swung round, eyes staring. His hands went to his throat and he started to rise. Dillon grabbed for an ankle and pulled him down. The kicking stopped surprisingly quickly and, finally, he hung there, arms outstretched. Dillon pulled off the mask and Sollazo stared right through him, straight to eternity. The Irishman took him by the hand and started up.

It was Kathleen Ryan who saw Sollazo's body first as he surfaced to starboard. 'Would you look at that,' she said.

Hannah joined her at the rail. 'Oh, my God.'

Barry and Mori hurried over. The Sicilian, without hesitation, pulled off his jacket and shoes, jumped over the rail and swam to Sollazo. He got an arm around him, paused and turned and looked up.

'He's dead.'

Dillon had released the body at ten feet and swam under the rail to the port side. He surfaced, unfastened his inflatable and tank and let them go, pulled off his mask and fins and peered cautiously on deck. Barry, Kathleen and Hannah were at the rail and he could hear Mori calling. 'Throw me a line.'

Dillon hauled himself over the rail and slipped down the companionway to the saloon. He got the Emergency Flares cupboard open, found the Walther and went back up.

Barry was standing at one side of Hannah and

Kathleen engaged in unfastening a lifebelt. As he threw it over Dillon said, 'Easy does it, Jack.'

He stood in the entrance to the companionway, a supremely menacing figure in the black diving suit, the Walther in his right hand.

'Get over here, Hannah.'

She did so. Barry still leaned over the rail, glancing back over his shoulder. 'Still the eighth wonder of the world, aren't you, Sean?'

'Don't do it, Jack,' Dillon said gently.

But Barry did, half-turning, Browning in hand and Dillon shot him twice in the heart. Barry was hurled against the rail, the Browning skidding across the deck, and he toppled over into the sea.

Dillon ran to the rail, Walther extended. Mori stared up at him, an arm around Sollazo, and Dillon took deliberate aim and shot him between the eyes. There was silence, only seagulls calling, whirling above them in the mist. Dillon sat down against the rail.

'Jesus, but I could do with a cigarette.'

Hannah went down on one knee beside him. 'Are you all right, Sean?'

Kathleen Ryan said, her voice strangely dead. 'Martin, push the Walther over this way.'

Dillon had put it on the deck beside him. He looked up and Hannah turned and there she was, Barry's Browning in one hand. The look on her face was that of the truly mad.

'Not there, Martin, not there in the first place. The cunning old bastard, my uncle. Only told me the other day, but clever, you must agree. It's there waiting for me and I'll fly in out of the sea to get it. Soon now, Martin, soon.'

'I know, Kate, I know.'

'Wouldn't hurt you, Martin, my lovely Martin, so down you go the both of you.'

'I think we'd better,' Hannah murmured.

'Anything you say, Kate.' Dillon smiled, stood up and kicked the Walther across.

Hannah went down the companionway and Dillon followed. 'Close the door,' Kathleen called.

He did as he was told, was aware of her footsteps on the companionway, the key turning in the door. It was only two or three minutes later that they heard the outboard motor start up.

'What do we do?' Hannah asked.

'Simple,' Dillon told her, 'now that she's gone. These things have a forward deck hatch, always do. I'll be back in a minute.'

He went out into the galley and saw the hatch at once above his head, stood on a stool, unclipped it and pulled himself through. A moment later, Hannah heard him on the companionway and the door opened. She followed him out on deck and they saw the green inflatable disappearing into the mist. Dillon went into the wheelhouse and switched on the engines. He turned back towards Scotstown.

'Here, you take the wheel and I'll go and change.'

When he returned, Hannah said, 'She's crazy, Sean, over the edge.'

'She always was a bit that way,' Dillon said. 'Something there, something really heavy, and I never knew what. Now she thinks she killed her uncle. By the way, is that Jack Barry's raincoat on the peg there? If so, I might just find those two Walthers he took off me.' He searched the pockets and turned. 'There you are, one for you and one for me. I'll take the wheel.'

'What did she mean that the gold wasn't there in the first place?'

'Remember I told you I felt there was something wrong when I went through the files and the newspaper clippings.'

'Yes.'

'Now I know what it was. Michael Ryan had a replica truck at Folly's End and Benny was to dump it on the coast road to put the police off for a while.'

'So?'

'It didn't strike me at first, but there wasn't a single mention of that truck in any police report or newspaper file. Now why would that be?'

'Oh, my God!' Hannah said.

'Exactly. After the robbery I took off for the

Irish Rose on the motorcycle with Kathleen. Michael followed in the truck, only he was late. Told us the automatic clutch was giving trouble.'

'Which it wasn't.'

'Of course not. He was late because he called at Folly's End and switched trucks. The bullion never went down with the *Irish Rose* because it was never on board. It's locked away in that hidey hole at the back of the barn at the farm, at Folly's End. Isn't that the biggest laugh you've had in years?'

THE LAKE DISTRICT

1995

15

Kathleen Ryan coasted in out of the mist and grounded on the slipway beside the jetty. She didn't bother tying up, simply left the inflatable where it was and went up to the quayside and crossed to The Loyalist. She went round to the yard at the rear and found Barry's station wagon. When she tried the door it was locked. She stood there thinking about it. She had to get out of it, had to keep moving, so she crossed to the back door.

Kevin Stringer sat at the table drinking tea and reading yesterday's newspaper. He looked up in surprise. 'What are you doing here?'

'Jack Barry's keys for the station wagon, where are they?'

'On the sideboard.'

She reached for them and put them in her pocket. 'I need my shoulder bag. I left it in the bedroom. I'll go and fetch it then I'll be off.'

She went out and left Stringer there, very disturbed. It was quiet, no staff due in for a couple of hours, and for some reason he knew fear.

He heard her coming down the stairs and she came in. She'd got rid of the reefer coat she'd worn on the boat, was wearing a long raincoat and her old black beret. The bag hung from her left shoulder.

'Do you know where Ladytown is?'

'It's on the far side of Newcastle on Dundrum Bay. You just follow the coast road.'

'How far?'

'Twenty miles.'

'Good, I'll be away then.' It was noticeable that the American accent had disappeared and now she had reverted to the hard Belfast accent of her youth.

Stringer got up and moved to block her way. 'What the hell is going on? Where's Jack?'

'Dead. Martin killed him – Martin Keogh – and he killed Sollazo and the other fella. He's still on the boat with that woman. I locked them in the cabin and came back in the inflatable.'

Her voice was flat and monotonous and Stringer felt strangely light-headed. 'Not Keogh – Dillon. Have you lost your wits, girl? They can't all be dead, not all three.'

'Oh, yes they are. Anyway, I'll be off.'

'You're not going anywhere.' He put his hands on her shoulders.

Her eyes seemed to burn in that pale face and she cried out, 'Don't put hands on me, you Taig bastard,' and she pulled the Browning from her right-hand pocket, jammed the muzzle against his side and fired.

He gave a terrible groan and staggered back. 'Damn you, you've done for me.'

She shot him again and he fell against the table and dropped to the floor. 'Good riddance,' she said. 'If I had my way, I'd shoot the lot of you.'

She put the Browning back in her pocket and went out. A few moments later she drove away in the station wagon.

Dillon eased *Avenger* into the side of the jetty and Hannah scrambled over with a line. He cut the engines, went over the rail to join her and tied up.

'Right, let's get moving.'

He took Hannah's hand and they ran across the street in the rain, going round the side to the yard at the back. Hannah peered cautiously in through the kitchen window.

'There doesn't seem to be anyone there,' she said, 'and I see the station wagon has gone.'

'All right, in we go,' Dillon told her and took out his Walther.

There was the immediate pungent smell of cordite and then, of course, Stringer's body. Hannah dropped to one knee and searched for a pulse. She looked up and shook her head.

'He's quite dead.' She stood. 'She doesn't take prisoners, that girl. I wonder where she's gone?'

'Look, she gave her uncle those pills to get him away from Barry and Co., to a hospital from where they thought they'd be able to do a runner. He died and she blames herself, but she is running and on her own now,' Dillon said.

'To the Lake District in England?'

'Where else, but how to get there?'

'Fly to Manchester and hire a car.'

'A possibility or maybe a private flight. Several old airstrips on that coast from the Second World War. You only have to look in *Pooley's Flight Guide*.'

'It's a possibility,' Hannah nodded. 'And there was that strange remark she made back there on the boat. "It's there waiting for me . . ."'

'"And I'll fly in out of the sea to get it,"' Dillon added.

'She's mad, Dillon, you do realize that? Did you notice she didn't sound American any more?'

'I know. She was talking pure Belfast just like the sixteen-year-old girl I saved on a dark street ten years ago, but never mind that now. We'll go into the office and call Ferguson.'

* * *

Ferguson at his flat in Cavendish Square had only just awakened and he sat up in bed and listened calmly to what Hannah had to say.

When she finished he said, 'Give me your telephone number.' She did so and he scribbled it down. 'I'll call back. Give me fifteen minutes.' He put the phone down, picked it up and rang his office at the Ministry of Defence. When the duty officer answered he said. 'Ferguson here. Put me on to Flight Information.'

When the telephone rang in the office at The Loyalist Hannah answered at once. 'Brigadier?'

'There is a Royal Navy Air-Sea Rescue base at Crossgar on the Down coast only ten miles from you. You're expected. From there you will be flown in a Sea King helicopter to the Air-Sea Rescue base at Whitefire. That's on the Lake District coast near St Bees.'

'What then, sir?'

'I'm leaving the office now for Farley RAF base. I'll be there in thirty minutes. They'll have a Ministry of Defence Lear jet waiting for immediate departure. They tell me we'll make Whitefire in forty-five minutes. We'll helicopter to this Folly's End place from there.'

'Fine, sir, looking forward to seeing you.'

'Stop being sentimental, Chief Inspector,' Ferguson

told her. 'Just move your arse,' and he put the phone down.

'Now what?' Dillon asked.

She filled him in quickly. When she was finished she said, 'What about Stringer?'

'Let the staff find him. Ferguson will handle the RUC later. Let's get moving, girl dear,' and he opened the door and led the way out.

Kathleen Ryan found Ladytown with no difficulty and she pulled over in the village square, got out and spoke to an old woman who was walking by with a poodle on a lead.

'Would you be knowing where there's an airfield near here?'

'I would indeed, love. That would be Tony McGuire's place.'

'And how would I get there?'

'About two miles on. Let me explain,' and the old woman went into detail.

It was a sad sort of place, obviously run down and neglected. The sign on the gate said, 'McGuire's Air Taxis' and the paint was peeling. The Tarmacadam of the drive was pitted with holes and she bumped along towards the administration buildings. There was a tower and two hangars and no sign of any planes.

She parked outside what looked like a Second World War Nissen hut and the door opened and a small, wiry man in jeans and an old black leather flying jacket appeared. His grey hair was close-cropped and there was a watchfulness to him.

'Can I help you?'

'Would you be Tony McGuire?'

'Who wants to know?'

'Michael Ryan's niece, Kathleen.'

McGuire said, 'I haven't heard of Michael in years. I thought he was dead.'

'Alive and well and waiting for me over in the English Lake District and, the thing is, he told me that if I needed a quick trip over there the man to see was Tony McGuire.'

'Did he indeed?'

'Oh, yes, told me he'd used you often in the old days.'

He stood there looking at her, a slight frown on his face, and then he said, 'You'd better come in.'

There was a stove in the office, the pipes going up through the ceiling, a camp bed in one corner, a map desk and an office desk cluttered with papers.

McGuire lit a cigarette. 'So what do you want?'

'A quick trip to the Lake District.'

'And when would you want to go?'

'Now.'

He stared at her, shocked. 'That's a pretty tall order.'

'You do have a plane, don't you?'

He hesitated then nodded. 'Just one at the moment. The bank foreclosed on me and took my best plane, the Conquest, in lieu of debts, but I do have a Cessna 310.'

'So we could go?'

'I'll show you.'

He led the way out and crossed to one of the hangars and rolled the rusting door back revealing a small twin-engined plane.

'How long would it take to get to the Lake District in that?'

'Probably about an hour.'

'Good. I'll take it.'

'Steady on,' he said. 'First of all it needs re-fuelling and I'll have to do that by hand and that takes time.' He turned and looked up at the sky. 'And the weather stinks. I'd need to wait to see if it would clear.' He turned to look at her. 'And then we have to decide where we're going.'

'As close as possible to a place called Marsh End. It's south of Ravenglass.'

'All right, let's go back to the office and I'll

check in *Pooley's Flight Guide*. That shows every airfield and airstrip in the UK.'

He leafed through the book for a while and then paused. 'I remember this place, Laldale. It was an emergency field for the RAF in the Second World War. I landed there once about fourteen years ago. There's nothing except a load of decaying buildings and an airstrip.'

'So we can go?'

'Well we'd need to land somewhere with Customs and Security facilities first.'

'Three thousand dollars,' she said, 'and we fly there direct.'

She pulled up the false bottom of her shoulder bag and produced several wads of American dollars, obviously to a much greater amount, and McGuire's throat went dry. He swallowed hard and managed to speak.

'Is this some political thing? I know what your uncle and his people get up to. I don't want trouble. I mean, those days are gone.'

'Five thousand,' she said and held the money out. 'How long did you say it would take?'

'An hour,' he said hoarsely.

'An hour there and an hour back. I'd say five thousand dollars was good pay. Here, I'll count it out while you go and re-fuel.'

She sat at the desk, took out wads of dollars and started to count. McGuire watched, fascinated and licked his lips.

'OK, I'll leave you to it. I'll re-fuel the plane.'

He almost ran across the broken Tarmacadam of the runway to the hangar and the one image that wouldn't go away was the sight of all those dollar bills coming out of her shoulder bag.

At the same moment, the Sea King helicopter landed at Whitefire Air-Sea Rescue base. The rotors stopped and, as Dillon and Hannah Bernstein emerged, a Range Rover pulled up and a Royal Navy Lieutenant-Commander got out.

'My name's Murray. You'll be Brigadier Ferguson's people.'

'That's right,' Hannah said.

'He's due to land in ten minutes. I'll take you along to the mess and you can have some tea.'

They got in the Range Rover and he drove away.

Tony McGuire came into the office and found her sitting by the stove.

'You all right?' he asked.

She nodded. 'Your five thousand dollars are on the table.' He went and picked them up, a bundle in each hand. 'Count them, if you like,' she said.

346

'What the hell, I trust you.' He went and unlocked an old-fashioned safe in the corner and put the money inside.

'Can we go now?' she said.

'I don't see why not.'

He turned and led the way out. As they walked across to the hangar she said, 'Can we get away with it?'

'Oh, sure,' McGuire said. 'There's more unrestricted air space out there than people realize and if I approach the coast of the Lake District at under six hundred feet I won't even show on radar.'

'I see.'

They went into the hangar, she climbed over the wing and took the seat directly behind the pilot's. McGuire climbed in and closed the door. He fired one engine, then the other and turned.

'OK?' She nodded. 'Here we go then.'

He taxied out on to the runway, bumping over holes, and turned into the wind at the far end. There was a slight pause and they moved forward. He boosted power and they lifted up into the mist and rain.

In the officer's mess at Whitefire, Dillon and Hannah were having a cup of tea when Lieutenant-Commander Murray came in with Ferguson.

'Here you are, Brigadier,' he said.

Ferguson gave him his best smile. 'I'd appreciate a word with my people, Commander. Ten minutes? After that we'll leave in that Sea King for the destination I've indicated on the map.'

'As you say, Brigadier.'

Murray saluted and withdrew. Ferguson turned and smiled. 'Is that tea? I really would appreciate some, Chief Inspector.'

'Of course, sir.'

Hannah found a clean cup and poured. Ferguson said, 'You have been having a ball, Dillon, haven't you?'

'Well it's been complicated, I'll say that.'

Ferguson accepted the cup of tea from Hannah. 'And your usual kill ratio, I see. Barry, Sollazo and Mori. Really, Dillon, you constantly remind me of the tailor in the fairy tale by the Brothers Grimm who boasted of having killed seven at one blow, only in his case it turned out to be flies on a piece of jam and bread.'

'Jesus, Brigadier, have I disappointed you again?'

'Don't be silly, Dillon. What about the girl?'

'She's quite mad,' Hannah Bernstein said. 'Whatever mental state she was in before is one thing, but this business of the death of her uncle has put her right over.'

'So you think she'll turn up at Folly's End?'

'She doesn't have anywhere else to go,' Dillon told him.

'All right, calm down.' Ferguson put his cup on the table. 'Let's go and see, shall we?'

Mary Power was feeding the chickens at her back door, a black and white sheepdog at her side. It was late afternoon, darkness tingeing the sky on the distant horizon. She finished with the chickens then went in search of Benny and found him in the barn sitting at the tackle table cleaning the barrels of a shotgun.

'There you are. Did you see to the sheep in North Meadow?'

He nodded eagerly. 'I brought them down,' he said in his slow pedantic way, 'and put them in the paddock.'

'You're a good lad, Benny.'

He reached for an ammunition box, took out two cartridges, loaded the gun and snapped the barrels up. For a moment it pointed at her and she cuffed the side of his head and pushed the shotgun to one side.

'I've told you before. Never point it at anyone. Guns are bad.'

'But the fox might come again,' Benny said slowly. 'Last time he killed twelve chickens.'

'Well you get the bastard when he comes, but don't shoot me,' she said. 'Now come and have your break. Cup of tea and that nice fruit cake I made.'

He put the shotgun on the table and followed her out.

The Cessna 310 came in from the sea at four hundred feet and banked to starboard. A few moments later it dropped in at the end of the runway at Laldale and taxied towards the far end. McGuire turned into the wind and switched off the engines. Kathleen reached for the door handle.

He said, 'I'll get that for you,' and opened it. 'You first.'

She went out over the wing, put a foot on the little passenger ladder and reached the ground and McGuire followed her. The mountains were shrouded in mist, and the rain was a persistent damp drizzle.

'You know where you're going?' he asked.

'Oh, yes, I can walk.'

'You're sure you'll be all right?'

'It's just three or four miles.'

'Only I was thinking about all that money in your shoulder bag. I mean anything might happen.' He reached and grabbed it from her.

He stood there beside the plane scrabbling in the bottom of the bag and found the rest of the dollars. 'Jesus Christ!' he said.

'Bastard,' Kathleen Ryan told him. 'You're all

bastards,' and she took out the Browning and shot him twice in the heart.

McGuire bounced against the wing and fell to the ground. She picked up the bag, slipped the strap over her shoulder, turned and walked away.

At Folly's End, Benny was forking hay in the loft of the barn when Mary Power went in search of him. 'I've done lamb stew. Do you want dumplings?'

Benny nodded eagerly. 'I'd like that.'

Suddenly, the air was filled with noise, an incredible roaring. Mary turned in alarm and ran into the yard, Benny following her, and the Sea King helicopter descended into the meadow beside the farm. The rotors stopped and Charles Ferguson, Hannah Bernstein and Dillon got out.

Dillon ran forward and Mary said in amazement, 'Martin? Martin Keogh, is that you?'

'As ever was, Mary. Has Kathleen been here? Kathleen Ryan?'

She looked bewildered. 'No, should she have?'

Dillon turned and shook his head to Ferguson who still stood by the helicopter. Ferguson leaned in and spoke to the pilot, then stood back and the Sea King rose into the air and banked away.

Ferguson came forward and smiled at Mary Power who stood outside the barn door, Benny at her shoulder.

'Who are you?' she demanded. 'What's happening?'

'Brigadier Charles Ferguson, Mrs Power. Is the truck still in the barn?'

She went very pale. 'The truck?' she whispered.

'Yes, is the truck still in the barn?' he said patiently.

It was Benny who answered. 'Oh, yes, truck in the barn till Uncle Michael come back. Benny show,' and he turned and ran inside.

It was raining hard now as Kathleen Ryan tramped along the Eskdale Road, a strange forlorn figure in her raincoat and beret, hands thrust into her pockets. She reached the gate with the sign Folly's End, paused then turned in and approached the farmhouse.

It was almost dark, fading fast and there was no light in the house. She stood there in the yard, remembering this place ten years ago, her uncle and Martin and she ran a hand over her face. Was it then or now? And then she saw a glimmer of light at the door of the barn.

Mary Power and Benny sat at the tackle table. Benny was polishing an old pony saddle, Mary watching him. The door creaked open, a small wind lifted straw in the hay bales. Mary looked up and found Kathleen standing there.

'So you've come back, Kathleen Ryan?'

'I had to,' Kathleen told her. 'It was meant to be from the beginning. Is the truck still here?'

'Oh, yes, it's always been here. Your Uncle Michael changed his mind. Told Benny not to dump the spare truck on the coast road after all. He came here after the robbery and exchanged them.'

'I know about that, he told me. He was afraid the crew of *Irish Rose* would try to steal the bullion. More than that, he was afraid he would have problems with the Army Council in Ulster. There was a man called Reid.' Kathleen shrugged, looking very tired. 'He could have caused trouble. Can I see the truck?'

'Benny show,' he cried, got up and moved to the back of the barn.

He tossed bales of hay to one side as if they were nothing, then pulled on the false wall, swinging it back. Kathleen went forward, turned the locking bar and opened the doors and there was the bullion in its boxes.

Charles Ferguson said, 'Miss Ryan I believe?'

She turned and found Ferguson, Hannah Bernstein and Dillon standing there. She stared at them blankly and then something stirred.

'Martin, is that you?'

'As ever was, Kate.'

'I've come for it, Martin, come for the gold like

Uncle Michael wanted. We'll beat the IRA at their own game.'

'It's over, Kate,' he said. 'We're into peace now. We've got to give it a chance.'

'Peace?' She frowned as if having difficulty at taking the idea in at all and then her eyes blazed. 'Peace with the Taigs?' She was like an avenging angel and her hand came out of her raincoat pocket holding the Browning. 'You saved me, Martin, in the alley with those three bastards, remember?'

'Of course I do.'

'But you weren't there the other time when I was fifteen and there were four of them.' It was as if she was choking. 'Dirty, rotten Taig bastards. To hell with them for what they did to me. And Uncle Michael, he hunted them down personally. He killed each one himself.' The gun shook in her hand. 'We have to stand and fight. We have to face the Catholic scum.'

And only at that moment did Dillon realize how truly mad she had become, but before he could speak it was Benny who interfered. He staggered forward, looking distressed, arms waving.

'No, Kathleen, guns bad. Mustn't point guns.'

His hands fastened on her shoulders and she screamed, 'Get away, Benny,' and her finger fastened convulsively on the trigger of the Browning and she shot him.

Benny cried out and fell back and Mary Power

screamed, 'No!' picked up the shotgun from the tackle table, thumbed back the hammers and fired both barrels. Kathleen was lifted backwards off her feet into the hay bales, the Browning flying from her hand. Dillon ran to her and dropped to one knee.

She grabbed for his hand. 'Martin, is that you?' Her body jerked once then went very still.

Hannah crouched beside him as Dillon stayed there holding a hand. 'She's gone, Sean.'

'Yes, I can see that.'

Benny, incredibly, got to his feet and stood, a hand to his side, blood oozing between his fingers. He looked shocked and dazed. Hannah examined him quickly and turned.

'Straight through his side. There's an exit wound. He'll live.'

Ferguson gently took the shotgun from Mary Power. 'Oh, God, what have I done?' she asked.

'Not your fault, my dear,' Ferguson told her. 'You've nothing to worry about. I'll see to it personally.' He turned to Hannah. 'Chief Inspector, I'd be obliged if you'd take her inside. And Benny. Do what you can.'

Hannah went and put an arm round her and led her out, giving her free hand to Benny to guide him.

Dillon stood looking down at Kathleen Ryan. 'You poor silly little bitch, I always knew there was something more.'

Ferguson said. 'I gave the Sea King an hour. He'll be back soon. Are you all right?'

'Of course I am, Brigadier.' Dillon found a cigarette and lit it. 'End of a perfect day, wouldn't you say?' and he turned and walked out.